I0718378

THE COURTSHIP OF
HARRY'S WIFE

D. B. Burns Mysteries
THE COURTSHIP OF HARRY'S WIFE
Book One

THE COURTSHIP OF HARRY'S WIFE

By
Jeanette-Marie Mirich

The Courtship of Harry's Wife
Published by Mountain Brook Ink
White Salmon, WA U.S.A.

The website addresses shown in this book are not intended in any way to be or imply an endorsement on the part of Mountain Brook Ink, nor do we vouch for their content.

This story is a work of fiction. All characters and events are the product of the author's imagination other than those stated in the author notes as based on historical characters. Any other resemblance to any person, living or dead, is coincidental.

Scripture quotations are taken from the King James Version of the Bible. Public domain.

The Team: Miralee Ferrell, Nikki Wright, Cindy Jackson
Cover Design by Lynnette Bonner

Mountain Brook Ink is an inspirational publisher offering fiction you can believe in.
Printed in the United States of America

Dedication

Who can find a virtuous woman? For her price is far above rubies. The heart of her husband doth safely trust in her, Proverbs 31:10-11

For my grandmothers, Euphemia Campbell Jackson and Delilah Belle Mays Brown. Women of courage, grace, and faith, who bathed their world in love by serving the needy, sacrificing for the poor, and opening their homes to the hurting. One was known as the angel of her neighborhood while the other filled her home and our hearts with joy.

Acknowledgments

When beginning a new novel, I feel like the Yankee players did when Casey Stengel ordered them to, "Line up in alphabetical order by height." I need the experts to come alongside and tell me straight out whether I'm to bunt or hit one to right field. The coaches guide players around the bases. I have a cadre of coaches who brought this book home. I am grateful to them all.

I am blessed by a kind, gifted husband who cheers on my attempts at meshing ideas with characters. Thank you, Rod, for your laughter, enthusiasm, and humor. You are also a terrific research assistant who doesn't mind dusty archives or roaming Normandy beaches.

Lorin Oberweger of Free Expressions Literary Service was the instigator of this tale. Lorin challenged me with a writing prompt and urged me to continue seeking joy and excellence in writing. Jason Black of Pen to Punctuation helped develop this tale. Eva Marie Everson encouraged my storytelling with her editorial skills and laughter. Lydia Schweitzer, my loving Oregon neighbor, made cogent suggestions. I have a group of prayer partners who have prayed over the novels I create. I'm grateful for Linda Crabtree, Judy Spoelman, Nancy Garten, Bev Daugherty, Shielda Gates, Allison Doty, Holly Lightvoet, Sharon Pera, Sherry Bennett, and Babs Caraway. All have listened, prayed and helped me focus on the importance of a moment-by-moment relationship with God.

Cheryl Hodde graciously accepted the challenge of critiquing this book with a writer's eye. Her suggestions and challenges made a great difference in the manuscript. Thank you for your encouragement.

A special thanks to Patrick Carney for his sharpshooter expertise, amazing knowledge of guns, and for the tutorial on target shooting.

Mountain Brook Ink is a unique combination of publisher and staff who love the Lord, who love books that encourage the reader to look beyond this world for solutions, and a team who have held my hand through this process with grace and amazing editorial skills. A heartfelt thanks to Miralee Ferrell and Nikki Wright for their expertise and kindness.

Chapter One

I DON'T KNOW WHAT MADE ME do it except loyalty. Harry had been dead only two weeks, but there I was, marching down Washington Avenue decked out with tan high heels and the special green dress that looked like something Sophia Loren would have worn in the sixties. I jiggled in undignified places I'd only let Harry see. But he'd made me promise to wear it while traipsing down the street like a "you-know what." And so, I did.

But I kept my dark glasses on, the ones with the rhinestones.

The dress exposed cleavage, which made me even more uncomfortable because men can't think about anything else when bosoms are involved, especially when it comes to a 36 C in a size four. Sorta makes you wonder what the good Lord was thinking when he created my figure.

The day sweltered, and it was only 9:15 in the morning. The pavement stretching in front of the courthouse shimmered. The red, white, and blue ribbons that days earlier twirled around the trees sagged to the ground. What looked great on the 4th of July was tacky by the 7th. But everyone knows summers in Kentucky are not for sissies.

Right as I dabbed my handkerchief to the place above my bosom, Judge Henderson stepped out of the courthouse looking dapper in a three-piece suit. He ogled. No other word for it. His mouth popped open and his eyes fixated between my neck and my waist.

I nodded once in his direction and kept going. I was fifty-three and a grandmother, for goodness sake. I wondered if I couldn't have fulfilled my vow to Harry by doing this at midnight, but was that fair to Harry? No. He said he wanted the smart alecks in town to get a gander at why he didn't go drinking with them.

God rest his soul.

I straightened my shoulders. No Burns has ever been cowardly. Not since the Civil War when cousin "Dump" skittered behind the oak trees near Perryville and was affixed to them like a leech on an ankle.

I shouldn't have made the promise when Harry was dying but . . . you know how it is. You want to please when someone's hooked up to plastic tubing looking peaky.

"You won't play Lady Godiva for anything," he had challenged.

To which I said, "You're right. I'm a real lady."

"Oh, sure you are," he'd drawled back, wiggling his eyebrows.

The curtains in Maylene's beauty parlor twitched, bringing me back to the present. The blush started at my clavicle, burned its way up my bare neck, my face, and then settled at my ears. All I wanted was to lay low and head for France before the holidays engulfed me.

I decided to stroll down to the drug store instead and pick up a bottle of eyedrops. Since the funeral, my eyes had been nothing but red and swollen. It is one thing to shake all those hands and get a sore jaw from smiling—it is another to sleep next to a cold spot.

Not that I had time to dwell on it, especially right then. The mayor's wife, her face pliable as iron, came barreling toward me. Behind Charlene's broad derrière were her look-a-like daughters wearing the same pinched-nose expression. Raylene and Kaylene might have been fifteen, but they already had their mother's attitude down pat.

I smiled so hard my eyes crinkled. Charlene Higgenbottom bobbed her head like Miss Wilderness Road, back in the day. Lord knows she still does the Queen of England wave when riding in the Christmas parade.

"Mornin', Miss Charlene," I drawled, nice and

sweet as my heart went rat-a-tat in my chest.

"Why, Miss Delilah. I didn't think ah'd see you this soon." Her chin ratcheted up then she looked down her nose from her too close eyes. "I mean, this early in the mornin'."

"Taking my constitutional," I replied, still walking. Her hand reached out and clutched my arm. My breath caught in my throat.

Charlene tilted an eyebrow. "We were sorry to miss Mr. Morgan's service." Her voice was as tight as my dress.

"Thank you," I said in my quiet Sunday voice. I didn't really know what else to say, being the widow and all. I am not good with small talk, so I started to move along when her fingers clamped down a tad tighter.

"I heard it was a lovely service." Her eyes narrowed.

"Yes," I said. "Senator MacPhearson came in from Washington for the eulogy." I stared back at her. "The governor, of course, spoke as well." I kept my voice cool as iced watermelon even though my hands were perspiring from the tension.

It had been quite a gathering, what with the mayor's absence a deliberate thumb-your-nose at his political opponent. Harry's letters to the editor curled Mayor Higgenbottom's toes. Harry had a way with words, which was why he won that literature prize, the one for poets.

Harry preferred, however, to farm. When we moved to teach at the college, he turned our yard into a garden with fruit, vegetables, and whatever else caught his fancy. It suited him, his hands feeling the dirt. He'd go to classes with it rubbed into the thighs of his chinos like he was a hired man. I kept his shirts ironed and starched though. From the waist up, he looked natty.

Footsteps behind Charlene and me sounded like the slap of wipers on a car window. Leather soles if I'd ever heard them. I turned back to see who was walking up, even though I felt certain the leather belonged to Judge Henderson. Loafers, Italian and expensive.

"Mornin', Miss Charlene, Miss Delilah." His voice sounded like chocolate mousse in crystal.

Judge Lyle Henderson's expression looked like he'd died and gone to heaven. He grinned for land's sakes, but his face had turned beet red as if he'd run a mile. Didn't make sense, the man being a long-distance runner and all.

Since he *is* the local Cary Grant with his suntan, shiny eyes, and chin dimple, Charlene Higgenbottom's bosom puffed up, reminding me of Harry's prize-winning chickens, the ones our neighbors complained about.

Wouldn't you know our neighbor was none other than the mayor's fussy sister? Eventually Higgenbottom had a new ordinance drawn. Police came with a warrant and practically arrested those Bantams. Then Harry started writing poems about the whole thing. That was what won the Pulitzer, his poems about the legal hassles with his birds.

"Would you excuse us, Charlene?" The judge removed Charlene's tentacles from my arm.

I rubbed where her fingers had left a mark, glad no one could see my eyes, which had gone squinty. She was right to grab ahold of me because I was about to take off at a gallop. The judge kept my other hand in his. We eased down the street. I don't know what came over me, but I went as docile as a lamb.

"I've been meaning to have a chat with you." He spoke in a baritone that gave most women palpitations.

"About?" I knew good and well I had not returned his five phone calls.

"Your promise."

"Oh." I swallowed, buying time.

"There is a bet between Harry and the mayor." He

stared intently into my eyes. "I hold the wager. Harry said that if you'd walk down the street in your beautiful summer dress the mayor would have to erect a statue. You won the moment you stepped out of the door. So now Harry's monument to those chickens of his goes up in the town square with Mayor Higgenbottom breaking the champagne bottle."

I would have clapped my hands, except he was locked onto one of them.

"And you, Miss Delilah, are having brunch with me." I eased my hand away because I didn't like the sound of that.

"I don't think Harry would approve."

"I have it in writing." The judge touched the place above his heart. "A poem, in Harry's hand."

Judge Henderson alarmed me because he was holding a poem by Harry I hadn't seen. I wasn't about to play tug-of-war in front of Toliver's hardware with Big Ike Mitchell lounging on the bench by the sidewalk. I walked sedately. The judge slowed down so I could maneuver in the floozy dress.

By 9:30 we walked into the Chicken Coop Diner. It was the place to eat if you went to town. I hesitated at the entrance, but the judge put a hand on my back, gently shoving me through the door.

Chapter Two

BETHANN TATE LOOKED UP FROM POURING Sheriff Bellows' coffee. Her eyes widened as if she saw that actor who once ran naked through the town sprinting by all over again. She spilled the rest of the fresh roasted coffee all over the counter. Heads turned. The judge kept moving with me right beside him.

"Lovely day," he said in his courtroom voice as he waved to the patrons. "Good to see you, Tom . . . Eddie . . . Doc." He walked me past the large ceramic rooster by the cash register, then along the red Formica counter.

The Chicken Coop had a country motif—chicken wire, oil paintings of chickens with Harry's poems interspersed, all tastefully hung. At The Coop, they served breakfast and lunch, their specialty being the best fried chicken in four counties. My stomach rumbled with hunger. I'd been so nervous about the stroll I had forgotten to eat my Raisin Bran.

The judge parked me genteelly into a booth far from anyone else. It was his and Harry's favorite. He leaned over the slick red Formica and whispered, "This was the first place on Harry's list." The judge looked like a man too pleased with himself.

"What?"

"Ah." His blue eyes closed briefly. When they opened, his lips turned up looking sneaky. "You don't know, do you?"

"Know what?" I slid my sunglasses down to the bridge of my nose, puckering my brow with suspicion.

"Harry made a list of where I was to take you on our dates."

"We are not dating," I almost shouted, then covered my lips with a hand, which I finally untangled from his. I plopped my glasses onto the table leaning closer to him. "Let's get a few things straight. I only came in here to get out of the sun."

Which wasn't the whole truth, nothing but the truth, so help me God. I went in because I couldn't bear the thought of going past Inman's furniture store. I perspired just thinking about it. I fanned myself with the red-checked paper napkin, making the silverware clink and clatter on the table.

Earl Inman had shown up at Harry's service in a somber gray suit with a flamingo pink shirt. Who wore such a thing to a funeral? In the reception line his eyes wandered over me, first high then low. I stomped on his toes hard, then watched him limp off. His eyes stayed glued on me, however, until the preacher escorted him out the door.

BethAnn sashayed over, her hips moving like a gyroscope. BethAnn had the weathered face and calloused fingers of someone who knew the word "work" up close. With a stainless-steel pot in one hand, two mugs in the other, and the menus under her elbow, she looked a mite burdened.

She winked at me as she slid the red with black menus across the table. Staring up from the cover was a parade of chickens—big and little chickens crawled across the front and each page—ending with the large one on the backside. Once a month the town council met for lunch in the back room, where the mayor paged through a menu. Harry had found it satisfying.

"Coffee?" she asked, as if we were anybody else but a famous judge and a poet's widow.

"Yes, thank you." I used the voice Harry had always called overly polite.

BethAnn leisurely positioned the white mugs with a rooster's silhouette on the table. She poured the coffee in a thin waterfall. Her feet were planted, ears cocked.

"Miss Delilah, what is your pleasure?" Judge Henderson canted his head left and curved his lips.

"One eggs benedict with homemade hollandaise

will suit me fine."

My mouth almost watered in anticipation. Carter MacDougal, the owner/chef at the Chicken Coop, knew his sauces. And sauces were my downfall. I'd offered to pay Carter for a lesson or two, but he always made excuses. Nothing I said could manipulate Carter into letting me into his kitchen sanctuary. Instead I came in once a month for breakfast.

On a slow Wednesday a couple of years back, Carter stood with a hand on his left hip and waggled his stirring spoon my direction. "You wouldn't be coming in here for my fancy hollandaise and béarnaise sauces if'n you could fix them yourself," he'd said.

I'd laughed until I saw Charlene and Mayor Higgenbottom. The mayor had laid down a miserly tip, right in front of the poster from his missionary sister-in-law begging for money. Carter studied the handful of coins spinning on the counter by the register then let his down-turned lips do his talking. You could feel the heat building and it wasn't from the fryer. The Higgenbottoms were within earshot, which Carter noted with a tight smile.

"You brighten up the place, Miss Delilah," he went on. "And Lord knows this town needs a little lightening up and generosity." His comments and stiff stare at the mayor's miserly tip didn't endear me to the Higgenbottoms and that was a fact.

I chewed on my lip at the memory as BethAnn extracted a pencil out of her apron and pulled a pad from her breast pocket to write our order. She wore her red gingham uniform with black banded short sleeves as though she'd starched it that morning. She wasn't stiff or formal though, only her uniform. I reckon she was lonely, living out on the farm after her man passed from liver disease. Maybe for therapy she took her time ironing, heavy on the spray starch.

"The eggs benedict comes with fruit on the side and fried potatoes," BethAnn said in her heavy drawl, interrupting my imagination. She hailed from

Mississippi. Her words sounded dark-chocolate decadent.

"The fruit and a coffee," I added in my mountain twang. "Hold the potatoes."

Mama always said fried food made your brains sluggish. I didn't need extra calories, either. Especially since I planned to devour that hollandaise sauce. And what with sitting around for months jabbering with strangers wearing white uniforms while Harry eased out of this life, things had gotten a little snug.

BethAnn nodded then slid her hips over toward the judge. Sort of like she was doing the hula.

"And what can I do for you, Judge Henderson?" she asked, in a voice that—in my thinking–wasn't referring to the food.

Judge Henderson kept his gaze on the menu and said he'd have two eggs over easy, whole wheat toast, and a small glass of orange juice. "You can throw in Miss Delilah's fried potatoes too," he added.

"You get them as well." BethAnn's voice went all breathy.

"Well, double it, then. I'm running in the half-marathon in Louisville soon."

Which I knew was a lie, since he'd done it in May. Not that I was surprised. Lawyers are paid to lie.

BethAnn patted her blonde bun, then poked the pencil behind her ear. "Oh," she exclaimed, as she backed away from the table. The judge flustered BethAnn, who managed the sheriff, the mayor, and assorted dignitaries with ease.

"Hmm." I glanced at the judge. "I thought the half-marathon was run before June."

"I enjoy fried potatoes," he said with a grin. "I'm going to take yours home in a doggy bag and have them tomorrow."

I knew he did all of his own cooking because over the years his two boys had complained about the concoctions they had to eat. I'd thought they were finagling for dinner. I'd set two, sometimes three extra places, then give the judge's secretary a call.

We were finishing breakfast when Madison, the FBI special agent from Lexington, came in. I recognized him because he showed up on a case that made national news, the kidnapping of the sheik's race horse. Although I'm not sure if it's a kidnapping when the victim is a horse. Perhaps we should call it horse-napping.

Madison plopped on a stool beside the sheriff still sitting at the counter and they had quite a conversation, their head-bobbing similar to those plastic dolls people put on their car dashboards. In a few minutes, both put down their coffee mugs then aimed their eyes our direction. I could see them plain because I was facing the front of the diner. The judge's eyes were elsewhere. It made me think something wasn't right, but the judge was in such a nostalgic mood, I didn't point out their interest. They slid out of their seats, paid the bill, and left in a hurry, heading toward the court house.

After breakfast we stopped to pick up eye drops at the pharmacy, which was the farthest distance in my promise to Harry. I took my change, then reached for my eye drops. The judge tucked them into his pocket and extended an elbow for me to grab.

"I'll walk you home," he said.

I grabbed a deep breath. So much for home lickety-split. He paraded me down Main Street.

"If we scoot along Harrison then meander down Dunkin's Alley, we will miss the traffic." I hoped to avoid extra encounters with my neighbors.

"Head up, eyes front." He grinned. I suspect he took my hand again to keep me from bolting.

"When do I get to see Harry's poem?" I asked as we turned the corner to Washington again.

"I'll show you his letters and the poem when it's appropriate."

"And you decide the *when*, I gather?" I was a little steamed, my voice edgy.

"No, Harry has dates on them," he said quietly. "That's when I'm to show them to you."

Well, that shut me up nice and proper.

We walked along the sidewalk past the ice cream parlor near the college. Even a fake fruity ice cream cone painted in soft pink and brown looked inviting.

"Not yet," said the judge as he watched me study the lettering on the poster. "We will stop on our second date."

The man sure talked presumptuous. I wanted to straighten out a thing or two, but our conversation wasn't for public consumption. I needed to wait until we were in a more private place. In some sophisticated city, I could invite the judge into the house to have a talk. Heaven knows in our small town I couldn't, especially with my widow status.

Half a block later we found ourselves amid the venerable brick and mortar of Boone College. The first house on our right was the president's, Federalist in design and surrounded by large floral gardens terraced up the hillside. The president's wife, Mrs. Benson, kneeled amongst her David Austin imports. She saw us, waved her clippers, then eased onto her feet. The house was on a slight rise and she was aiming to walk over the berm instead of down the drive.

"Uh-oh," I murmured.

"Courage," said the judge.

He walked over, offering his arm to stabilize her scrawny little legs. It was a gallant gesture, the knight waiting on the queen herself.

Mrs. Benson dimpled up. The judge didn't squire around women like a playboy, but he knew how to treat a lady and Mrs. Benson was a lady who hailed all the way from Charlotte, North Carolina.

We got along fine too. But she was a sympathetic person, all wrap-arms-around-then-pat-your-back.

In parting Mrs. Benson pecked me on both cheeks. I saw the judge turn away and blow his nose on the handkerchief from his pocket. She walked back to her roses, the judge playing escort. He skirted down the hillside around the cabbage roses and we took off, aiming toward the shade trees along the sidewalk.

We only had to go around the corner, then the three blocks to my drive. Maybe I could make it that far. It wasn't only that my feet were throbbing from the sling back heels, it was the emotions blendering around like berries for a fruit smoothie.

The judge and I talked about the kids, his two and my four. I managed not to bring up the covert interest the sheriff and the FBI special agent had shown earlier in the judge.

Dogs are an essential conversation topic in our neck of the woods, so I broached it. Everyone knew the judge loved dogs and that he had a new puppy. This time his dog was what Harry called a lady's dog, a fuzzy Shih Tzu.

"How're you doing with the dog training?" I asked as our feet concussed the cement.

"Bartles is an exceptional dog." His chest swelled. "He rings a bell to tell me it's time to do his duty."

I laughed. "What a relief to laugh after the crazy morning. Since Harry's death my emotions are in lock down." Only time I remembered laughing over the past few weeks had been with my young grandson Austin. "Funny name for a dog."

"I always wanted an English butler. This is as close as I can get." The judge swung his jacket over his shoulder, holding it with two fingers as if it were air.

I limped from my unaccustomed hike in party shoes. I hadn't wiggled into pantyhose, so I stepped out of my shoes. Good thing the trees kept the sidewalk shaded so my feet didn't burn. Only a fool wore pantyhose on a ninety-degree day with the air so thick moisture drooled down the back. The judge smiled at my orange polished nails and we went on, me skirting the sticks on the sidewalk, the judge still talking about his dog.

Next door to my Queen Anne Victorian, George

Salas sprawled in his lounge chair wearing little else but an undershirt, Bermuda shorts, and a pair of flip flops. The garden hose in his hand spurted out water in a casual arc. You'd think George would have something else to do than sit for hours letting water squirt out in the yard. Twenty minutes in one spot suited him. I'd timed his rotation one day while sitting and watching Harry breathe.

George waggled his hose at us. We waved back dodging the water drops plopping on the sidewalk near our feet. George gave us another wave, this time aiming the hose toward his house when his wife Mamie stepped onto the verandah. I don't think he saw her, but she got a face full of cold water. She hollered loud as a contrary bull then scooted back indoors before he could do more damage.

Chapter Three

WE ROUNDED THE CURVED PART OF my drive and there was Olive Patrick's Cadillac parked sassily in front of my carriage house.

"Well, I can imagine what Olive Lorraine wants," I huffed.

The judge raised his eyebrows.

Olive Lorraine Patrick, along with her husband Neely, owned Patrick and Patrick Real Estate company down by the Jiffy Lube. Not a great location but they owned the block. Anyway, she wasn't here to commiserate on my losing Harry. She'd said all she needed to say at the funeral buffet when she handed me her card declaring she would call when things settled down.

She wasn't in the car, which meant she'd wormed her way into the house. I should have told Josephine to bar the door. Hadn't thought much about Olive Lorraine's threat to visit. Woman hadn't darkened the door of our house since we'd come to town.

The judge's eyes were glimmering like he knew something I didn't.

"Okay, what?"

"It appears you have a visitor." He patted my hand like I was a half-wit. "Thank you for your company, Miss Delilah." If he'd had on a hat, I do believe he would have tipped it.

I clutched his arm as tightly as Charlene Higgenbottom had glommed onto mine. "Oh, no you don't." I dragged him up the stairs. "One good deed deserves another, and you're not deserting me now."

"So be it." The judge laughed. The man's laugh made you want to join him, dad-rat it.

I put my high heels back on before I crossed the verandah. I wasn't going to be caught dead walking around barefoot in front of Olive Lorraine, even if it was my house.

"Josephine," I bellowed from the foyer. The house was silent, not a footfall.

Now, I have a big house. Three stories, not counting the basement which we turned into a billiards room, to state it fancy. Over the years the neighborhood kids took up residency down there. The Salas kids and the judge's two boys were some of the occupiers, so the judge knew our house from top to bottom, but he lounged by the Chippendale sideboard crossing his arms all comfortable.

"Well, do something."

"I think I'll find some lemonade. Josephine always has a pitcher in the Sub Zero." He ambled off while I went in search of my unwelcome guest and Josephine, my housekeeper.

Josephine, our permanent house fixture, appeared when I was down after the twins came too early. They hadn't even taken a breath before they were in the arms of Jesus. Because they said I almost "expired" from the hemorrhage, Harry wouldn't let me lift a finger and hired a nurse. The nurses he hired got cranky when the kids ran, or hopped, or generally were children, causing our four to tiptoe around the house like thieves. I fired the first two then sat in bed like a princess.

Into the shuttered windows and gloom of my bedroom walked Josephine. It was my second week home. She took one look at me and said, "Mmm-hmm. You are the sorriest sight I've ever seen."

That took some gall, Josephine being hired to be sympathetic. I sat up in our big four-poster and crossed my arms. "They say it's a miracle I'm alive. And *Mr.* Morgan says I'm to rest."

She stood on the Kurdistan rug and waggled her head side to side. "Got to admit, you so pale I swear you crawled out from under a rock."

I raised my eyebrows.

"I say, move your sorry behind out of that bed and get a shower," her voice boomed. "Mothers don't have time to mope around feelin' sorry for theirselves. They's got children to care for." She marched right up to the bed. Her mahogany-hued fingers began to strip it while I was still entangled in the sheets and trying to get my bosom covered because she was a stranger.

She was as right as August rain, of course. We hit it off then and there. She's been an institution here ever since. It'd take an A-bomb to dislodge her.

I glanced left then right in my front hall. Josephine had evaporated. I figured she was tracking Olive Lorraine and counting the silver. Olive Lorraine wasn't someone you let mosey through your house. She's got a calculator for a brain. You could detect it in her picture on the billboard near the bypass. Daddy always said to look in people's eyes and you can see their heart—hers was parsimonious. Living with a poet I've learned a word or two.

On the second floor in the hallway leading to the conservatory, I found Olive Lorraine peering at a painting of thoroughbreds at pasture near Versailles. Her glasses were perched on her nose as she tried to read the signature.

Josephine sighted me and shrugged. I narrowed my eyes at her, giving her my best no nonsense look. The least she could do was appear sorry, but no, she looked gleeful. Her pearly white teeth glimmered in the light from the chandelier. She took a step back and began to walk away.

"Chicken," I mouthed. She grinned but continued to the back staircase.

Olive Lorraine was transfixed by one of my sister Suzanne's best oils. I cleared my throat. Olive Lorraine straightened up right smart, turning the color of a pickled beet.

"You have some very expensive paintings in the house." Her pale blue eyes were wide open, as if she were astonished. "I didn't know Mr. Morgan had such fine taste."

Was she disappointed the paintings weren't barnyards with chickens? We didn't have renditions of chickens in the house. Chickens were Harry's aberration. His poetry was mostly about the land and people. Harry loved to get his hands in the soil, and he wrapped words around the experience.

"He did. Do you want a house tour before you leave?"

"Well, I-er-had Josephine take me around a little." She waved her hand in the air to indicate she'd spied through all the rooms. Her metal bracelets clinked together so hard they made an echoey sound in the long hall. "I didn't know you quilted." Her high-pitched voice grated on my ear. "The wedding ring quilt is very . . . colorful."

That meant she'd been on the third floor. Good. Maybe she hadn't wandered around Harry's library. She didn't stop long for breath.

"You still make your own clothes too." There was a sneer in her words.

I made the flowered dresses I wore to church. Can't get a good fit on a simple cotton dress unless you go to Paris and have some fancy seamstress whip one up.

"Nice hobby, sewing," she pressed through the silence. "Josephine took me around the first floor, as well. And I've never seen a table like the one in your dining room. She said it came from Brittany. That's in France, isn't it? It looks quite elegant."

My lips tightened around the edges. "Then if you've toured the entire first floor, you must have been in Harry's library." Anger made my voice rise. The library had been where Harry died, and although not a shrine, I felt it was where I could best talk to him when I prowled around the house at night.

"Yes. I saw his newest book with the embossed leather cover. Now that he's dead, I'm sure it will be a best-seller."

Tact wasn't part of Olive Lorraine's persona.

My throat contracted. "Usually that's what happens," I managed, holding up my end of our conversation. "A poet dies, and everyone wants a little bit of something to remember him by." I sounded hoarse talking around the bulge climbing up my throat past my vocal cords. I wanted to grab her arm and haul her down the staircase.

"You have several paintings by this artist." She pointed to the painting, ignoring the watering in my eyes.

"Yes. We admire her work." I used my polished voice rather than the musical rhythm of Horsetail Falls where I grew up.

I am self-conscious about my Eastern Kentucky accent, but the way I spoke never bothered Harry. He always told me that he was my mirror, and when I felt awkward, to look at him. So, I would. All I could see was love when I looked at him. It was a comfort.

"They must be worth a fortune." She drew her purse up to her chest as if protecting her cash.

"Probably. Suzanne Burns sells in galleries in New York and D.C."

"Oh," said Olive Lorraine. Her eyes caressed my armoire next to the painting. "You have some unusual things. I didn't expect to see French antiques. Since Mr. Morgan preferred farming, I thought it would be more . . . country." She looked puzzled. "I can't find a chicken anywhere."

"No," I stated dryly. "They were evicted." That momentarily silenced her. "I've a pitcher of lemonade in the kitchen. Why don't we find a glass before you . . . leave?" I didn't want to be rude to Harry's old sweetheart. What would he think if I threw her to the curb?

I couldn't have been more direct, but the woman seemed epoxied to the floor. Extracting Olive Lorraine was going to be a problem. She kept pausing to study a painting or running a finger over a piece of furniture.

Where was the judge? I didn't bring him in to play hide and seek.

Spying the 1752 English Highboy in our bedroom she crossed the threshold. I jumped in front of her.

"Sorry," I said firmly. "I haven't changed the sheets." I didn't move, so she backed out the door.

The bedroom I shared with Harry was private with a capital P. I wasn't going to let Miss Snoop go any further. Didn't she realize she was intruding? Or was it all natural, this poking into others' lives? She should have been a surgeon and cut off appendages willy-nilly. An arm here, a leg there. Did it matter to her if she was dissecting my life with Harry?

We were walking down the "grand staircase," as Harry called it, when she stopped on the landing and looked out the hexagonal window to my rose garden. I did have flowers amid all of Harry's tomatoes. I could see her counting them, her irises moving back and forth as if she were watching ping pong.

"There are sixty-three grandifloras and floribundas, twelve climbers on the trellises and pergola with three dozen miniatures scattered about," I said, my voice flat. I was getting tired of being polite.

Her mouth formed an O. I'll bet she thought I'd drawl, "That un's pink, this'n red." I pulled a mayor's wife friendly move, sliding my arm through hers to keep her walking.

"The water ponds have koi, because Harry loved to see the fish dodging the water lily leaves. If the raccoons or hawks didn't get them, they'd grow until they were too big for the ponds, so we carted them over to the Louisville Zoo. Are you wanting an inventory, Olive Lorraine?" At least she feigned surprise. I learned that word from one of Harry's students.

"I came, really"—her words took off at a gallop—"to offer my sympathy. Such a big house to wander around in all alone." She spoke that last word as if it had five syllables.

"We fill up when the children are here."

The judge came out of the parlor looking mighty pleased with himself.

Olive Lorraine lifted her chin and gave him a coy smile. "Morning, Your Honor," she said all whispery.

"Good morning, Olive." He dipped his head like a nineteenth-century gallant.

A wickedness came over me. I tried to stop the words from sneaking past my throat lump, but they popped out anyway. "I'm thinking of renting out rooms like a boarding house." I said the words loud enough to see both their reactions. I could tell Lyle got my joke from the smirk that flitted across his face.

She staggered, knees buckling, but I held onto her, keeping her upright. The judge lifted his lemonade glass in a salute. He was no help at all. I should have let him swelter all the way back to the courthouse.

"The upkeep on a house this size must be monumental," Olive Lorraine rallied. "Sometimes it's best to consider the economics. Without Harry's income, however will you manage?"

"Harry always quoted the man who said, 'Live like nobody else when you're young so you can live like nobody else when you're old.'"

I'd let her figure it out. We bought everything with cash, which was none of her business.

We were almost on the last step when the grandfather clock in the hall chimed 11:00. Mercy me, Mademoiselle Bousquet, my French tutor, was due in ten minutes. My heart rate settled into first gear.

"Judge Henderson." Olive Lorraine stepped onto the yellow pine flooring. "What brings you to Mrs. Morgan's doorstep?"

"Lemonade." The judge raised his glass. "Josephine has been supplying me for years." His fried potato bag was missing. I had the awful feeling he would be here for breakfast tomorrow and Josephine was going to heat them up for him. He craved her onions, cheese, and bacon mixed in with fried potatoes. He'd said so last Saturday night when he was over digging in the sandbox with my grandson, Austin.

The judge sauntered toward us from the doorway, towering over Olive Lorraine's five-foot roundish figure. He paused for her interrogation to continue. He was enjoying himself.

"I was saying to Mrs. Morgan, a house this size is really for a family. Much too large for only one person."

"Like mine?" The judge's baritone was almost a growl.

Olive Lorraine dismissively waved her hand in the air. "I've been telling you, I'm ready when you are."

Why would a happily married woman flirt? Not certain if this was about selling his house or batting her eyelashes, I grabbed her hand trying to keep her moving.

"So nice of you to come to comfort Mrs. Morgan," Judge Lyle Henderson said while I was fumbling to get her out the door. "I believe she will call you when she decides about finding renters. I imagine lively college students would be a blessing to a widow lady like Mrs. Morgan."

Olive Lorraine opened her mouth then shut it quickly.

He outmaneuvered her as he opened the front door and walked her down the steps.

I cut and ran for the kitchen to find Josephine. I was practicing my speech when I passed the butler's pantry. She stood, humming a gospel song, surrounded by the casserole dishes that kept coming like unwanted mosquitoes. We were both in the choir and knew the soprano and alto parts. If I hadn't been so cheesed off, I would have joined with, "You and me sister."

But I didn't. I tapped one Jimmy Choo shoe.

Josephine shook her head. "I didn't think Miss Real Estate would take up residence, so I didn't rescue you. I've fried chicken for lunch. The judge said to set an extra place. Think I'll invite Sidney when he's through watering Mr. Harry's zucchini. Odd number at a table is bad luck." She patted the backside of the only chicken in the house, a colorful ceramic rooster that stood about three-feet-tall.

Josephine didn't believe in bad luck any more than I. She filled the air with words getting me flustered. She wasn't going to worm her way out of inviting the judge to lunch, no sir. Erecting barricades to keep out intruders suddenly seemed a good idea. Next thing I know Olive Lorraine will be pushing that little wheely thing around the yard to get the dimensions of the house.

I stared at the driveway from the kitchen window and watched Olive Lorraine slide into her freshly waxed Cadillac. The judge waited until she backed out toward the street before he returned. I'd have to get rid of him too. I didn't want him to find out about Mademoiselle Bousquet and my French lessons.

"Well, thank you, Judge." I came up beside him. "I imagine you want to gather up your fried potatoes before you return to the courthouse. All those criminals must need sentencing."

"I've taken a leave of absence until January." A tiny green line circled his blue irises. I could see it distinctly. I was five-foot seven without heels, and with heels, a stork-like five-ten. We were standing three inches apart. I stared into his baby blues and waited. I'd known the man for twenty years. Something was on his mind. I could see it cogitating behind his turned-up lips. The doorbell reverberated down the hallway and into the kitchen where we were standing. I stood rooted by the Sub Zero.

"Don't you think you should let Mademoiselle Bousquet in for your French conversation?" The judge pointed toward the door.

I glared at Josephine. She shrugged her shoulders.

"I suppose so. How did you know about my lessons?"

"Fairly obvious, since there are French books in the parlor, French audio tapes by the stereo, and she walks down the sidewalk on Tuesdays and Thursdays and stays until one."

I squinted my eyes. "You seem mighty interested in the comings and goings of my household."

The judge's lips twitched. "You might say your comings and goings are the talk of the neighborhood."

Chapter Four

Life was getting messy. I answered the door with the judge trotting along with me, his eyes all scrunched up with laughter. He was wrong about the caller. It was the special agent and Sheriff Bellows.

They were holding their hands in front of themselves, in what Harry called the fig leaf. They looked mighty uncomfortable, so I knew it wasn't good news.

"Judge," said Special Agent Madison. "We need to talk to you. In private."

The judge opened the door wider. "Mrs. Morgan, would you mind giving us your parlor for a visit?"

I nodded and backed away. The judge grabbed hold of my hand and tucked it into his.

"Josephine," he hollered toward the back of the house. "We're needing glasses of lemonade in the parlor." His baritone was robust enough for any gathering.

"I'll go get the pitcher." I steamed at his presumption.

"Not on your life, Mrs. Morgan," whispered the judge. He ushered the two law enforcement gentlemen into my green and pink living room.

The pair halted in front of the fireplace. Their heads moved upward to look at a painting. Another one of my sister's canvases was parked above the mantle. On it were eight horses leaving the starting gate at Keeneland. This particular one was an oil that had won a prize in France. When Harry admired it, she gave it to him.

He wrote her a poem.

They called it even.

I could hear Josephine coming down the hall pushing the squeaky tea cart. As she aimed toward the parlor entrance, she hung on, steering it firmly as the cart veered to the right. Josephine had placed a pitcher of lemonade, a plate of icebox cookies, and five glasses on the wicker top. She parked the wheeled cart in front of me—I sat on the divan beside the judge—then she settled in the wing chair. If the sheriff was surprised, he didn't show it. Everyone in town knew Josephine was family.

We went through the charade of politeness, showing law enforcement where to sit, then drinking our lemonade and passing the cookie plate before the FBI special agent cleared his throat.

"Judge, did you ever hear from your wife after she left town?" The sheriff smoothed his uniform pants crease on his knee.

The judge shook his head, no.

"Did she write to the boys or have her alimony sent somewhere?" The sheriff looked puzzled.

Again, the judge shook his head.

This was old territory. Clarisse ran off with a smarmy obstetrician years ago. No one had heard from her since. Not her parents, brother, or her children. Not surprising she wouldn't contact the judge, except for more money. She'd tried every which-a-way to get cash before she vacated.

It happened so long ago you'd think I'd forgotten that October morning. The day she left I heard the tires of her Stingray squeal out of the drive about 9:00, peeling down the street with teenage recklessness toward town. I remember thinking she wasn't dressed for the gym where she usually spent her mornings.

At that time, Harry and Lyle Henderson had coffee in Carter's old diner before it became the Coop. That's where they were, seated across from one another in the crunchy yellow seats when the bank manager came panting in like he'd completed a marathon. He stammered to the judge that his wife was at the bank cleaning out his safety deposit box.

Harry said the judge looked as surprised as a

monk at his first revival meeting. At that point, Harry stood up and walked out, while the two other men continued a whispered conversation.

Harry said it didn't take two and two to figure out the missus was on the lam and going to bankrupt the judge. Who, of course, wasn't a judge at the time. He was a defense lawyer. Harry trotted right over to the BG&T Bank and waylaid Clarisse as she came out of the vault. She had a giant purse and a duffle bag full of the judge's grandmother's silver service, stock certificates, and the antique jewelry passed down through the judge's family since before the Civil War.

Harry stopped beside her and offered to carry her heavy bag. Instead of handing over her loot she thumped the bag on the floor by the teller and demanded a withdrawal slip. Harry leaned on the counter and started to talk about the classes he was teaching. The teller worked in slow motion. Harry kept talking. After ten minutes, the judge appeared.

The judge was all cool and calm, Harry reported to me later. He asked Clarisse what she was doing. She said she was going shopping. The judge peered into the bag then took the withdrawal slip she had scrawled on, looking it over as if it were evidence. He tore it into tiny pieces. He pulled out his check book and filled out a check. A crowd gathered and the bank manager herded everyone to other tellers.

After handing the teller the withdrawal slip, the judge picked up the duffle and carried it back to the entrance of the vault. Clarisse's eyes were glued on the money the teller counted out in crisp one-hundred-dollar bills.

When the judge returned, he invited Clarisse to come to the bank manager's office. She didn't have much choice, seeing Harry and Lyle were her escort. There was a lot of yelling. She stormed out all red-faced but kept hanging onto her big purse and the money the judge had given her. By the time Lyle and she got to that hot red Stingray of hers, the bank manager stood leaning on the driver's side door. Clarisse almost hit him with her purse.

Without a word the judge took the car keys from her hand and opened the passenger door. She slid in. Harry's recounting of the bank scenario made sense because the rest of it took place before my eyes.

I was raking leaves when the Henderson car pulled up in the drive across the street. Clarisse was screeching before the door opened. It was embarrassing, the words hurled his direction. His face was set like thunder, but he opened her door and let her march into their brick Federal. He followed. Pretty soon I saw clothes thrown out of an upstairs window.

It was colorful, all her lingerie blanketing the boxwoods. That was all the judge tossed out, her underthings. I tried to skedaddle into the house so I wouldn't embarrass them when she slammed the front door yelling, "I'm *never* coming back. And you can keep the boys. I wanted girls and you know who is responsible for their sex."

I turned hot around my neck when I had to tell the FBI special agent that when he interviewed me. I wouldn't have gotten involved if Clarisse hadn't taken off with a doctor the Feds were investigating for Medicaid fraud.

I didn't like it that Special Agent Madison was back after so many years, quizzing the judge in my parlor. The FBI special agent leaned forward, clasping his hands between his knees. "There has been a discovery concerning your ex-wife." Madison let the words agitate in the air for several seconds. "Our report states she drove off with Dr. Dwight Timmons, the gynecologist. She picked him up at his office at 10:20 a.m., October fifteenth. Seems no one has heard from her or him in the past eighteen years."

"You know the reservoir out Paducah way?" Sheriff

Bellows slid in. Judge Lyle Henderson nodded slowly. "Been a lean rain year. It's down a bit. Islands are appearing in the middle of the low water, with, of course, tree stumps poking up to confound boaters." Bellows, a natural storyteller eased into his news. "Well, yesterday they were dredging out the channel and up come a car. License plate still attached, you see."

The sheriff took a big pull from his lemonade. The judge didn't say a word, but he chewed his back molars.

"There were two bodies inside," the FBI agent said. "Skeletons actually. From the pictures of the skulls, it looks as if both were shot in the head."

The judge blinked.

"We are thinking it might be Clarisse and the doc."

I gasped, my heart pounding like a mallet flattening chicken fried steak.

"We won't know real soon because forensics takes its sweet time." If they were suspecting the judge of nefarious activities, they weren't letting on.

The judge fingered his empty glass and looked at the table. "I see."

Josephine didn't waste a beat. She rose up nice and tall. Her dark face was a mask hiding her emotions. "If that's all you gentlemen have to share, I'll be escorting you out the door. Judge Henderson here needs a moment to think on your news."

Realizing they'd been dismissed, they stood as if they were attached at the hips and thanked her for the lemonade. We got up as well and walked them to the door. I thought they'd invite the judge down to the station, haul him in, to do an interrogation. The judge being a court officer perhaps made them cautious.

We didn't say anything when they left. Josephine tidied up while Judge Henderson and I stood together in the foyer like mutes. The thought that he'd have to tell the boys before news hit the airwaves hung heavy.

The law did the do-si-do in the driveway to turn

their vehicle around, and I spied Mademoiselle Bousquet dodging the car by jumping over the boxwoods onto the lawn. Good thing I trimmed them in May, or she would have been high-centered.

The judge seemed lost in thought. I didn't interrupt his cogitating when I opened the front door to welcome my newest guest. Mademoiselle Bousquet stood in the sunlight allowing the rays to make her golden hair shimmer. She almost purred when the judge greeted her in French and kissed her on both cheeks. He took Mademoiselle Bousquet's hand in his and escorted her into the parlor. The man was turning out to be a dancing partner for all my guests.

"I didn't know you spoke French." I lifted an eyebrow.

"I spent a year in France courtesy of the US Navy before I went to law school." His eyes remained on my pretty visitor. "I was stationed in the south and spent my time wandering the countryside on my bicycle."

I could picture him in shorts and a T-shirt peddling through the vineyards and kissing all the dark-haired French girls.

Mademoiselle and the judge continued with a conversation I struggled to follow. I *think* they were discussing her classes. Mademoiselle and I usually talked about furniture or food, things I could point to. "'*Le stylo est sur la table,*'" I had down.

Maybe *they* should be dating. He wouldn't have bought a dog if he wasn't lonely. That would leave me to grieve properly. Of course, I could *help* their romance. I'd matched up more than one couple and things seemed mighty fine in the matrimony department.

Mademoiselle settled on my divan and lifted her limpid gray eyes to his. The look on Mademoiselle Bousquet's face was embarrassing. No woman should drool over a man. She looked as if she needed to blot her lips.

Let me be honest here, the judge has an effect on

women. They swoon. From the looks of things, Mademoiselle Bousquet was part of his fan base. She was too young for him, being thirty, but heaven knows older men seem to prefer younger women.

Judge Henderson never had *any* effect on me while Harry was alive, even though he practically lived here while Harry was casting his gaze heavenward. Since we got Harry's diagnosis of pancreatic cancer, the judge would come over after supper a couple of nights a week and settle over the Scrabble board with Harry. When I could no longer support Harry's weight without struggling, the judge began coming over every night and helping Harry get into bed. Guess that is what friends are for, helping us totter to the bathroom when we're on the lean side of this earth.

I started to well up again and the judge, who was perched on my big wing chair, reached into his pants pocket and extracted a freshly ironed hanky. I shook my head and sniffed. He stood up and thrust it into my hand before he strode off to the library, his jaw all tight.

Mademoiselle Bousquet's eyes followed his retreating figure with an intensity that made me wince. Harry entered my life before I'd ever dated. I never had to hunt for a man.

When Harry came into Meier's Fine Tailoring and Shoes, I was a fresh nineteen and hadn't kissed but one boy and that was in the school play for all the world to gawk at. When you work two jobs to get tuition money for college, there isn't time for fooling around. So, when Harry insisted he'd walk me to my geology class, I thought it was a friendly gesture, not knowing he would wait around to walk me home. Next thing I knew, he strolled into the diner where I worked nights.

He ordered Tully's meatloaf and mashed potatoes with dark gravy. The next night he ordered a strawberry milk shake and a hamburger, hold the onions. I handed him the ketchup bottle for his fries and our fingers touched for the first time. I could hardly breathe.

I'd been crazy about Harry since the second day he appeared with his hair slicked back and his eyes looking into mine instead of somewhere disrespectful. I ran the counter for Tully. Harry would sit there for hours staring and smiling. Tully demanded he order more than a meal and pay rent for the stool he loitered on, but Harry ignored him. That went on for two weeks. One Saturday, when it was quiet, Tully invited him into the alley to have a little talk. Harry rolled up his sleeves.

"Not that kind of talk," Tully laughed, holding up his hands in surrender. "Dee Dee," he said to me, "you hold down the fort while I take Romeo here"—he jerked a thumb Harry's direction—"out for a little chat."

Tully, my second-cousin-once-removed wasn't someone you messed with. Harry scrutinized him and didn't back down. They went out to the alley, necks all stiff with tension. I'll tell you, I had a hard time serving the burgers with one ear pointed outside. They took their time but returned with their arms around each other's shoulders.

After their alley bonding, Harry bought me a steak dinner. Until then I had a bowl of cereal for breakfast and a package of ramen noodles when I could.

I shook my head to remove the memories. Josephine's fried chicken wafted into the parlor. Mademoiselle cleared her throat, no longer letting her eyes creep toward Harry's library and the judge. She looked at me. I smiled. She smiled.

"Bonjour, Madame Morgan," she began.

"Bonjour, Mademoiselle."

The lesson went downhill from there. My feet throbbed, and I worried about the judge and the FBI man. I took my shoes off and spied red toes. If I was in a cartoon they would have throbbed visibly like volcanic eruptions on the screen. I almost laughed but quickly said, "Oui," to Mademoiselle's question. Which

I think was the right answer. I finally excused myself and went in search of a bathroom. Two cups of coffee, a lemonade, and stress wasn't a prescription for a woman who'd birthed babies.

Mademoiselle had disappeared when I returned. I figured she'd be with the judge, but he was in the library, alone. I kept looking until I found Mademoiselle in the kitchen. We commenced to talk about food. I was in safe territory when it came to food. I'd read *The Art of French Cooking* while I tried to master the sauces.

Mademoiselle left early for her private tutoring lesson with a professor's wife. When the front door closed the judge came in with a "lean and hungry look," to quote Shakespeare.

My gardener Sidney slunk in the back door and dusted off his hands before sidling up to the sink to scrub them.

Without warning he got on his high horse. He does that occasionally, being a man who lives alone.

"Chicken," he shouted, his white arms gesticulating like a drum major. "I ain't eatin' no chicken."

No one ever turned down Josephine's fried chicken. Josephine's eyes narrowed as if she'd seen mice droppings. She put her hands on her slightly rounded hips, an indicator that you might want to back up a little.

"And what is the matter with my chicken?" she asked, her voice crackling with fire.

"You know what them things eat?"

Josephine blinked. She was thinking hard.

"They ain't nothin' but buzzards that cain't fly," he said, sitting down in the chair. They'd been to this dance many a time but never over a chicken dinner.

"If you don't like my chicken," Josephine huffed, "you can make your own lunch."

Sidney smiled, having made his point about chickens and fixed himself a ham and cheese sandwich.

The judge ate as if he'd never seen a chicken before. Between the two of them, Josephine and the judge gobbled up the plate of chicken. I was counting on sampling a breast if I got a little hungry, but there was always the macaroni and cheese that keeps metastasizing.

"Call it off, Josephine. I've got to put a halt to all this food coming in."

"Is you ungrateful, Miss Dee Dee?" she asked.

"Of course not. I just don't think I can get rid of any more mac 'n' cheese at the mission. They said they were full to overflowing with the last ton."

What I wanted was cottage cheese for lunch. Something light and not fattening. I was a little vain about my clothes—I didn't want to buy anything larger—let alone cut out a pattern and park myself at the Bernina. Looking in the mirror before doing my sit-ups in the morning, I thought a little bump below my ribs was emerging. If I was getting a muffin top, I was swearing off pimento cheese for life. I won't even sneak any when I'm wandering around the house at 3 a.m.

The judge praised Josephine's prize-winning chicken, then grew quiet. I think he was afraid we'd load him up with mac 'n' cheese. After his second glass of water he rose from the table.

"I've run out of handkerchiefs and have to mosey home to get more."

I would have handed them back, but they were soggy.

The judge left without so much as tossing a grin over his shoulder. I loaded the dishwasher and fumed. He got to traipse off to his quiet little life while he'd whipped mine into a frenzy with his letters from Harry.

Chapter Five

I FIGURED THINGS SHOULD SETTLE DOWN to some kind of normal. I'd done what I promised. The next thing on my list—selling Harry's old truck, a classic turquoise 1969 Ford F100 with an ooga horn.

The time had come to change out my Jeep for something with good visibility and style. A European sports car. Harry and I had talked about it one rainy afternoon not too long before he died. He trusted German engineering. So, tomorrow, I'd drive into Lexington and look at a few. Tonight, however, I had a guest sleeping over.

Which beat having Josephine sleep in the guest room. The Sunday after we buried Harry she declared, "'If'n you think you are sleeping in this big old barn alone, you got another think comin'." She brought her suitcase in as the kids headed out.

Josephine seemed to be waiting for me to collapse. When you face the death of someone you love, you begin the mourning early. I wasn't about to land in a heap. Sleep turned out haphazard though.

Every night I'd head up the stairs and put the pillows in a line down Harry's side of the bed so I wouldn't feel an empty spot when my toe wiggled that way. I set my mind on sleeping, even took the pills Doc Claiborne handed me, but by two or three o'clock I'd be in Harry's library on my knees praying. I'd spent the last few months praying by Harry's bed, so it felt familiar.

Tonight, hallelujah, little Austin would sleep in the bedroom with me. Josephine rolled in the small bed into my bedroom and set it up while I did paper work in my study. A ton of lawyerly stuff and bills demanded to be looked over. I spent the afternoon sorting and filing in my color-coded files.

I liked things to be organized. My gaze landed on the books in the shelves above my desk. First editions, but not worth much since they were recent publications. I scribbled a note-to-self about symbolism in cover art.

While I made paper piles, Josephine thumped around upstairs. Besides putting the child's bed in the turret, she had little else to do on the second floor. Maybe it was her new aerobic exercise workout in order to get so tired she'd sleep.

Harry grew on Josephine over time. She mourned him too. After her Savannah was born and her without a husband in sight, she swore off men. "They ain't fit to dampen a handkerchief over."

Harry agreed with her.

Which didn't help the minister at the church much, as he had his eye on her.

Josephine kept every man at a distance because of her hurt. Made me sad sometimes, thinking about her loneliness with only Savannah and her mother in the clapboard house they shared.

I walked Josephine to the kitchen door. Her suitcase was in her hand, her eyes sorrowful.

"You call me if'n you have any troubles," Josephine said as she stood one foot on the back porch the other one on the floor.

"You go home to your child and your mama. Leave me be, Josephine." I kissed her cheek. "Lord knows you've done enough around here for twenty people. Time has come for you to rest. You're grieving too."

She finally left, driving off in the Camry Harry bought her. She waggled her fingers at me as she swung around the driveway to exit. I waved back, sad and relieved at the same time.

She passed our son Paul who was dropping Austin off before he headed back to the farm where they lived. Austin was three and the right age. He didn't whine for his mama and was content when with me.

Because I couldn't face another mac 'n' cheese

dinner, I headed to the front door to wait for the pizza delivery man to get out of his little car. I reached the verandah when the judge stepped over the boxwood hedge and ambled up my walk. His little dog's leash was in one hand and he carried a bottle of wine in the other.

Did the judge come over because he saw my guest arrive? Maybe he was lonely, even with his fluff ball of a dog. The judge didn't have grandkids yet. But he loved ours . . . *mine*. Since the day Austin arrived at the hospital, all wrinkly and red, the judge had loved that little boy. He and Harry toted him around on errands to hardware stores like he was a prize poodle.

Now what in the world was I going to do with the judge? I couldn't let him in because the town gossips would circulate the news on the tweeter thingy on their phones. I stood on the verandah waiting. Austin took one look at the judge then scooted out the door and down to the lawn. His face lit up and the judge's did the same when their eyes met.

As soon as my grandson got within range that little dog jumped up, licking Austin smack on the lips. Austin didn't mind. He squatted down on his thin little legs and let that puppy love all over him. They rolled in the grass together, the boy laughing until I thought he'd split something. I didn't think they'd come up for air if George hadn't poked his head over the fence.

"Is it time, Judge?" he called out.

"The pizza man has arrived." The judge grinned broadly at Austin.

George pushed open my wrought-iron gate and strode through as he used to when he and Harry talked politics. So, the judge invites the neighborhood over so he can mooch dinner? His manners wore thin on me.

I counted in my head the slices of pizza and divided them into fourths about the same time the pizza man walked up behind the judge with two cardboard boxes instead of one. I thought I'd ordered one pizza, one half cheese, the other half with ham and green olives. Being a little forgetful at the moment, I might have ordered one each.

"I thought you might order pizza, so I called your favorite take-out to see," the judge said to me. I raised my eyebrows. "Ordered for you, George. All meat with extra cheese," said the judge. The judge looked beyond George. "Where is Mamie?"

"Mamie had to sort out the DAR mailing over at the Hamiltons'. Er, you know how it is with these DAR ladies. Harry's letters to the editor set them against the Morgans. I'm afraid they've included Delilah in their shunning."

George walked over the grass to my limestone walk with the grace of an athlete. When George levitated out of his lounger, he looked more muscled than plump. I hadn't studied him seriously after they moved next door. When he'd join us for lunch I usually ate and ran when the kids were home.

"I couldn't visit you by myself, Miss Delilah," the judge said quietly. "It wouldn't be proper, since you are now a widow." He handed me the wine.

"My family may be from Appalachia, but we aren't drinkers," I said stiffly. "My daddy says, 'Drinkin' is for fools and the broken hearted.' He's carted many a friend home to sober up and feed good vittles into. Daddy is a lay preacher at the Baptist church." I blushed at the pride I heard in my voice. "Thank you for thinking of me," I finally said.

The judge lifted his eyebrows at my comments, then stepped onto the verandah beating the pizza man by a foot or two.

"I wanted to talk to you about my phone call with the boys, however that can wait until we finish dinner." He dug into his wallet for the pizza man's money.

"Hey." I thrust my hand into my apron pocket for the twenty smooshed in there.

"My treat." The judge grinned, then slipped the

pizza man an extra ten. "Harry said you haven't paid for a meal in almost thirty-three years. Why break a record?"

I ate one slice of pizza and a half cup of lettuce with only tomatoes and olives to make it tasty. The judge looked at my plate and raised his eyebrows.

"Looks like a meager helping, Miss Delilah," the judge said as he wolfed down the piece of pizza I coveted.

"I think I need to go lightly these days. Not enough exercise to lob off the calories." Or the muffin top, which from my viewpoint, threatened. I'd spent my life whippet thin. I didn't relish growing out of my clothes.

"GiGi." Austin spoke around a mouthful of cheese pizza. "Do we get ice cream for dessert?"

"Of course, with chocolate sauce and sprinkles."

George smirked at the prospect. I planned to have one dainty scoop, the kind you use for scooping out cookie dough.

"What does GiGi mean?" George asked Austin.

"Grandpa gave it to GiGi." Austin waved a hand in the air. "It means Gorgeous Grandma."

Lyle's mouth twitched.

And the name stuck. All the little kids in the neighborhood began calling me GiGi, including the Salases' daughter Alexa. When Harry got amorous, he'd call me GiGi too. He said he liked cavorting with a gorgeous grandma.

"Did you see the news tonight, Judge?" George mumbled around a piece of pepperoni. "It seems the FBI are interested in a car they pulled out of a lake somewhere near Paducah." George kept chewing while I fiddled with a lettuce leaf, chasing it around the plate.

"There's some speculation it was your old car." George swallowed then pursed his lips. "Mamie got a phone call from Charlene Higgenbottom. She said the FBI were in town this morning."

"Yes," said the judge.

"Well, that's interesting."

"Could be."

I quit pursuing the salad, leaving it to wilt on my plate. The three of them finished the two pizzas. The judge and George took Austin into the parlor to show him card tricks while I cleared and filled the dishwasher.

The judge's dog played under my feet. From the look in his eyes, Bartles hoped I'd drop a bite or two. He sat on his rump and begged. I fed him scraps of pepperoni and ham then lifted the puppy into my arms. The fluff ball dog had the softest, silkiest fur I'd ever felt. The judge got him the day the hospital bed arrived, and we'd moved Harry downstairs for the ease of it.

Harry and I had an affection for dogs. They were our farm dogs. The kind of animal you can let roam and hope they don't chase a skunk. Harry's favorite was Wags, his dog when he was ten. "Every boy needs a dog he can tell his dreams to," he'd said. My eyes got misty. I don't think Bartles was the kind of dog the judge could have a tête-à-tête with. Don't most men want a dog with substance rather than a lap dog to be a companion? However, maybe caring for this little thing would take his mind off the FBI special agent and the bodies in the red Corvette.

"I talked to the boys this afternoon," the judge spoke into my worry. I hadn't heard him come in and almost dropped the dog onto the hardwood floor.

"Bit jumpy tonight, Miss Delilah?" He stepped close. I put Bartles down. The pup bolted. "The boys said it explained why she never remembered their birthdays." His voice was all scratchy, his eyes as damp as mine. "Over the years I forgave Christmas, but their birthdays? Who forgets their child's birthday?" He handed me a handkerchief. "I resupplied my pockets," he explained, using one himself.

The judge wasn't a weeper, but when your best friend passes, his wife is blubbering all over heck and gone, and your kids are hurting, a wise man can sniffle.

"Cam will be heading home at the end of the month." He blew his nose. "He thinks by then, forensics might have some answers."

"Good." I washed my salad tongs in the sink.

"The law can be deliberate, Miss Delilah. Don't know if we'll have answers, perhaps only conjecture. Beau sends his regards from California where he's playing Marine in the desert." The judge tossed me a half smile before heading back to the parlor.

About eight I walked with them to the verandah. With a hint of tropical mystery, the liquid scent of jasmine washed over me. The smell of summer.

The judge and Austin said their usual goodbye, a weird handshake they'd made up. It contained slaps, wiggly fingers and a grunt or two. When they finished, George glanced across the street toward the judge's house.

"Looks like you have company, judge. You should have invited them over."

The judge jerked his head up. There was a silhouette of someone in his front room, but there wasn't a car in the drive. It's hard to see since from my front door to the judge's front door a good three quarters of an acre sprawled.

"I think I've uninvited guests." The judge's words were clipped short. He thrust Bartles into my arms and began a jog to my drive. "Get in the house Delilah, and lock the doors," he shouted.

He had never used my Christian name without the "Miss." It was unsettling.

"Hey, wait," George hollered. "I'll get my gun." He grabbed his phone from its holster and dialed 911.

"Looks like robbers at Judge Henderson's house," George shouted. Then after a moment, "What do you mean everyone's out at the truck accident in Perryville?"

The judge hesitated on the front walk and George

took off like a shot. As he ran toward his yard, George continued his alert. "Get someone there pronto."

I contemplated Bartles and wondered when he had last relieved himself. I wasn't going to have pee on my carpets. I sent Austin through the back door into the kitchen with orders to stay there, so if anything exciting happened he'd be out of the way. When I heard the back door close, I took the dog around George's side of the house and under my pergola. The judge came storming up when I was heading toward my BBQ.

"What do you think you're doing?" he shouted.

"Taking the dog outside. Seems someone forgot to let him do his duty."

I was a little huffy about it I admit, but the judge looked astonished that I'd be quarrelsome.

"You care more about your Aubusson than your life?"

"Don't be ridiculous." I stared him down. "You probably have a burglar. With your paper salesman friend, you two will truss him up with toilet tissue and haul him in to the police."

I smiled at my witticism. The dog peed by my sea green ceramic planter. I'd have to find a bag if he did his other duty. Tracking dog doo into the house isn't my idea of an elegant finish for the evening.

Fortunately, George returned before I could say anything more. George held the gun in his hand as if he'd had practice. Had he been in the military like Harry?

The men looked at one another, squared their shoulders then took off in kind of a lope down the drive. Kentuckians tend to take care of themselves. I figured the judge and George should be all right. My breathing was a little shallow. I collared the dog and went in the back door by the laundry.

Then, I locked things up tight.

Chapter Six

AUSTIN TOOK UP HIS REGULAR SPOT at the game table in the curve of the front room's turret but protectcd by a wall, so if bullets flew, he would be safe. I placed my chair so I could see the activity at the judge's. Being Federal, his house was laid out symmetrically. The front parlor on the right, the judge's office on the left, dining room behind the parlor, kitchen behind that. I could picture it all with Clarisse's fancy mahogany furniture. Beautiful, like Clarisse is.

. . . Was.

The silhouette moved to the judge's office on the left side of the entrance.

The judge went in the front door, George right behind with his gun drawn. My lips scrunched tight together. The thunder drew closer as streaks of lightning flashed off toward Perryville.

Austin played with Mexican Train, pushing over the dominoes making sharp noises on the wood floor. I jumped each time a stack collapsed. Bartles licked my ankles. I reached down, picked him up, and then plunked him on my lap. He made a dent on my green floozy dress, flopping down as if tired. The dog began to snore. I wriggled in the dress I'd had no time to fling aside. If I had on my jeans the dog drool would be absorbed by denim.

Lights came on in the judge's study. I jumped to my feet, dislodging the pup. A shadow person bailed out the side window and made for the alley, then took off like a jackrabbit. The escapee was in full throttle by the time another figure climbed out of the window. The second person promptly fell on top of the camellia guarding that part of the landscape, then got up slowly, rubbing his knees. He wandered toward the front to meet up with the judge standing on the brick stairs.

Austin and I had our noses pressed against the glass in the turret. My legs chattered on the pine planks like ill-fitting dentures. Sirens shrilled from Main. Two police cars screeched down our street, lights blazing. The judge being a court officer, the sheriff must have made him a priority.

The police jumped out of their cars, guns drawn. The place looked weird lit up with the flashing lights, like pictures of Mardi Gras parties. Two of the deputies darted around the side yard to the back of the house. The rest congregated in front. In a few minutes the judge, George, and the police went inside.

Feeling guilty for neglecting Austin, I made a snake of dominoes across the floor and into the hall. That's where we were when the judge tapped lightly on the door before letting himself in with a key hidden under the jasmine planter. He stood in the doorway looking down at us, George behind him. I was on my knees as if I were scrubbing the floor while Austin pushed a domino around like a race car complete with roaring sound and squealing tires.

George stared at me over the judge's shoulders then bent to rub his knee. I hustled to my feet and brushed off my skirt. Antsy, I grabbed the judge's mutt and tickled its tummy.

Mama used to say, "A woman mustn't tap her foot or look agitated when she wants a man to talk. It only aggravates him. He will tell you in due time." Well, I've patience enough for a mother of ten, but not at the moment when the police are picking through the judge's house.

"Too early to say if there is something missing from the break-in." The judge rocked on his heels. "I'll need time to sort it out. My guess is we probably interrupted the robbery."

"They may be back." George spoke with excitement, fingering his gun.

"I saw one person exit the house, not a gang," I

offered.

"There was a vehicle revving its engine in the alley. They made a clean getaway." George waved his arms in the air.

"Why would someone trash my office?" The judge scratched his head. "Books are on the floor, drawers opened, things stirred around."

"Your case files are locked up tight so they're not missing, right, Lyle?" George asked.

"Right." The judge had furrows between his eyebrows. "Seems logical somebody might want info on paperwork for the upcoming cases I haven't yet given to Judge Endicott. Most of the town doesn't know I'm on leave."

Bartles licked my right ear. I took off my earring to give him more opportunity. Harry used to like to do that too.

Blast these tears.

The judge searched his pockets for an un-wadded handkerchief. He handed one over with a flourish, like you see on BBC costume dramas—the waving of the hanky.

Austin cuddled against my leg, protecting my flank.

The judge's face went soft. He squatted by the little boy and looked him in the eye. "Austin," he said in a voice melting with kindness. "Your gigi is a little sad today. That's why we've come."

Distant thunder rumbled. The clouds were boiling and black. George gestured at the sky. "Looks like we'd better head for Lyle's to check on things." We headed toward Lyle's house as the wind picked up and pushed the maple trees sideways. Along our path magnolia blossoms snowed the ground. We picked up our pace, the judge racing Austin down the sidewalk and then holding his hand as they crossed the street. The police were leaving by the time we arrived at the judge's house. The sheriff emerged from his squad car when he saw us, hailing the judge with a shout.

Sheriff Bellows tipped back his hat and brought his eyebrows together. "Lyle, do you think this might have anything to do with the news broadcast?" he asked, looking all serious.

"I doubt it, Sam. Clarisse disappeared eighteen years ago. I suspect it's the Marlowe case. He's got a lot of relatives itching to get it thrown out so he doesn't stand trial for manslaughter. They must think I'm still presiding."

Austin yawned. *Way past his bedtime.* I took Austin's hand from the judge and started to walk toward the road.

"I'll see you home, Miss Delilah," George said.

George walked me across the street then escorted me to the door. We didn't see Mamie on the verandah but we both heard the door slam shut on their side of the fence.

The storm rolled in about 9:30. It shook the house, blasting rain against the bedroom windows. So much for Austin sleeping in the little bed. We set up camp in the basement where I keep emergency supplies because tornadoes spin through the area every few years. It didn't take long for Austin to fall asleep.

I slept solid until a small body wiggling and a hand whacking my shoulder made me open my eyes. I settled my sleeping companion a few inches away.

That's when I heard them.

Footsteps.

Footsteps crossing the floor above my head.

Footsteps in Harry's office.

If the judge was checking on me, he was going to get an ear full. Did he think I was a pea-brained incompetent? But if not the judge . . . perhaps a drug gang hitting the neighborhood?

I grabbed the flashlight by my pillow and eased out of bed. We had a handgun in a lock box on each floor. The box in the cellar was velcroed to the pool table bottom. I ripped it out of its nest, then searched for the lock box key where the ammo was stored. I found it taped to the back of the navy-handled pool cue. Armed and dangerous as Harry used to say when referring to our bedroom activities, I tiptoed up the stairs. I planned on giving the judge a start. I could manage fine on my own, thank you.

The thunder and lightning were gone, but the trees groaned, saying the winds remained. The candelabra lights that usually flickered welcome in the foyer had no flicker to them. Power was out. In the darkness, a pinpoint of light danced around Harry's study. I'd heard robberies happened when someone died but stealing from the dead and depriving his widow was plain ornery.

I circled through the dining room and into the parlor. Harry's study was across the hall. I was going to jump out and yell, *hands up bubba*. I moved toward the foyer entrance, past the couch and coffee table when my gun hand brushed against a flower arrangement. A maroon ceramic vase hit the floor and shattered around my bare feet.

There was no place to hide. If I moved, I might as well invest in Johnson and Johnson band-aids. Footsteps aimed my direction.

"Don't come in, Judge," I said, still hoping it was the judge. "I've got my Beretta locked and loaded." It sounded impressive to me.

There was a sharp intake of breath then a light dazzled my eyes—the police-line-up-kind-of dazzle where you can't focus. I was riveted to the floor because I'd broken the vase. The footsteps receded fast down the foyer. The front door opened before I could take off in pursuit. What good was martial arts training if you stood as still as a mesmerized jack rabbit?

I inched my gun toward the table to put it down since it wasn't needed. One moment the Beretta was pointed at the floor, then raising it I bumped the edge of the table. The next thing you know it went off. I dropped the gun into the fragments of ceramic, a wet sympathy card and a spray of pink roses. Shoot! I'd probably blasted a hole in the striped wallpaper. If I was not careful my foyer would look like a carnival shooting gallery.

A cool breeze ran over my toes and up my PJ legs. Whoever had invaded my house had left the door wide open. I reached over the low mahogany table for the couch pillows so I could throw them on the floor to avoid lacerating my toes on the ceramic slivers. Footsteps thundered on the verandah.

"Miss Delilah?" the judge called out.

"You can't come any closer! There's broken pottery all over the rug."

"I heard a shot."

"It was a mistake."

"Did someone fire a gun at you?"

"Noooo. I . . . shot by accident."

"Ah." He didn't say anything for a bit. "When the power went off, I grew worried about you two." His voice was knotted with tension. "I was on my way over when I saw someone run from your house."

"I had an intruder. Seems our neighborhood is on the list of the meth heads." His flashlight waved over the hallway floor and shone its circle into the parlor. "Hold it right there," I ordered. "I can't move and I've my PJs on."

"Well then, I'll find you something." He laughed. "Come on, Bartles, to the rescue."

His round light made for the big stairway right beyond Harry's study. The judge must have been carrying his little dog, because I didn't hear the tick-tick of nails on my hardwood.

After a few minutes, the judge thrust his hand around the doorjamb and flapped my robe into the room. I grabbed at a sleeve, pulling the floral and zebra print tightly around me. Now to move. He anticipated my attempt to vacate by striding across the Aubusson and picking me straight up beneath my armpits. Taking three long strides he put me on the hall floor like I was a delicate flower.

He put his hands in his pockets. "Where's your gun?"

I jerked my head to show it was behind me.

"Do you greet all visitors with firearms?"

"I'm from Appalachia. All revenuers are greeted with courtesy." I'm not usually sarcastic, but at two a.m. one can get a little cranky. "I need to check on Austin."

"Go right ahead," said the judge, as if it were his house.

He went with me. Austin was half out of his lion bag and curled up in a ball. I smooshed him past the lion's face pillow and straightened. Austin started to snore.

"Would you like a cup of coffee?" I whispered to the judge.

"No."

I moved back up the stairs. By now my feet were getting cold from the draft. I rubbed one on top of the other and then hurried to close the front door. A shadow of a person wiggled on the verandah. He was half-hidden by the big wicker chair.

"Yipes," I hollered.

"It's me," George shouted back. "Woke to a gunshot. When I looked out the window a man ran across my lawn." George's Sig Sauer pointed at my verandah floor boards.

Harry didn't anticipate his assigned knights lurking around the house after midnight. As soon as I shoe-horned George and the judge away from the house, I needed to have a talk with Harry.

"We need to call the police again," said the judge. He phoned while I cleaned up the vase fragments, water and flowers, then we waited for another revolving red light.

Chapter Seven

I GAVE MY STATEMENT TO A peach-fuzzed deputy I didn't know and had never seen a single day in my life. I somehow remembered to tell the police to check the hidden drawer in Harry's desk for his gun before I yawned. Thought I'd only rest my eyes a little but fell asleep on the divan while the judge and the night-shift patrolman scoured Harry's office.

When I finally jerked awake the sun shone brightly through the windows. Someone had tucked me under the crazy quilt I'd made for our anniversary. It smelled of lavender. I fingered the line of silk ribbon embroidery framing an image of Harry before sitting up.

In the kitchen, Josephine talked to a baritone-voiced man. Not just any man, mind—she chatted with the judge. Austin was talking too, his mouth full of something. The judge must have watched me snore over the last few hours.

"Pushing his limits," I whispered. Since Josephine kept an eagle eye on Austin, it was safe for me to get my act together. I grabbed the draggy ends of my robe's sash and cinched it around my waist before hiking upstairs. The front doorbell rang. Josephine's footsteps, then George's voice interrupted my stair hike.

I don't believe in coincidences. *Could somebody be after something at the judge's? Did they figure the judge had given it to Harry? Harry didn't have hiding places around the house. I did.* I kept my jewelry tucked away in my bedroom. After my shower I pawed through the chest hidden in our closet. Nothing amiss.

When I entered the kitchen, Austin and the judge sat side by side devouring pancakes. Josephine had a stack ten high on a platter and was set to flip more.

My stomach growled as the briny scent of cooked bacon wafted from the platter to my nose. George helped himself to a cup of coffee.

I hoped he hadn't stayed the night too. Slamming-door-Mamie would be in a snit. They had been a little distant after George retired. Maybe he had spent too much time at Harry's bedside, and she felt ignored.

"Hey," I said to Austin. "How did you sleep last night?"

Austin shrugged his skinny little shoulders then glanced up at the judge. "He slept fine," the judge stated. "He woke me up about seven asking for pancakes."

"Oh," I mouthed.

"Yep," George said in his flat New England voice. "I prowled around the neighborhood with a couple of cops for an hour or two while Lyle spent the rest of the night with Austin."

George looked pleased with himself. George, no longer parked on his lawn chair and "waiting for the grim reaper," as Harry once said, looked years younger. A purpose other than watering the lawn would keep him living. I worried about Mamie. It wasn't wise to make a wife jealous.

"This morning I went searching for Harry's collection of round-to-its," the judge said.

He forked another pancake onto Austin's plate, then helped himself to one. I settled in my place at the foot of the kitchen table before taking a sip of orange juice from a champagne flute. I smiled sweetly at the judge.

"Well, I think a few are in his office on campus with one or two in the shop behind the carriage house."

"What are round-to-its?" George asked.

Josephine waved her pancake turner at George. "Best I explain." She eyed the judge. Maybe she knew about bloviating lawyers. "Must have been after Mr. Henderson first moved across the street the tradition started." She turned a pancake. George slid into a chair at the table.

"The judge and Mr. Harry regularly passed them things back and forth. One of the men would say they needed to get around to fixing the fence or the leaky toilet. In the mailbox the next day would appear some roundish concoction painted the colors of who knows what. I think it was their leftover paint. You know what I mean?"

Josephine closed her eyes. "Mr. Harry said since his time was limited, he'd better get rid of his stash. He gave me one the week before he died." Her voice skipped a beat.

I cleared my throat. "He wrote a little message with each one. I know he had one for you, Judge. Didn't he give it to you, that last day?"

"No," said the judge. "I looked for it this morning. He said he'd made it out of a lug-nut, an antique, and a washer."

Sidney spray-painted the round-to-it gold, then I stuck a small rubber caterpillar on it because the judge said he needed to get around to weeding.

Josephine stood over me to make certain I had more than one bite. I was getting weary of her hovering. "We've got us a problem, Miss Dee Dee. That no-good robber broke a window in Mr. Harry's study. It's in so many pieces it can't be fixed. A sheet of wood might do for temporary."

"Taken care of," George said around a bite of bacon. "I've spoken to Lester at the window shop. Had to put a fire under him, so I mentioned to him we can't let water damage Harry's library, because someday it might be a museum. Lester said he'd be here at ten."

"A shrine for Harry? He'd hate it." I chewed on the soft skin by my lips like it was Juicy Fruit gum. "Maybe even the town's statue is a dumb idea. Harry was a simple man. He had the gift of common sense, which isn't so common anymore." My voice trailed off as tears splashed from the corner of my eyes.

Harry would look at a thing and be able to wrap words around it. First thing on his heart was God. Every morning about five there he'd be rocking in the prayer chair that sat in our bedroom turret, his eyes closed, his lips moving, but not saying anything aloud.

"There aren't many men like Harry left," I managed around my tears.

My napkin needed to be wrung out.

I took the handkerchief the judge dropped by my coffee cup.

"I'd better warn you, ladies"—George waved a hand—"that an alarm man is coming at eleven. A lady living alone should have an alarm system."

Now George was taking over as well.

I wasn't going to argue. How could I protect Austin if all a robber had to do was bust in a window? I gazed around the room. Where was the judge's dog? Slinking around the house somebody might step on it.

"Where's Bartles?" I asked.

"You don't need to worry, Miss Delilah. The dog is visiting Mamie," George offered. "She's been begging for a dog and Bartles seemed to fit the bill."

Mamie didn't strike me as a woman who liked pets. She had George and that seemed enough of a bother to her.

At 9:08 as I put on my sun hat to go out to the yard there was a delivery man in his little brown shorts and shirt on my doorstep.

I signed the receipt he shoved toward me. The judge placed the box on Harry's desk. It had Harry's publisher's return address on it, but it wasn't for Harry. It was for me.

I didn't open it. I'd wait until I was alone.

Austin and I pulled weeds for a while. Little boys have a hard time knowing a weed from a daisy, so I pointed out the dandelions. Their golden heads bobbed in a puff of hot air, making them easy to spot. I handed him a small trowel and a plastic bag, letting him do what he wanted.

The judge said he'd wait for the glass man. As Austin and I went outside, he plunked down in Harry's office in the over-stuffed chair by the turret window. There were two turrets on my house, one on each side of the front.

Now what was he up to?

Maybe the judge thought I didn't know how to change a tire or balance a checkbook. Harry brought home the paycheck. I gave him an allowance. He was a poet, for pity sakes, and sometimes he daydreamed a little.

I'm not falling apart even though the three of them behaved as if my living in the looney bin was right around the corner. I needed to discuss with Lyle Henderson his constant companionship first, then tell Josephine to adjust her attitude.

I do know some widows who get a bit flighty and need a keeper for a while. However, I come from the mountains. Making do is part of the vocabulary.

I raked out the grass that snuck into my rose beds, hoping the judge didn't grow curious about the box on Harry's desk. Some things are private, and that box was one of those things.

By the time the window man arrived the heat had turned melting hot, so Austin and I decided to wash the car. We squirted each other with the hose. If you do it in front of the car the sides eventually get clean.

The judge came storming out of the house, glowering at us. He had the what-will-the-neighbor's-think look on his face. My drive is long, the trees on each side of the yard thick so nobody could peek at me. I surveyed the hose I held and caught a glimpse of my wet shirt sticking to my bosom. I think the judge's face being red had more to do with my looking like a college girl on spring break than on the local gossips fricasseeing me on their cell phones.

He stopped by the light post at the end of our sidewalk and before the drive then spun on his heel, his back toward us. After a few moments he turned, his head shaking. "I owe you an apology, Miss Delilah." He walked closer, rubbing the back of his neck. "I've been worried that you would get into trouble so um, I've been bossing you around."

I opened my mouth to tell him I wasn't about to do anything foolish when he held up his hand.

"I'm not saying this right. When Clarisse left, I realized I'd let her run the house, the kids, and I guess me for a very long time. Easier when I was shipped out with the Navy to just let her manage everything. It was the undoing of my marriage. I decided to immediately alter how I dealt with my life. I'm now in the habit of being in control. I'm sorry I've offended you. You can call me on it if I get irritating."

Austin scrubbed the tires with a sponge and soapy water not paying any attention.

"Well, that certainly changes things. Apology accepted." I bobbed my head his direction. "Why don't you and Austin finish up here while I get changed." I passed him and went to the rear of the house.

"Josephine, I'm heading to the farm to take Austin home then off to Lexington. I won't be home for lunch."

"And exactly what are you going to do in Lexington two weeks after Mr. Harry's passing?" Josephine stood by the back steps. "You shouldn't be prowling around the countryside when you're in mourning, Miss Dee Dee. You need some time to sort things out. 'Sides, I need to protect you after letting Miss Olive Lorraine rampage around the house. As to the intruder, well, with George's alarm, you will get help from the police and your nosy neighbors."

I peeked out the window long enough to see the judge and Austin playing tag in the back, with Austin winning. "I've some shopping to do after I take Austin home."

"Them grief people say not to make any decisions for a while." Josephine put her hands on her hips. "And what are you shopping for in Lexington?"

"Oh," I said, gazing at my fingernails. "Something

Harry and I talked about."

"Uh, huh. That wouldn't be a car, now would it, Miss Dee Dee?" The woman had radar like a bat.

"Well, I'm thinking about selling the Jeep. Occasionally I'll use the mini-van and the boys might like Harry's truck. A smaller car with good gas mileage seems sensible."

"Ain't nothing sensible about you tearing off to Lexington by yourself and buying a skateboard-sized car. They ain't safe and that's a fact."

"I'm going anyway."

"I expected you'd say that." She marched to the back door and flung it open. "Mister Judge," she hollered. "Miss Dee Dee needs your assistance."

"I do not."

"You most certainly do."

Next thing I knew, the judge was driving my van with the kiddie car seat in the back, while I fumed in the passenger seat. We were headed to the farm when some yahoo pulled out from a gravel road and nearly hit us broadside.

"You stupe," roared the judge.

"Stupid. We don't say stupid. Mommy says calling people stupid is naughty," piped up Austin.

I bit my lip, trying to keep from laughing, but laughed anyway until my eyes teared. The judge turned pink all the way down his V-neck shirt front.

"Thank you, Austin," he said quietly. "You are certainly right. And thank you, Miss Delilah, for brightening my day with your laughter."

Okay, maybe the trip to Lexington wouldn't be so bad after all. We had sweet tea at the farm and after hugs, we discovered a flat tire on my van. I handed the judge tools while he dealt with the tire. A very interesting event to Austin, who squatted down behind the judge and watched. We washed up and waved goodbye one more time.

The judge opened the car door for me. "Lunch is on me. Raisin' Cane's. I like their chicken."

The restaurant was clear to Nicholasville. My hair was stringy from the sweat, my white pants had a scuzz of dirt at the hem and a hand print by my knees.

I stammered, "I'm filthy."

"That makes two of us." He dusted off his hands. "We're not dining with the queen." People from our neck of the woods didn't go twenty miles from town for lunch, so the gossips wouldn't see us.

I hesitated. "Okay."

He gave me a smile in return. "Third date," he said quietly, "should always include a drive."

Chapter Eight

"I THINK," I BEGAN AS WE rocketed past Bryant, "that you and Harry must have had a discussion about my incompetence."

The judge turned to stare at me and almost drove into the ditch. "Whatever made you think that?" he finally sputtered.

"You're hovering. You act as if I can't tell a cock from a robin. It's getting a bit wearying."

"Are you telling me you're offended by my attentions, Miss Delilah?" The judge's mouth puckered and looked as if he'd chewed on a sour cherry.

"Just suspicious."

"Harry is . . . *was* my best friend. He'd do the same if I left a widow."

"I suppose so," I said with reluctance.

"That should clear the air," he said with sarcasm. "You do have a problem with unwanted visitors. I suppose you include me in that category?" He raised an eyebrow awaiting my response.

I looked out the front window.

"Your break-in wasn't a coincidence. I don't believe in them."

"Well, neither do I."

When we returned from lunch Josephine was walloping the verandah rug with a broom. You could hear the whap-whap-scurry from the carriage house.

"Uh-oh." I stepped out of the van. "Now we're really in trouble."

The judge didn't run for cover. He walked right up the steps and faced the music.

"I don't see no flashy new car." She hit the rug hanging over the bannister with her broom, stirring up a dust cloud.

"We had a flat tire, Miss Josephine," the judge said. "It side-tracked us a bit."

"Long enough for you two to be traipsing around the countryside and Miss Mamie whispering about it."

My glance skittered the direction of the Salases' house.

"I'll make her a lemon meringue pie," I offered. "We'll sit and talk. A little kindness will put a stop to the gossip." It was a feeble suggestion and I knew it.

Josephine snorted. "That will do a lot of good with them DAR ladies. You catering to their chit chat will only add logs to the inferno. What you got to do, Miss Dee Dee, is go visit your sister." She thumped the broom against the leg of the wicker love seat for emphasis. "And you, Mr. Judge," Josephine pointed the broom handle at him, "you got to stay on your side of the street, no matter who is roaming through the yard—robbers, murderers, what have you." She glared at him. Josephine had gotten as sassy as I get. "I'll be sleeping here for a while. That will put the rumors to the grave."

Wish she hadn't said "grave." I'd gone three full hours without tearing up.

"No need for pie diplomacy." The judge patted my hand. "I'll take care of Mamie." The judge marched down the steps aiming toward the Salases'.

I wanted nothing to do with another caretaker. I shooed Josephine home. Her mama needed her medications for the Alzheimer's disease that had been eating away at her brain since she was sixty.

Heading for my library I saw the metal alarms on my windows. They reminded me of padlocks on old-fashioned jail cells. I gave a disgruntled sniff, like some elderly person told to stop snacking on chips and eat fruit instead.

I should go to the mountains. Smelling the pines always clears the air. Mama mentioned on the phone they were heading to Washington D.C. for a meeting and Meemaw would be alone.

The box on Harry's desk nagged. I cut open the sticky tape. When the judge tromped into the study I jumped in front of the half-open box.

"Mamie invited us to dinner. She said seven." I opened my mouth to protest when he cut me off. "I accepted, of course. No cause to offend her. George is heading to the store for steaks."

Oh, help. I'm going to need elastic waist pants.

"What are you hiding, Delilah?"

"A box from Harry's publisher." I said it as if it didn't matter a hoot.

"And it's none of my business?"

"Yep."

"I'll see you at seven, then."

The desk phone rang before the judge could step out the library door. "They're coming for the judge!" Josephine shouted into my ear.

"That's ridiculous," I said. Heaven only knows where that woman got her info.

"I heard it from my second cousin, Gerald. You know, the maintenance man up at the county offices? He listened in as the sheriff talked to the dispatcher."

"I wouldn't put it past Bellows. He wants to run for mayor after Higgenbottom gets to the legislature." My words turned the judge back into Harry's office.

"Did you hear me, Miss Dee Dee? You got to get the judge out of town." She was breathless from her yelling. "Take him into Owsley County. No one would ever find him up in the hollers."

I let my synapses range around. Harry would never desert a friend. Was *I* supposed to take care of the judge? Is that what Harry had in mind and not the dating business? In my head I nodded agreement with Harry, but my heart looked on the judge's predicament as a burden.

I looked at the judge who seemed to be on another planet. "Josephine says the cops are looking for you."

"Don't talk about it. Scram." Josephine's yelling

pierced the air. I felt sure the judge could hear her, even though I pressed the phone tight against my ear.

"They know where to find me." He headed for the door, making arresting him easy by walking out in public instead of hiding in my house.

"Maybe we should consider an alternative to you getting arrested." My voice dripped with reason.

"What'd you say?" Josephine asked from the other end of the line.

"Do you have someone with your mama?" I asked.

"Yes."

"Well, get yourself over here. I'll need you for stalling."

"I'm not going anywhere." The judge turned and narrowed his eyes.

"Of course not." I put the phone back into its holder. "I think seeing you in the slammer would be interesting. That way you could stop snooping and following me around."

"I've not been snooping."

"You want to know what I'm doing every hour of the day like a spy on TV."

"I want you to be safe."

"Uh-huh."

"The break-in last night . . ." he began.

"Hold it right there." I held up my hand. "We don't know who was here last night. Could be robbers or Higgenbottom's squirrely brother trying to get something on Harry." I wasn't going to tell him about my other suspicion, that Clarisse's body resurrecting started this whole thing off. "We should call George. He's got a first-rate mind and we need to piece a few things together."

"I'll coerce George into paying a visit." The judge strode over the verandah. "Then I'm going for a run to clear my head." He skirted around my automatic sprinkler pumping water onto the lawn.

He returned with George before I had time to figure out the instructions for the alarm system.

"Judge." I didn't beat around any bushes. "What did you do after Clarisse took off?"

His face colored. He cleared his throat. "I sat around and tried to figure out what I did wrong."

"Any witnesses?"

"What?"

"They're trying to pin a murder rap on you. If you had witnesses to say you never left town, say so now. You learn from mystery shows to always have an unbreakable alibi."

"That's a long time ago, Miss Delilah." George shook his head. "Before Mamie and I moved here."

"Right," I said. "Was Lupita working for you then?"

"No." His eyes slid sideways. A sure sign a person was prevaricating. What was the matter with him? I didn't want to carry little lunches to him while he sat in a cold jail cell awaiting trial. He needed to wake up.

He glared at me. "I prefer to keep my cogitating private." His mouth tightened and his eyes narrowed. "Since Madison appeared, I've had a millisecond to think this through. Only one reason the FBI would be involved. It's the unfinished case with the doctor." He spoke like fly paper stuck to his tongue. "I can see the headlines now." His hands traced a banner above his head. "A racy little story about a sitting judge, nefarious doctor cheating the government, and piece de resistance." He beat a drum roll on my wooden front door. "The disappearance of the doctor's mistress, said jurist's ex-wife."

Ex-wife? When did they divorce? Harry had never breathed a word on the matter.

I changed tactics.

"Who was around back then?" I muttered as I paced. The men watched me storm by like pelicans on a pier watching for fish.

"It helps to have little cards so we can make a time-line." George smiled as he spoke.

I'm wondering more and more about George and his toilet paper selling job.

That got me thinking about Harry and his journals. Notebooks and journals filled with the daily weather, crop reports, and how his vegetable starts were doing in February, accumulated after Harry turned eight. Most writers keep notes. Harry kept logs.

"Harry's journals," I said too loudly to be polite.

I dashed into his study. I unearthed some white 3x5's for George in Harry's desk drawer then let my eyes roam over the bookshelves. The Bobbsey twins followed me more bemused than curious.

"Got to be in the black ones," I mumbled. I tend to process aloud, which drove Harry to distraction. A poet needed free airspace. "Harry changed the journal colors every decade. Twenty years ago, I think he was into black. Judge, search the bookshelves by the fireplace for Harry's black journals. They should be dated the year Clarisse left. I think that would be the years we're looking for. George, write down, 'Clarisse took off from the house about 10:15 a.m. on the fifteenth.'"

George scribbled. The judge hunted through the shelves as a car pulled into our drive. The vehicle didn't have the purr of Josephine's Toyota. If the sheriff was going to take the judge from my doorstep, he'd hear about it from me. I stood from kneeling by the bookshelves and crossed my arms.

Into Harry's study walked my daughter Molly. Behind her was the judge's son Cam. They were holding hands. Well, that got my attention.

Cam cleared his throat. "I need to speak with you, ma'am."

I glanced at the judge. We both knew from the way Molly tightened her grip on Cam's fingers what was coming.

"Molly and I have been seeing each other for a while." He smiled over her head while she stared at the floor. Cam's fingers turned bluish from her grip. "We love each other and want to marry." His shoulders sagged with relief.

I glanced at the judge. His eyes crinkled at the edges with smile lines.

"I know, Mrs. Morgan, that this is too soon after Mr. Morgan's passing to consider planning a wedding. We can wait a few more months before the official engagement."

From the way Molly gazed up at him they were going to cross lines right soon, if they hadn't already.

Putting down the black journals, I turned. "Well, Judge. Do you think they need our permission?"

The judge grasped his son's hand and pumped it like pumping well water. "You have our blessing, Son," the judge said. He kissed Molly's cheek.

The words, "I couldn't be more pleased," spilled out of my mouth. I sounded like a prissy old lady. "I'm delighted, and Molly, if your father were here, he would pop the champagne, not that we have any."

"Actually, Miss Delilah, a few weeks ago Mr. Morgan asked what I aimed to do, since I loved his daughter."

Cam visited on the Saturday they had upped Harry's morphine. Harry would have seen their love because even toward the end he had his wits. And love is hard to miss.

I had missed the signals, though. My thoughts were about Harry's comfort and helping the children cope.

The judge palpated his pocket. He was out of handkerchiefs. "Drat," he said. "I think I'll have to order by the gross."

I hugged Cam and told him to start calling me Mom right as Josephine clomped into the doorway.

"Well, it's about time," she huffed, dropping her suitcase by the door. "You two have been sneaking around here like teenagers. If you's in love, let everyone know, but if you's in lust, you are goin' to have to deal with me, and it won't be pretty."

"Josephine, you wouldn't consider being my best man, now would you?" Cam teased.

"I might take you up on that, Mr. Cam, if I didn't have to keep Miss Dee Dee in line. Not every day you give a daughter away. She might be a hot mess."

I didn't protest. I might be.

"So, when's it go'n be? Don't make it before September. Miss Dee Dee and I have to get things arranged. It will take at least a month or two."

"They want to wait," I said.

Their faces drooped like puppies caught piddling on the carpet.

"I figure, if they can wait a year, they must not really want to be together." I kept my face straight and waited for their response.

"Ma'am er, Miss Delilah. I don't think I mentioned a year." Cam's voice squeaked apologetically.

"Fine," I said. "September is a good month. I think we can manage it by then. Of course, if you'd rather delay . . ."

"No," they both shouted. "We can't."

George laughed.

"We hoped," began Molly, "we could wait until Christmas."

"No," the judge interjected. "You've been friends for years. It's time you crossed the Rubicon."

Molly buried her face in Cam's broad shoulder.

"What is it Ecclesiastes says about a time to mourn and a time to dance? Well, there's going to be dancing . . . and joy. We need a lot of joy around here, and if the judge isn't in the hoosegow, he can walk Molly down the aisle," I said.

"First things first," Josephine added in a solemn voice. "We got to get the judge out of town. Tonight. Then we'll plan the wedding."

"What's going on, Dad?" Cam asked.

"The death of your mother has the police focusing on your father," George stated. "All their suspicions will be proven false. Your father isn't capable of murdering a woman. One can always tell." George thumbed through the black journals I'd dropped on

Harry's desk. "We need evidence and an alibi," he added. "Here, you two, start looking for the month of October, eighteen years ago."

My guests plowed through the journals while I grabbed Josephine by the arm and dragged her into the parlor.

"We need a plan," I said. "When they get the DNA and figure out it's the doctor and Clarisse, if the judge doesn't have an alibi, he'll get sidetracked by court appearances and depositions."

"He'll get railroaded. According to my sources"— Josephine puffed out her chest— "the mayor is trying to get his finger into the legal system here."

That settled it for me. If Higgenbottom made the judge his next target, it would be a pleasure to upset his apple cart.

"If we take off now, we'll be in the mountains before midnight."

"You'll be an accessory if they catch you."

"We're old friends going to visit my sister's studio." I smiled. "The judge mentioned to Harry he wanted to buy a painting of hers."

"You sure think fast, Miss Dee Dee."

"The problem is," the judge said from the foyer, "I'm not cooperating." He thrust his hands into his pockets and stared at us.

"Just like a man," snorted Josephine. "Has his own mind about things."

The judge didn't smile. "At this moment, my mind says to go run five miles. If you ladies will excuse me." The judge jogged out the door.

"I guess he figures getting to do laps in jail isn't on the schedule," I said loud enough for him to hear.

Chapter Nine

WHILE JOSEPHINE WENT TO RUSTLE UP some mac 'n' cheese for the lovers, I walked into the study. My mind rabbited around, unable to sit. If all the black journals were ten years ago, or thirty, then I'd have to unearth the red ones. They were in the attic.

"Mom, what's in this box?" Molly asked as she began to open the one on Harry's desk.

"Oh, something your Dad's publisher sent." I stepped smartly over and thumped the lid back in place. "I'll get around to it later."

The house resembled the whack-a-mole game one can get at those cheap pizza joints. Every time you thought you'd gotten them to go away another popped up, grinning. I didn't know when I could haul the box into my office to hide the contents.

The small hand on the clock inched toward six when Josephine came to the study. There were piles of books from the desk to the window, but no sign of the old journal.

"Short of tying up the judge and throwing him in the back of your van, you come up with anything yet?" Josephine asked.

"Nope."

"Well, if that don't beat all. You done lost your creativity? Time was, Miss Dee Dee, that you would have thought up something right smart. I think I'm going to have to do it." Josephine looked at George. "Mr. George," she said. "You go home to your wife. Don't want to start no rumors. 'Sides, I don't think you've rustled up them steaks, yet."

George levitated from the desk chair and made a sharp exit. No one lollygagged around when Josephine gave orders.

"You two love birds need to see to my dinner,"

Josephine stated. Molly grinned at Cam. They headed toward the back of the house, hand in hand.

"That leaves us." Josephine had a serious gleam in her eye. "So, Miss Dee Dee, is you too tired to save that man's life?"

"Josephine, you are a drama queen."

"You know what they do to court officers in jail? The judge sentenced some of those men and they ain't forgetting it."

I gulped.

Josephine licked her lips. "So, I says we get him out of town and away from that nosey FBI man." I must have looked blank because Josephine crossed her arms. "Harrumph," she snorted. "I didn't expect you to fail me."

"Give me a minute. Go serve the kids and let me think." Wheels churning, I dashed up the stairs to grab a dress for Mamie's dinner.

I didn't want to lie. I'd read the Good Book and knew what the Lord said about liars. He said a few things about gossips too. I always treaded close to the precipice. Then there are the kids. I was not leaving them in the house alone when they were hot and bothered.

I threw on a pale blue dress, one I'd never worn in town. I had two wardrobes, a simple one for home, one for travel. The blue was tasteful—a dress I could wear to tea at The Russian Tea Room while sipping with my little finger curled. With this outfit Mamie would be polite.

When I came into the kitchen, Molly's eyes grew wide. "Wow, Mom. Where'd you get that?"

"Um. Your father bought it in New York."

"You look terrific, Miss Delilah," Cam stuttered in his surprise.

It wasn't in my mind to look terrific, it was in my mind to get the judge out of town. There was a little something he hadn't mentioned. He had disappeared about an hour after Clarisse burned rubber down the street. I'd taken care of his boys that afternoon and all evening. Heaven only knew where he'd gone.

"We've got to get your daddy out of here, Cam. Until things cool down a little." My words were as tight as a shrink-wrapped package.

"He won't go." Cam focused on stabbing an olive from the jar, which kept floating away in its brine. "He's a court officer and obeys the law."

"Miss Dee Dee," Josephine interrupted. "Didn't you always want to see them quilts in Paducah? We could see if anyone recognizes the judge or Clarisse. Somebody knows something."

"It's too obvious if we head directly south. We need to stick with the plan of visiting my sister."

"Well then, you tell that judge you're worried about that tire going flat in the mountains. He's a gentleman and he ain't about to let you take off into danger." Josephine had a point. "Oh. I'll have to call off the Spice Girls lunch," she whispered to me.

Four of us met for a leisurely lunch once a month. It was tomorrow. I'd miss Janice and Lupita's laughter. However, rescuing the judge was vital.

Molly was half-finished with her salad when I took her into the parlor. "Listen, young lady. I may be gone a few days." With Cam and Molly dating for some time I knew it wasn't my business, but I decided to put in my two cents. "You and Cam can't be in the house *alone* together."

Her eyes rolled.

"Mom, you don't really think we're going to abuse your hospitality, do you?"

"If the opportunity arises, yes I do. Your daddy and I couldn't even hold hands without a nuclear explosion." Molly looked skeptical. I brought in the big guns. "Your Gran made your dad sleep in the barn when he visited the farm. The sleeping arrangements made him laugh, but he did it. I want you to have the sweetest wedding night possible. Which won't happen if you step over the kissing stage into the panting in the backseat stage."

"Too much information, Mom," Molly said in a funny voice.

"Think about it, sweetheart." I kissed her cheek.

"Thanks." She laughed. "You're not as formidable as Josephine and Daddy. He threatened to haunt Cam like Marley's ghost if he so much as pinched my bottom."

"Oh." I felt behind the times. "No bottom pinching until the vows, then."

"Mom," she said in a dreamy voice. "We want a simple morning wedding. Maybe in the back yard with Dad's vegetables as centerpieces . . ." Her expression softened. "Oh, don't cry, Mom."

Too late. The deluge began. I wanted Harry in the worst way. I kept seeing Harry at the end of the aisle in our white clapboard church. His eyes shone so bright you'd think they were diamonds. Daddy whispered in my ear, "I've never seen a groom look like your Harry. It's as if he swallowed the sun, moon, and stars."

Molly went in search of Kleenex in the bathroom. I preferred the judge's soft, monogrammed handkerchiefs. When Molly returned with the tissues, she stood on one foot, obviously uncomfortable.

"What's on your mind?" I asked as she plumped up a cushion and descended to the divan.

"Mom, Cam and I want what you and Dad had."

The judge came in while we were sobbing in each other's arms. "Towels," he muttered. "I need to purchase highly-absorbent towels." He stalked off in his running togs to find his son.

At 6:35 I peered out the front window and spied Sheriff Bellows and Special Agent Madison pulling into the judge's drive. I steered the judge into Harry's office.

"We *need* to find the journal before we go to George's." I pointed at the shelves.

"We do? I think I need to shower and shave, and see what Bellows is doing on my front steps."

"You can't go over there," I fussed. "If they arrest you, whatever will I do?" The words popped out of my mouth, which I covered up with my right hand. "Never mind," I mumbled around my fingers.

His eyes laughed at me.

"I'm sure it will be fine." I waved my hand in the air to convince him. "You can post bail and be out in a few hours. It will look bad in the paper, though—local judge arrested for the murder of his ex-wife."

The judge started to laugh. "Delilah, you have an over-active imagination." He kissed me on the forehead and marched out the door to his fate.

Ten minutes later Madison drove off. I breathed a sigh of relief. I was about to go into the study to deal with the box left by the UPS man, when Sheriff Bellows came to my doorstep. His eyes about popped out of his head when he saw me through the screen.

"I wondered if I could trouble you, Miss Delilah." He stuttered like Cam. I don't know what has come over the men in this town. "I've a need to speak to Cameron Henderson."

"Now, Sam," I began in my sweetest voice, "that boy is here for a quick visit. If you want to talk about the judge's situation, well, I've a mind to listen in."

"Looks like the judge has you pegged, Miss Delilah. He said you'd try to waylay me." Sam Bellows slapped his thigh. "No, ma'am. I'm here for Cameron. A little matter of a DNA swab. We need to ascertain if it's his mother they've got in the morgue in Frankfort." That was a mouthful for our locally raised sheriff. He must have read it somewhere and put it to memory.

"Please come in, Sam, and forgive my rudeness."

"I'm overlooking it, you being protective of a friend and all."

I took him to the parlor, motioned for him to sit, then headed into the kitchen.

"Cam, please follow me," I said. "Sheriff Bellows wants to speak with you." I ushered him into the parlor.

Cam's hands flew out of his pockets. He clasped them together like a Benedictine set to pray.

Cameron Henderson stood up tall, squared his shoulders and studied the sheriff as if he were one of the bodies in his anatomy class. I could see Cam's jaw tightening. One was the spider and t'other the fly. Don't reckon I could tell which was which. I was about to head to the Salases' so I backed away when the judge walked in my front door. The man was too familiar. He sashayed right up to me and bowed like he was asking me to dance.

"After dinner I'm taking you to your sister's, Miss Delilah. I suggest we invite Josephine so the town won't roast us both with their vitriol."

The sheriff sucked in air, gasping as if he'd inhaled a fur ball. Cam whacked him smartly between his shoulder blades.

"Speaking of the town hierarchy," Bellows said. "Need to ask what day the unveiling for the statue's sketches is scheduled. Our mayor," Bellows spat out the word mayor as if he'd swallowed a gnat, "wants to have the streets cordoned off for a pet parade, so no one can get to the artist's reception. I might be able to help you, Miss Delilah, if you will allow me."

I was a mite surprised, since the sheriff and I were of nodding acquaintance, nothing more. I'd expected him to take the judge to the station for questioning, not be helping on the front line of the Higgenbottom wars.

"Thank you," I managed. "I'll let you know when the date is set."

We were heading down the front steps when George moseyed through the gate between our houses. The expression on his face was plain comical, because his mouth was puckered up as if he'd eaten a sour ball.

"We have to cancel the dinner party," George said. "Mamie has poison ivy in places she won't even tell me. Got it in the Hamiltons' garden. They were having tea when she tipped over her chair into the flower bed. All I could see were some red bumps growing along her arms, onto her neck and ears." George's face resembled the sad-face clowns in the circus. "She is one unhappy lady."

I was more than relieved. Mamie with hives and all wouldn't be for the faint of heart. I began to rearrange my evening, thinking of cottage cheese with blueberries on the side when the judge stepped forward. "George, want to come along on a road trip?"

George almost sprang off the verandah he got so excited. "Where to?"

"We're heading to Appalachia where Delilah's family lives. Her sister has some paintings I'm thinking of purchasing."

I knew Bellows could hear us from the parlor, so I was content to let the judge project his lies like a vaudevillian.

"How long will we be gone?" George asked.

"A few days. Better pack some things for warmer weather, in case the temperature rises. I'll give you a jingle when I get home." The judge waggled his eyebrows up and down at George as if giving a secret message.

"I'll be with you in a jiffy," George hollered as he galloped across the lawn.

"Off to count up the traffic fines," Bellows said as he pocketed his swab from Cam's cheek.

Judge Henderson took off to speak to Mamie about the four of us heading out together. It wouldn't look right if Mamie was upset with George for escaping when she was miserable and thinking I was after her husband.

It took five minutes, but I finally had everyone out of the house. I marched into Harry's study. "Harry, you've left me in a pickle." I paced the room with my voice raised. I knew he could hear me fine. It felt better to shout. "First the judge's acting looney, now George's thinking he's a spy or something."

I went to the bookcase between the fireplace and side window and pushed on a lever hidden as a book. The case slid back without a sound.

"I can't believe you up and took off when you knew this mess was about to descend. And don't tell me you didn't know. You could see things coming, for instance that tornado nearly obliterating Berea." No one had predicted Berea's house roofs would be in the middle of the street and rafters scattered in yards like discarded Tinker Toys except Harry.

I picked up the publisher's box and carted it into my hidden office. It was heavier than the last one.

"Now, I'm not blaming you for Molly and Cam's secret love. I had too much going on right then to notice, what with you up and dying on me."

The box went onto my desk. I opened it and began to pull my novels from its recesses and place them behind the fancy brass wire that served as my upper cabinet's front doors. I tidied the books into a neat row and clicked the doors shut. The spines of my novels added color to the shelves. I gave a hesitant smile, trying to rein in my pride. The receipt at the bottom of the box went into the file in my right-side bottom drawer. When I left the room, I spoke my magic word. Silently the bookcase eased back into place. Only three of us knew about my hidey hole. Well, two now since Harry had gone to his reward. Josephine could keep a secret.

"I haven't even started on Josephine's attitude," I continued with my complaint. "She's bossing me around like I'm feeble-minded. Is that what you had in mind? Getting me certified?" I would have ranted a bit more but there were steps in the foyer.

By the time we aimed toward my van, I'd changed into casual pants and a shirt, Josephine had packed my overnighter, and the judge completed his trips of loading the car with our bags. He also had his dog, dog food, doggie treats, a dog carrier, and a box of little bags I called dividend picker uppers. There was a suitcase for the dog's toys, bedding, and blankets. Bartles' luggage took up more space than the rest of ours combined.

Cam offered to spend the night at the Salases' and watch over Mamie. She almost cooed having a medical student as an attendant. I made a quick call to Sidney. He arrived with a paper bag for a suitcase and his ever-present gardening boots. Alarm system or no, I wanted a man in the house to guard Molly. Sidney was the best I could conjure.

After handing Sidney a set of house keys, I climbed into the van loaded with maps, snacks, and a thermos of coffee. Bartles decided I had the perfect lap. Reading a map with a dog rearranging himself on the paper proved difficult.

The judge drove down our street, on to Jefferson then toward the Lexington road. We clipped along at about sixty-five in a fifty-five-zone. I fiddled with maps, a flashlight, and the dog. The judge glanced in the mirror. He crossed into Garrard County then whipped the steering wheel right. We headed toward a side road that pointed south.

"Hey," I declared as the flashlight fell out of my fingers.

"Change of plans, Delilah." The judge smirked. "All roads lead to Paducah, to misquote history. I waited for Deputy Fergis to quit tailing us. Now we can find out what happened to Clarisse."

He pulled a smooth turn and took the road to Lancaster. "You'll need to turn off your cell phones for the duration. The FBI can track us when we use them."

George dug into a briefcase stuffed beside him. "Burner phones. We'll set them up so we can talk to one another."

I was concentrating on wedding plans and figuring out how to alter a dress, when Josephine spoke from behind me. "What on earth did you do, Mr. George? You ain't no paper salesman, that's for sure."

I turned my head around, imagining George as an American version of James Bond, and laughed.

George coughed. "Well, I worked for the government."

"Which one?" Josephine asked.

"The red, white, and blue one," George snapped.

"In that case," she said, "a smart man like you will know to keep out of my hair."

"Coffee anyone?" I asked in my sticky-sweet voice. The judge pursed his lips. "The sunset is pinking up nicely," I bubbled. I let the dog lick my ear, then settled him on the seat beside me while I poured four coffees into the floral mugs I brought from the kitchen.

"I've a plan," Josephine said after sipping her coffee. "We need to find out who saw what all them years ago. Someone knows something, that's for sure."

"Most likely," said the judge. "We've reservations for the night near Bowling Green. We'll change cars there. Our names have been changed too. That will keep Madison from showing up. George, did you bring the IDs I asked for?"

"No problem, Lyle." George dug into his expandable briefcase. He brought out a fist full of plastic cards. "Hand me your flashlight, Miss Delilah." He pointed the light to the shiny cards. "From now on out, Lyle is Robert Holmes and Josephine is Elvira Smith-Hughes." He smiled at her. She frowned back. "My name is George Mudd. I saved the best for last." He waved toward me and handed over a Tennessee driver's license with my picture and the name Alessandra Teasdale on it.

"I don't think you spent much time buying steaks at Kroger. Do you print money in your basement too?" I asked as I slipped the card into my wallet.

"Not saying." George laughed. "Learned this from an illegal immigrant operation. All I need is a photo and I'm set."

George was packing, and not just a suitcase. I could tell by the bulge beside his left arm. I studied the judge's silhouette. "You have a permit for your sidearm, Judge?" I inquired.

"Yes. So does George. He also has an ID that states he's a Federal Officer."

George glanced down at his briefcase and nodded solemnly.

"At least that's one thing you're not lying about," I muttered.

"Humph," Josephine said, "likely as not we'll get shot for being with these two."

After an hour, we pulled into a swank B&B. The owners knew the judge. They came out all smiles and kisses on each of his cheeks. They were French. Pierre and Franck served mint juleps, little crackers with cheese spread, and a plate piled high with fruit. Being short on sleep, I wasn't interested in the food or conversation.

"We've put you in your favorite room, Mr. Henderson," Pierre said, looking from George to the judge.

"Er..." The judge scratched his chin. "We'd better have one with twin beds."

"Miss Alessandra," the judge said as Franck handed me my room key, "desires to visit France someday." He looked at our host and smiled.

"It can be arranged," said Monsieur Montret. "It would be my pleasure to escort you myself," he added with a wink.

The judge took my hand in his.

"Oh," the judge said, "I think Miss Alessandra will have no trouble finding the right escort."

Chapter Ten

"MY, MY, MY, WASN'T THAT SOME breakfast," Josephine commented when we took off in a blue SUV. "They stay up all night cooking?"

"Our hosts will be happy to know it pleased you." The judge's right hand tickled Bartles' chin. Bartles looked content planted in my lap.

"Now, ladies and George, we need a plan if we're going to piece Clarisse's journey together and clear my name."

"They might have stopped for gas on the way. We should check gas stations," I said.

"They must have stopped for food." George flicked his fingers toward a café as we passed. "They snuck off before lunch. I'd place my bet on a food stop before Paducah."

I shook my head. "What was around eighteen years ago? Most of the Mom and Pop places have closed and fast food joints have lit up the roadways."

I craned my neck to see if anything was old enough to have been here for twenty or more years. It was hard to get my eyes focused. Everything was a blur since the judge had the car on rocket speed.

"As I remembers it," Josephine piped in, "Miss Clarisse nibbled on rabbit food. She would choose a salad, hold the bread and dessert. Look for a place with a salad bar."

How she knew that tidbit beat me. Clarisse had never set foot in our house. Maybe Josephine's spies at the country club informed her of the town notables' culinary habits.

"I need to make a few calls to set things up for our investigation," Josephine said mysteriously. She whipped out her burner phone and dialed. "Hello, DeWayne? That you? . . . How you been?" Josephine was off and running. "That so? Well, what a shame." She waited a heartbeat before saying, "Hey, I'm calling to ask a favor. Miss Dee Dee and I are on a trip and we're heading your way." She paused. "Well, now that's mighty kind of you for the invite, but we've other plans." I could hear the smile in her voice. "I wondered about the car they drug out of the lake . . . That's the one. You know anything about it? . . . Oh, he did? Well, I'd be mighty pleased if you'd let me talk to him while Miss Dee Dee is perusing the quilts at the museum."

I turned around and gave her my squinty eye. She grinned back at me. "Thank you, DeWayne." She disconnected. "While you are keeping yourself out of trouble, Miss Dee Dee, I'll be speaking with my cousins. Nobody pays much attention to the hired help, but we are all ears."

Which was the way I felt. Aside from the ruse of going to my sister's for a painting, my contributions were zilch.

"Good thinking, Josephine," George said. "Now who had an interest in the doctor? The police? Feds?"

"If he hadn't run off, he was going to be indicted for Medicaid fraud and tax evasion. The FBI was in town the week he disappeared." The judge thumped the steering wheel with his right hand. "They acquired a subpoena and were going over his office books, computers, and checking places he rented. He had storage units stocked with antiques and paintings scattered in three counties. The Feds thought he was investing in tangibles he could resell."

The judge's foot tromped on the accelerator.

I grabbed the door handle. We passed three cars like they were standing still.

"His wife claimed she didn't know a thing about the furniture and art." The judge nodded his head. "Nothing could be proven against her, so the Feds disappeared shortly after that interview. Lack of evidence."

"What about his checking accounts, safety deposit box, savings, stocks, and bonds?" George leaned forward to peer over the seat.

"His wife got them. When the doctor didn't appear after six years, Penelope divorced him. She is now Mrs. Ted Whitley of the Versailles Whitleys. She reigns over the best thoroughbreds to grace Churchill Downs." The judge was a wealth of information.

"Who else did he double cross, besides his wife, the government, and all the people he owed money to, like my daddy?" Josephine asked. "There were rumors that he was involved in drugs. The prescription kind of drugs that are resold by street punks," she concluded in a strained voice.

"Not that we heard of." George coughed and slanted his eyes out the window.

"Red, white, and blue, my fanny." Josephine crossed her arms. "You been spyin' on the judge and the sleazy doctor's wife, Miz Penelope all these years?"

"I won't deny I came to town because of the case. That's not why I stayed, though. It's a great town for bringing up kids, and Mamie fits right in. She became president of the garden club among other things." The pride in his voice set me to praying for Mamie. It would go a long way if she was respectful of George.

Concentrating on my prayer list, my eyes were closed when the judge pulled the car off the road. I gave a little gasp at the sudden change in direction. He patted my hand as if I was Austin. We pulled into a service station. The gas attendant was a skinny teenager with a cigarette pack in his shirt pocket.

While the judge gassed up, George and I went into the small store and looked at one of those book carousels with maps on it. He carefully fingered one of Kentucky Lake and the rivers flowing into it. George's eyes smiled but nothing else. He plunked his money on the counter. His dollar bills were crisp as if they had come from the mint. I hoped he didn't create them himself. George seemed to have unusual talents.

The young lady behind the register looked for a price, flipped the map over and squinted at it.

"Thought we'd check out the lakes after we saw the news broadcast." George leaned on the counter. "Might be a nice vacation spot from what we saw."

The girl took a gulp from her oversized soft drink then wadded a stick of gum into her mouth. "You mean the one about the bodies in the lake?" she asked.

George shrugged.

"My daddy owns this place." She jerked her head toward the chest with ice cream bars. "With all the news people around he got to talking, so someone stuck a microphone in his face. He's the one you saw interviewed on the TV." She sounded pleased.

"So, he owned this place around 2002?" I smiled at her to keep her talking.

"Yes, ma'am. He reckoned the dead woman was one he seen then." She paused like a good actress waiting for our response.

"Well now," said George, attempting to slather a local accent over his nasal Boston. "Don't that beat all. Your daddy getting famous for being a witness."

"He got a couple of minutes on the news station in Louisville." She popped her gum.

"We missed it," said George. "What did he say?"

"That she come in to use the facilities." She pointed to the sign at the back of the store. "Daddy said the woman was real pretty. Had long blonde hair, sort of a Dolly Parton do."

I found it hard to believe someone could recall a face from nearly two decades ago. Seemed a mite of a stretch. I can't remember if I bought toilet paper last week. Truth was being stretched beyond recognition. A blonde? Was he mixing things up or did Clarisse wear a wig as a disguise? When she left town, her hair was dark brown and cut short, so when she exercised it stayed out of her eyes.

"That's right interesting," piped up Josephine.

"Your daddy must have a lot of stories about a place like this. Anything else he say about the two victims?"

The clerk narrowed her eyes. "He thought they were arguing. She wanted to keep driving to New Orleans, but he was set on staying around for a few days."

"I guess he won that discussion." George had lost his phony accent. George stepped out of the store and wandered toward the gas pumps, his ear glued to the cell phone.

I walked the dog. Bartles didn't object to my making him trot beside me. Daddy taught, "Let a dog know who's the top dog and you won't regret it. There's nothing sillier than a dog dragging a person down the street. Pets and children," Daddy said, "should be civilized. That way you can let them out in public and not be embarrassed." Bartles was on the road to being domesticated, but puppies need to be reminded who's the boss.

We reached Paducah near noon. "Where to?" George asked.

"I'm heading for the local museum." The judge pointed his hand toward town. "The attendants are usually retirees who've been around. I'll drop Miss Delilah at the quilt museum then Miss Josephine at her cousins'. What about you, George?"

"A downtown coffee shop is always a good stop." George wriggled as if he wanted to move, *now*. "And the newspaper morgue."

"If any of you need help, call me," the judge said. "I'll park the car by the flood wall. We can meet back there at 1:30."

He drove right to the quilt museum, although it's tricky maneuvering the one-way streets.

I was left to myself in one of the best spots in the US of A. "Look for old people," I said to myself, "they might know about Clarisse." There were plenty of blue-hairs walking around.

"I'm new in town," the receptionist replied to my

question regarding twenty years back. "Our curator was here then. You'll have to wait though. She's out to lunch and won't be back for an hour."

A quilter gets their nose so close to the hanging art it almost touches. I grabbed hold of my hands putting them behind my back so I wouldn't finger the work, then sidled up to a woman in a splashy print dress and leggings.

"Do you live around Paducah?" I whispered.

"We're from Manhattan, Kansas. My husband packed suitcases, put them in the trunk, and off we went. Practically kidnapped me." She giggled. Her face turned slowly back and forth as she studied the stitches. She couldn't keep her eyes on my face, just focused on the colorful quilts. "Do you quilt?"

I nodded. We moved in front of a trapunto quilt made in the Philippines. I had the urge to finger the pale applique.

"I'm finishing my hundred and twentieth," the Manhattan lady continued. "Some are tied, though." She shrugged and moved to a small art quilt made in Holland. "Not enough time in the world to get through all my stash."

Harry said they could shore up a levee with all the fabric I'd collected.

I left the unhelpful Kansas lady. Of the five people I talked with, no one had been around Paducah on the week of the fifteenth. The curator took a very long lunch. I looked at my watch, a silver one Harry had given me when we were first married. I'd have to hustle.

The judge paced along the wall as Bartles wound his leash around his master's legs. The judge untangled himself without a whit of humor in his narrowed eyes.

"You're late" He tapped his shoe impatiently.

"Yes. I'm sorry to keep you."

I used my floppy brimmed hat to fan my face. The rest of my wardrobe was as risqué as the slinky green dress. I don't know what Josephine was thinking when she packed. I would have thrown in sneakers and capris.

"You should have called if you were going to be late."

"I hiked over here as fast as I could and forgot to." I'd practically sprinted across the park that fronted the museum and was damp from the exertion.

"See that it doesn't happen again."

"Yes, sir." I whipped him a smart salute.

"Blast it, Delilah, you had me worried."

"The name's Alessandra, Mr. Holmes." I smiled at him and tickled Bartles' ears.

"And don't try to make up to me by flirting with my dog," he snapped.

George wandered over from the mural of a steamboat. "This is some wall." He gestured toward it. "That picture makes me want to take a boat down the Mississippi and see the sights."

"Where's Josephine?" I asked the judge.

"She had the courtesy to call and decline my luncheon invitation."

"I'm about to decline too, if you remain as prickly as a holly bush."

"Humph." He sounded like Josephine. "My apologies. It was probably difficult to tear yourself away from all the quilts."

"I was sleuthing."

"With fabric?" George asked.

The question wasn't worthy of an answer.

We walked silently to a New Orleans style restaurant and settled at a small table outside. It was muggy. You could wring the air and fill a bathtub. My hair escaped from the knot at my neck. A ring of tight curls formed around my face. I plopped on my hat to cover up the disaster. A waiter brought a water dish and dog biscuit for Bartles. The dog smiled at the offering.

"I poked through the town's museum. Couldn't

find anything more current than what happened on the Ohio for recreation right after WWII." The judge set his mouth in a firm line.

"I hit pay dirt." George smiled. "Eighteen years ago, October sixteenth, someone called a tip line and alerted the police about two men. Ended up they were arrested for drugs."

"Male or female caller?" The judge narrowed his eyes.

"Female." George dipped his chin. "With a strong Southern accent."

"Clarisse was from Baltimore and devoid of any drawl," the judge said.

He looked at me. Obviously, the judge prefers a scraped clean accent that sounds like a news person from Minneapolis. Heat rose up my face. I opened my menu and hid behind the words.

Water and my lemonade arrived with the waiter and I lowered the menu. "What may I get for you, ma'am?" he asked, twirling a pencil in his fingers like a baton.

"A small garden salad with ranch on the side."

"What, no cottage cheese?" said the judge with a slight smile.

"I'll have an order of your garlic cheese rolls as well." I planned to share.

"I'll have the oysters Rockefeller, the house salad, and a gin and tonic," the judge said.

The judge lifted an eyebrow at me to see if I wanted to comment. I didn't. If a man wanted to drink it was none of my business, unless I was married to him. Giving the judge my squinty eye would make him laugh.

"After lunch we need to head to the police department. They must have files about the doctor's disappearance." George glanced around him as if searching for an exit, even though we were outside.

Anxious to tackle the old files in the courthouse, we ate in a rush. A few minutes later, George went in to the police office first and flashed a policeman some ID. Hope it was legitimate. I think it's a felony to have forged government ID.

The judge and George started toward the file room. I asked the desk sergeant for the janitor. I wandered down a flight of stairs to find him. A man, dressed in clean tan pants and a blue oxford shirt, sat by the vending machine, a half-eaten candy bar in his left hand. A bucket at his feet and a long-handled mop tilted on his bench revealed his trade.

"Hi," I ventured. "Been working here long?"

"Who wants to know?" he responded, voice suspicious.

"Alessandra Teasdale." I reached out a hand.

"You a news reporter from Louisville?" He extended his hand and we shook.

"No. A friend of a friend who wants information."

"Lawyer? Private Eye? A snoop?"

"The latter." I laughed.

"Okay, Miss Alessandra. I reckon you look harmless. This about someone locked up in the jail?" He patted the bench seat and scooted over.

I sat and fiddled with my fingers. "I was wondering about a couple of men arrested for cocaine in about 2001 or 2002."

"I was here back then."

He was making my snooping difficult. I sat but put my purse between us. He wiggled over a couple of inches closer.

"You're talking about the hoods from Chicago." He chomped on the nutty innards of the bar.

"Yes."

"They had cash and drugs on them."

"Anything else?" I pried.

"They got sent up for that. Law around here don't cotton to the mob coming in and bringing drugs."

He leaned back on the bench, putting his arm around the top, close to my shoulder. If he expected a reward for talking to me, he'd another think coming. I stood up and nervously brushed my pants.

"Sorry," he said, rubbing a freckled hand over his thinning hair. "I get a little lonely down here." He winked and patted the seat again. My feet pointed toward the stairwell. "One of the men copped a plea," he said indifferently. "Said they were here to get money owed them by a visiting doctor."

"Ah," I said, waiting for him to continue.

"Seems they had a row with him at the hotel over yonder." He jerked his thumb east then looked at me sideways. "You sure you ain't a reporter hot on the story of the bodies in the car?"

"No," I smiled. "I've a friend who wants to know what happened because he's got family involved. Can't say much more, but you know how it is with family. You want to know the story, even if it's bad."

"Rumors circulated that one of the bodies might be a doctor who stayed at the hotel. Eyewitnesses reported that the good doctor was downing barbecue ribs with his girlfriend when the men were arrested." He shook his head.

"Girlfriend?" I asked.

"Yep. And some looker from what I saw. I was eating my lunch at the next table. Far too young for that old man, but they were cozy as two love birds when the sheriff questioned those drug pushers. Anything else you'd like to know?" he asked as he wadded up his wrapper and lobbed it toward the garbage can five feet away. It hit dead center.

"Nice shot." I glanced at my watch. "Thank you, but I need to get going." I shook his hand and headed toward the file room thinking about Clarisse, who didn't look young, just formidable.

I found George up to his eyeballs in tan and green files. "Doesn't mean someone else from their organization didn't do the deed," he said as I closed the door. "I knew Josephine hit the proverbial nail when she mentioned prescription drugs. What I didn't know was his involvement with a crime syndicate."

"I speculate that the two met up with him the morning of their arrest." George held up one finger. "The one seeking leniency stated they were sent to discourage the doctor from leaving the country without repayment of a debt to their boss. Apparently, the doctor handed over twenty thousand dollars in one hundred-dollar bills."

Sitting at a small desk, the judge choked on the bottle of water he sipped.

"There's more." Our informant smirked. "The hoods claim the doc had stiffed them for millions."

"That doesn't get us anywhere." I frowned. "If we could prove the Chicago gangsters weren't alone here and other gang members were around, the judge would be in the clear."

"If they suspected me, they would have taken me in for questioning," the judge said.

George pursed his lips.

I bent over the files George was leaning on. They appeared to be police logs. "Why did Clarisse and the doctor spend a few nights in this little town? Were they waiting to meet with the thugs?" I couldn't figure out why the doctor stalled.

"They wouldn't stay here to meet them," said the judge. "Not if they were afraid of them. They'd head for the coast and catch a fast boat to a place without an extradition agreement." He drummed his fingers. "We're missing something."

George whistled and thumped down a file he'd been reading. "I'm farther along than you think in the investigating department. A newspaper report says that the woman and the doctor were overheard talking about their encounter with the men from Chicago." George had a grin that went from one side of his face to the other. "A witness stated that the woman with the doc was a curvy blonde . . . named *Darlene*."

Chapter Eleven

Darlene Frogmiejer, one of Charlene Higgen-bottom's sisters, was a blonde. About the same time the doc and Clarisse took off, Darlene headed to an island in the Caribbean to do missionary work. Her letters were posted around town and in Maylene's Beauty Parlor. The pictures she sent were of starving children in Haiti, or pregnant mothers lining up for a medical clinic in the Dominican Republic and were accompanied by a request for donations. The good-hearted citizenry of our town never failed to put cash and checks in a box for the orphans.

"Judge, what was the amount of the check you wrote for Clarisse?" George asked.

"Twenty thousand." He spoke with deliberation. "George, would the local police have a report of the twenty thousand they confiscated? If so, is it possible to find out the serial numbers on the money the bank gave Clarisse and compare them to the cash picked up here?"

"Doubtful. During a robbery they'd note the numbers. The bills may have been a new shipment." George's voice grew thoughtful as his brow furrowed. "It's Saturday. The bank's closed. We can't get the information until next week."

"I need to call Cam and check on things," the judge said as we walked out of the courthouse. He dialed the number. "Mowing the Salases' lawn?" he spoke into his phone. "I'm sure Mamie will appreciate that, Cam . . . Oh, she is? Well, I'm sure the shots will help."

"What?" George paled.

"Mamie's eyes are swollen shut from the poison ivy. Lydia Hamilton put cute green plants into ceramic pots to give away to her friends. Being from California she hadn't seen poison ivy before. Apparently, she soaked in a bubble bath after her distribution effort and washed off the ivy's oils, but all the ladies who carted the pots home are covered in the rash."

"I'd better get home." George seemed apologetic.

"No need. Cam has things under control. My son said she was a bit 'garrulous', but darling Molly is feeding her." For the moment, the tension left Judge Henderson's face as the tight corners around his mouth smoothed. His tension could be caused by being a suspect and having to prove his innocence. Must be vexing for a judge to be on the other side of the law. Could be that explained his pique at my tardiness.

"You, my friend, have more detecting to do." The judge clapped George on the shoulder.

George shrugged. "In that case, I'll go to the barber shop. I need a haircut and a little information."

"Miss De-er-Alessandra and I will mosey on over to the Quilt Museum."

You could have picked me off the floor. I didn't see the judge as a connoisseur of art quilts. After he conned the lady at the desk into watching Bartles enjoy the lawn, he walked me through each gallery asking questions. When the curator lady arrived on the fly, the judge suddenly disappeared. One minute here, the next gone.

"Who was the distinguished gentleman I saw you with?" she asked me.

"A friend from home."

"I think I've seen him somewhere," she replied, her voice puzzled. Which set me to wondering. He knew about the one-way streets and that there was a historical museum in town.

"Call me Miss Mable, sugar," the curator said. A soft plastic thimble was on the middle finger of her right hand. When Miss Mable talked, she danced the orange blob around as if it were a day-glow soccer ball. "Everybody around here does. If'n you call me Mrs.

White, I'll scout around for my mother-in-law, who's been gone ten years, now."

For a woman whose figure resembled a plum, she moved at warp speed down the hallway. I trotted beside her.

"There was a picture in the paper of a woman the state police think might have been in the car in the lake. Have you seen her before?"

"I recognized the woman right off," she said in a soft drawl. "She was here. During autumn, being our slow season, I escorted her around myself. She was not a quilter. Couldn't tell a calico from a batik. She asked questions about the town, where the post office was, that sort of thing, but not about the quilts. I thought it odd. Told the sheriff a couple of days ago."

We wandered through the international quilt room as Miss Mable talked. The hand with the thimble scratched her nose. "When I called the police, the deputy thought I'd not remembered things accurately since it was so long ago. I went back to the sign-in records for the museum and it all came together. I recalled she drove up with an older man, not the thin-faced doctor from the paper's article." The thimble finger traced an arch on her cheek.

Another man? I decided not to tell the judge she was three-timing him. That would be a misery no man should have.

"I watch people. My husband says we don't need a neighborhood watch sign because everybody knows Miss Mable's got an eye on you." She laughed so hard her belly jiggled.

Afraid I was about to lose her on a rabbit hunt I said, "Was the woman a blonde?"

"No, dark-haired like the lady in the picture."

"Thank you." I stretched out my hand to shake.

"My pleasure." She nodded. As I turned away to search for the judge she said, "There is one more thing." My feet skittered to a stop. "I was unloading my car when I noticed the woman stomping her feet like a little girl throwing a tantrum. The couple were two places west of my space. Arguments happen here when husbands don't want to *waste their time* looking at our art." I didn't interrupt the flow but gave a half-smile. "She told him to go home and not bother her again."

Miss Mable paused. "He put her suitcase on the ground then drove off. I didn't think much of it until later, when the school children left. You know in Kentucky you can tell in which county the license plates were issued. I used to make a game of it with my kids. We'd squint to read the county on the plate. Her driver was a long way from home."

"What county?" I burst out.

"Don't recall. Not from around here. That much I know. That woman the paper called Clarisse Henderson was the one having the conniption fit. She explained to me that her car had broken down and the man had given her a lift. Since the man wasn't a local, I thought she was lying. There was no call to give me details." She paused in her reciting for a breath. "Ruby Teeter took her to the fancy downtown hotel in his little yellow taxi. A three-block walk, and she hails a cab." Mable White sniffed derisively.

"Well, I thank you, Miss Mabel." I smiled. "I can't tell you how much your observations mean to me. You see, the lady was a neighbor of mine. I know her children well. For their sake, I hope it isn't her."

I wrung my hands then stopped. I didn't know how the boys would cope knowing their mother was murdered. That would be easier to accept than desertion, but I didn't like the whole shebang. Something stunk. Had Lyle been with Clarisse in the parking lot? Had he hidden out here and bumped her off?

I glanced outside to check on Bartles. Josephine sat on a bench with the dog nipping at her feet. When I exited, Josephine smiled at me like an all-knowing character in a cartoon. The judge scooped up Bartles' deposit in one of his freshly pressed handkerchiefs, then threw the soiled linen in a handy receptacle. I wanted to ask him why he'd vanished, but he rose and took Josephine by the arm. Left to untangle Bartles' leash, I untwisted the coil four times before he was free while Josephine whispered to the judge. The pair of them bonding was fine with me. I needed to think about the judge, and his absence the day Clarisse exited.

George lounged under a shade tree beside the car. His hair was styled like a politician on the stump with waves and height. He wore dark navigator sunglasses.

"Everything's set for Monday," George said as we drew closer. "My colleagues will search and, if possible, have the serial numbers of the bank bills coordinated by noon."

The judge nodded.

A car pulled up beside our borrowed SUV and Special Agent Madison emerged. He had a grin on his face that rivaled Walt Disney on the Dumbo ride. His eyes raked the judge over as if my neighbor was a terrorist.

"Glad I caught up with you, Lyle," Madison said. "As always, I'm happy to see you, Miss Delilah." He bowed to me.

I wrung my hands again. The judge grabbed my fingers in his big ones and held on tight. Little did he know I suspected he followed Clarisse here when she vamoosed. Maybe he strangled her, and the doctor caught him in the act, so the judge had to shoot them both. I began to feel mighty uncomfortable holding hands with a man who could be a murderer. After all, Harry wasn't perfect, and he could have missed small, telltale signs about the judge. I slowly eased my fingers out of his as I cogitated. He lifted an eyebrow my direction.

"George's friends at Langley had a chat with my boss, so I flew in," Madison said. "I thought we'd compare notes. See if it leads us anywhere."

"We're rowing in circles." George pursed his lips.

"That's not what I hear," Madison said. "The grapevine says you've established motive for the O'Neal cousins to have committed the crime. By the by, it is now officially a double murder." He appeared quite satisfied with himself. "I appreciate all you've done, but my advice is to play it safe. All I want is for you to stop interfering with my investigation. Try to leave it to the professionals."

"So you can railroad the judge?" Josephine snapped as she marched right up to Madison and stared straight in his eyes, daring him to move. "I's got news for you, Mister FBI man. The judge ain't guilty of nothin', 'cept marrying a woman who run off. An' who could predict that?"

Madison knew he was outfoxed. He nodded to her and grabbed the corner of his lip with his teeth. "I've not come to arrest the judge," Madison said with studied calm. "We've no evidence Judge Henderson had anything to do with the murders. Even if he was seen leaving town about an hour after his wife." Madison's eyes swiveled toward the judge.

My mouth flew open. I picked up Bartles and hugged him to my chest. I knew the judge had left and thought it was court business.

"That right, Lyle? Witnesses say they saw you heading down Perryville road." Madison picked at a hangnail on his left thumb.

"I was."

"Care to expand on that?" Madison was aggressive.

"Not here. I've heard the hotel bar is cool and out of the sun. Miss Delilah has to watch out or her freckles will grow."

Which was the truth. I've a splatter of freckles across my nose and cheeks, down my arms, and up my legs. I inherited my persnickety skin from the redheads in the family.

"Good suggestion." George nodded then slipped into Madison's car.

"I'll check us into our accommodations and meet you both in a few minutes," the judge said.

I think his invitation to meet at the bar was a step in the right direction. I was getting into this detecting business. "We'll be with you as soon as we get settled." I gave a nod.

Josephine and I lugged our suitcases up the staircase, because the elevator bore an Out-Of-Order sign on its front like a badge of honor. I yawned as we came to our floor. A good nap was in order. Josephine had stirred the air with her snoring last night. Our room had high ceilings and a balcony overlooking the river. Josephine stood in the middle of our room and turned around slowly.

"Look at all them googahs. Gold jumping off the walls at you. Gold on the mirror frame, gold on the little lights by the bed. This much gold looks like somebody didn't know when to stop with the slatherin'."

"Something bothering you, Josephine?" I asked.

"Now that you mentions it. Cousin DeWayne set me to talking with his ol' football coach. The coach said he saw a Corvette headin' toward the lake that night." She took a deep breath.

"And?" I prompted.

"Coach Hosler claims he couldn't see into the car but another one came up behind it, following real close."

"What was the make?"

She shrugged. "He disremembers. Cousin DeWayne also told me that Aunt Claudine told him, that scoundrel doctor and Miss Clarisse stayed right here in this hotel. Aunt Claudine was a maid then. DeWayne hustled me over to Aunt Claudine's house by the cemetery. I sat on her front porch drinking her ice tea and gazing out at the nice green lawn with the white markers. Mmm-hmm, that tea was mighty good."

Josephine always took her own sweet time. Next,

she'd tell me where her cousins were buried and when. I hung up my clothes as she chattered.

"I asked her to think back and tell me all. Aunt Claudine said that the day after the doctor arrived, two white men with slicked back hair came in and demanded to see him. Later, when she was tucking in those little chocolates by the pillows—the rectangular mint ones—she saw a woman with short brown hair come out of a room down the hall from the doctor's. The woman, and Aunt Claudine swears it was Clarisse, wasn't the same one in the doctor's room. The one in his room was a blonde."

"Well, that's a mouthful," I said. "I suppose you should relay all that to Madison and the judge."

"You want to join me for the revelation?"

"Count me in. If things get tedious, I'll come up for a nap."

The hotel dining room was like a saloon in a TV western, all wood and red glass chandeliers. They even had flocked wallpaper at the entrance. The three amigos were sitting at a worn table sipping on something from small clear glasses.

"We're having gin and tonics," George said, holding up his drink. "If you ladies would care to join us, we'd be more than happy to order for you."

"Sweet tea will suit us fine." I sat in a chair near George.

The judge ordered our drinks as we settled into chairs.

Josephine had a glint in her eye. I sat up stiff as a post.

"Thought y'all'd realize you need every one of your brain cells instead of letting them turn to mush with alcohol." Her voice said no use arguing, I've made up my mind.

I didn't expect her to let their drinking slide. After her daddy lost his business he was known to indulge.

The judge took one look at his glass, pushed it to the middle of the table and lifted his finger toward the waitress.

"Functional synapses it is, Josephine," the judge said before ordering a glass of tea.

I closed my eyes and thanked God. When I opened them the judge's denim-blue eyes twinkled my direction. He raised an eyebrow and smiled.

"Lyle cleared up a few things while we waited for you." George leaned forward.

"Well?" I was itching to hear more.

"Seems he called Thomas Hazard as soon as Clarisse stormed out of the house. Had her followed." George looked amused not worried.

Thomas Hazard was the local private eye, but not like you see in a Bogart movie. He was small and weaselly. Rumor had it he could dress like a woman with no one the wiser. I glanced at the judge. He studied his fingernails.

"Did your investigator find Clarisse?" My voice came out stiff.

"Yes," the judge answered not looking my direction.

"And did you come to Paducah?" I pressed.

Josephine, who was next to the judge, jerked her head his way.

"Yes." He glanced first at me then at Madison.

"Well, if that don't beat all," declared Josephine. She scooted back an inch or two to get some distance between them.

"I groveled," he said, misery coating his words. "I'm not proud of it."

"Did you talk to Clarisse?" Madison probed.

"Argued with her," the judge said. "I asked her to reconsider. The boys needed her."

My lips curved into a smile. "And *you* didn't?" Of course a man who loves his wife and kids would come and beg her to return. The thought of his trip to Paducah as a reconciliation meeting settled it for me. He couldn't have done her in, if he wanted her back for the kids.

The judge choked on his ice tea. "No, I didn't." He looked me directly in the eye. "I was humiliated and angry, but I was willing to let her go. The boys, however, would be heart-broken to lose their mother, so I appealed to her maternal instincts."

"That all?" Josephine said.

"She refused. I came home. End of story." His gaze dropped to his drink.

Special Agent Madison sat up tall and took a sip from his glass. Was he trying to intimidate the judge?

"I took care of the boys that night," I said thoughtfully. "When they got home from school and found no one there they trotted over for dinner. In fact, I went over about eight and you still weren't home. I stacked your boys up in our bunk beds." It was so odd it was memorable. The judge or his housekeeper were always home when the boys arrived. I leaned across the table. "When did you get home that night? Or, did you get home that night?"

The judge's head whipped around fixing his gaze on me. "I left a message with my housekeeper to speak with you. Didn't she call?"

I shook my head.

He frowned. "I left Paducah about midnight. Got home about three or four. I drove around a while."

Although the judge looked me directly in the eyes when he said it, who knew if this was a tall tale. If he'd tell a fib about fried potatoes, for heaven's sake, what would he say to avoid a noose? I grabbed a breath. I'd reserve my judgment. Harry had been a good judge of character.

"Got any receipts that can verify you getting gas or a meal?" Madison asked.

"I don't keep eighteen-year-old receipts on file," the judge almost shouted. His hands clenched tight, as were mine.

"Can Lupita testify that you were home on the day after Clarisse disappeared?" George interjected. "She's a credible witness."

"She didn't work for me then. Mrs. MacCreedy did. She died more than seven years ago."

"Huh," said Josephine. "Not looking good, Mr. Judge." Then Josephine chuckled and shook her head as if to dispel her doubts.

"There are court records for the fifteenth and sixteenth that will state I was in town," Judge Henderson asserted.

I couldn't recall if the boys had dinner with us again that week or not. Harry would have recorded it in a journal. I *had* to unearth it. The journal might clear the judge . . . or it might not. That was the problem. When she refused, he might have shot his wife and thrown her in the lake. Act of passion, rage? But I had a hard time believing that could be the case. I rubbed my forehead because a headache stormed around between my eyebrows.

"I've some news," Josephine waved her hands dramatically, like a ham actress playing Lady Macbeth. She proceeded to relate her Aunt Claudine's story about the doctor and Clarisse having separate rooms. "And you know what that means?"

I shook my head.

"They had a falling out. Maybe she was regretting leaving the judge and was planning to come back home."

Chapter Twelve

WHEN WE LEFT THE MEN, I aimed for the stairs in need of aspirin and sleep. I took the stairs two at a time to flee the thoughts nagging me.

"What you going to do about the judge?" Josephine panted after me.

"Nothing," I said. "He could have bumped off his wife. Men have done it for less than adultery." I opened the door and did neck rolls and heard the creak and pop of my tense muscles. "I'm surprised that the sheriff and Madison haven't hauled him in. After all, the husband is always the first one they suspect. Do they know something we don't?"

"Probably," Josephine said. "You trust him to get us home safely?"

"Yes. I think it's time we looked elsewhere rather than at my neighbor." My head pounded so hard my teeth chattered.

"Mr. Harry trusted him," Josephine said as I put the old key in our room's lock. "And Mr. Harry was a good judge of men. Didn't he save old Clint Farmer from a trial when he was accused of stealing Charlene Higgenbottom's car?"

When Harry had stomped out of the house to post Mr. Farmer's bail, he'd actually slammed the front door. It had been a very trying time for Clint Farmer, a WWII vet, who shook in his boots when Harry brought him to our house. "Nasty bit of business, Delilah," Harry had said. "Clint Farmer was a hero, and we've got the mayor's wife all skittery because he was mowing his lawn when her car disappeared. He's near eighty-six," Harry shouted. "But because he's black, it makes her think he stole her car."

"Mr. Harry was right too." Josephine's words jerked me back to the pulse of the air conditioner. "That old man hadn't done a thing. Charlene failed to put the emergency brake on when she parked and went to her garden club meeting. Soon as she got in the house her old car took off like a shot and disappeared. They didn't find it for hours because it rolled straight across the road and over the embankment to the creek."

"You up for a wander through town?" she asked.

"Nope. I'm going to nap." I proceeded to strip off my clothes fast so she couldn't haul me downstairs. Josephine wanted to talk, and I wanted to get rid of the throbbing behind my eyes. I slipped under the duvet, felt the lineup of pillows for a squishy one, and eased my head onto it.

I actually slept. I woke to the thump of the air conditioner and the green numbers on the night stand's clock shining, 5:52. The ache behind my eyes was gone except of a little twinge that made me squint. After a shower, I had managed to dress in the only other pants Josephine had packed, black silk ones. I searched for a top that would match.

Josephine opened the door. "You sure were out. I poked my head in here and you were tucked up in the blanket like a newborn."

I smiled at her.

"I've got news for you." Josephine had a grin across her face that made my smile widen. "Mr. George said all the ladies covered with poison ivy have gathered over at his house. I don't think he wants to go home tomorrow. He asked the judge about a spare room. A spare room." She snickered. "When Mr. George heard Charlene Higgenbottom was one of the ladies, he begged the judge."

"We've crossed over into gossip territory, Josephine. I'm only mentioning it because I think the judge and George can work out their housing without my knowledge."

Josephine thumped her twenty-pound black purse on the bed and crossed her arms. "I'm just getting to the good stuff." She lifted an eyebrow to see if I would object before she barged on. "Since Mamie's eyes are glued shut our Molly decided to read *Burns'* newest novel to them. Turns out, D.B. Burns is their favorite author. Mamie has an entire bookshelf of Burns books. What do you think about that?"

"That's nice." I shrugged.

"Nice. I should say. Them DAR women reading your books and refusing to invite you into their homes. Maybe what you write ain't penetrating."

"I could try a sledge hammer."

There was a tapping sound on the door.

Neither of us moved. "Come in," Josephine said like a princess to a vassal. She turned to me. "So, when are you going to come out and confess?"

"Confess what?" asked the judge who had entered the room by the hall door.

He turned to Josephine. "What does Miss Delilah have to confess?"

"Not a thing." I glared at Josephine, then back to the judge. "Where's your little dog?"

"George is walking him toward the river to watch fishing. There is a late afternoon breeze cooling us down. If you ladies would accompany me, we'll take a history tour of Paducah, beginning with the murals on the flood wall."

I had to admit the evening was nice. After the walk, Madison joined us for a catfish dinner in the hotel dining room. We talked sports. I thought we would be heading back home in the morning but when the coffee came around Josephine took a sip and stared at the four of us. "I told DeWayne you all would be dee-lighted to come to church in the morning. Starts at 9:15."

"Thanks, Josephine." Madison shook his head. "But I've got to catch a flight to Lexington." Madison's verbal backward tap dance didn't impress Josephine.

The look she cast his way would have stopped an NFL linebacker. Josephine's invitation to church wasn't to be escaped.

"And you, Judge?"

"Oh, George and I wouldn't miss it. Would we, George?"

"No," George stumbled over the word. "Only problem is . . ." He paused, his eyes looking desperate. "Your dog, Judge. Somebody will have to take care of him. I will be happy to take the duty."

"Cousin DeWayne said drop your doggie at his house. His mama-in-law has a summer cold and will be the dog sitter. It's all lined up."

No escaping for George, and from his expression, he was not pleased.

"Any other excuses?" Josephine crossed her arms.

No one volunteered.

"Aside from a beauty parlor the best place to get the local news is in a church." I smiled at the men, which ended the discussion. I got some of my best story material by listening to others at church meetings.

Back in our room I made a phone call to check on Molly. "Mom," she nearly shouted. "How did you stand it all these years?"

"What are you talking about?" I asked as I eased out onto the balcony.

"Those women don't like you. I was in the foyer and heard them say that you were from some hick town in the mountains and had stolen Dad out from under Olive Patrick's nose. I got so mad I marched in and told them your secret."

Had Molly told them about my writing? I thought I'd kept my secret from the kids because I'd wanted to work without interruption. Now, with the country club women spreading my writing all over town, I'd get no peace.

"I don't think I've ever been so angry."

"Calm down, dear. I'm not worried about the

women in Mamie's circle. I've many friends in town." I thought of all the mac 'n' cheese and was grateful for their expressions of love. "I just don't have the committee women as bosom buddies."

"What will I tell Gran?"

"What are you talking about?"

"The DAR. I told them Gran was the State Regent. They almost fell on the floor. You should have heard Mrs. Higgenbottom. She said I must be mistaken. When I said we were descendants of Daniel Boone, Miss Mamie choked on her sweet tea." Her voice trailed off.

Thank heavens she didn't yet know I was D.B. Burns and couldn't spill the beans. I didn't know what to tell her. Comforting your daughter from dealing with prejudice was something I didn't know how to do.

"Mom." She interrupted my grief. "I was so mad I stormed out of the Salases' house and ran to Cam. I threw myself into his arms and cried. I guess without Daddy to protect you it's going to be hard."

"No," I said quickly because I didn't want her to worry. "It won't be. It's a matter of making up my mind to be thankful for what I have."

She started to sniffle, and I heard Cam in the background. "Molly, my sweet, sweet, Molly," in a voice so loving I began to tear up.

She was right about her daddy. Harry made choices that protected us all. In the country, it had been easy. Everyone came to the community church; white farmers whose family had worked the land for two hundred years, the Mexicans who helped on the large horse farms, and the African Americans who had small businesses. We lived life together. When Harry took the job at the college, all that changed.

"Well, little girl," Harry said after visiting a church where they got all stiff and pulled in their elbows as though they didn't want to make contact with anyone lower than themselves. "I think I'll dust my feet off and travel down another road." That is the way Harry felt about the unwelcome mat a handful of locals spread. I wanted to gather in all the naysayers and show how love embraced all.

It took us some time, but we eventually found people who gathered in folks with hurts, sin, and heavy loads. Nothing fancy about our church except the hats. It was a good place, pimento cheese and all.

The sun sets late in July and it lingered golden for a while before fingers of peach spilled across the moving water. We could see it from our balcony. I sat in a chair beside Josephine, listening to the slurp of the water along the levee and the call of the night birds. Shadows deepened. I closed my eyes.

"Penny for your thoughts, Delilah," said the judge from his balcony. I opened my eyes to see him sip from a tall glass with water dripping down its sides.

"No thoughts. I'm listening to the river. The slap of water against the levee and the sighing of the trees when the wind tickles them sounds like music."

"Maybe you should have been a poet too." He spoke quietly.

"Me? Oh, no. Somebody had to fold the sheets when Harry massaged words."

"I spoke with Cam a bit ago." The judge's voice was tense. "He and Molly want you to move in with them when they get married."

"That's not going to happen." I laughed. "They must think I'm as incompetent as you do."

"Now, Delilah." He narrowed his eyes. "I've never said you couldn't manage. I think a man should protect the women in his life."

"I'm not in your life, Judge." I spoke firmly, hoping that closed the subject. "I came on this trip to clear your name because Harry would want that. He wouldn't want you to go to jail."

He cleared his throat. "What I meant was, I'd be honored to have a conversation with the ladies on your behalf."

"Those women took scalping lessons from their

mamas." Josephine had a glint in her eye. "And I ain't letting Miss Dee Dee in striking distance of their tongues."

"On second thought"—George spoke from his lounge chair on the judge's balcony—"I'll have a talk with my wife and put a stop to this." He pushed himself vertical then headed toward the door, his face a mix of anger and fear.

Josephine began to hum. "I think I'll go for a walk." Which was odd since she prefers to lounge around when she can, and she'd just been on two walks. She went into the room to find her fan. The air was so humid you could wring out a bucket from a napkin.

The judge raised his glass in salute to Josephine and stepped over his balcony rail, then over mine until he stood in front of me. I smiled at him knowing I didn't have to worry because he was Harry's friend.

"It's mighty kind of y'all to take up my defense, but I'm fine." I smiled at my friends.

"Uh-huh," Josephine poked her nose out the slider. "Mr. Harry done his job for you, now let the rest of us. Even you ain't got a stiff enough spine to take their uglies."

"Hear, hear," encouraged the judge.

Josephine kicked up her heels as she closed the door. The night sounds swelled. The river pulsed along the levee as if it had life. Which I suppose it had. The Ohio's croon almost lulled me to sleep where I stood. I wanted to sit again, but thought the judge had more to say, so I waited.

"This is the first of Harry's letters to you. I think you should read it." The judge handed me a folded piece of paper. Harry's handwriting rose to meet my eyes. *"For Delilah, when you think she is ready."*

I opened the letter to find a short note.

My dear little girl,
I need to explain a few things that I couldn't say. I

have cared for you from the moment we met. There you were, all shiny and young, your face filled with kindness. I wanted to scoop you up and take you home with me right then. You are the tenderest woman I know. You have nursed me with a gentleness I don't deserve.

I could barely see the words through my tears. Harry deserved so much more than my meager attempts to remove his pain. Sometimes love comes only once. I was one of those people. Love came once— and it was precious and lasting.

It is my heart's desire to see you loved, contented, and happy after I pass. It is selfish and a bit controlling of me to write asking that you consider allowing Lyle to be part of your life. He is a good man. A man, who, with time, could love you. Please give him the opportunity.
Love,
Harry

I didn't need another man in my life. I still had Harry. I looked up at the judge, feeling my face go all rumpled.

"Do you know what Harry wrote?" I asked in a flat voice.

He shook his head.

A frown grew across his forehead. I handed him Harry's letter. He had the manners to blush when he finished. Without a word he handed me the paper.

"Harry didn't know that you prefer to be the eligible bachelor and not commit to anyone."

"That I what?" sputtered the judge.

"Well," I began, trying to say it delicate like. "You seem to like dating and having lots of women friends." I wasn't going to say he seemed a coward for not remarrying. Did Clarisse ruin him for another woman?

"You think"—he got redder by the second— "because I haven't remarried that I don't like women enough to commit to a lifetime relationship?"

"Well . . . yes . . . that's what I thought." I drummed my fingers on the top of the rail.

"Great balls of fire, Delilah." He was so mad, even his nose turned red.

I took a step backwards. He reached out and grabbed both of my hands in his. "I'm Harry's friend, and yours, I hope." His stare was riveted on my face. "I've not remarried because there hasn't been a woman I wanted to share my life with." His voice choked. He pulled me into his chest, hiding his face. We stood together as the night birds called to one another, then he kissed me so tenderly I couldn't breathe. Lord, help me, I didn't think about Harry, not one little bit. I thought about the judge's lips on mine and the whack-whack of my heartbeat. My feet had gone all tingly by the time he kissed my forehead.

"I apologize, Delilah." He sounded sincere.

"You don't have to," I mumbled, light-headed.

"Yes, I do. Day before yesterday everything between us changed. I have no right to be less than a friend to Harry and to you."

I wanted him to kiss me again, killer or no. Harry hadn't been able to participate in a real kiss for a while before his death. Harry's kisses had become lean, polite ones because he couldn't breathe well. The judge's were inviting. I chewed on my lips, feeling like a traitor to Harry.

We stood looking at one another kind of surprised and not knowing what to do about it. I put my hands behind my back, afraid I'd start wringing them again. A little breeze blew river air around us. I got all shivery.

The judge took me in his arms, holding me like Harry's best friend would. Like he'd held me after all the funeral guests had left the buffet and I stood alone in the reception room. This is safe, I thought, letting my head rest against his chest. His heartbeat was too fast. It thumped so hard it was almost pushing my ear up and down.

"Delilah," he whispered into my hair.

Just his speaking my name made my knees wobbly. "This isn't going to work." I pulled away from him. "We've a wedding to put on, a murderer to catch." Come to think of it, I might be standing with him right now. "We can talk about Harry's letter at another time." I waved it in front of him like a matador's red cape.

"I agree," said the judge.

He stepped back and climbed over the railing. I stood and watched him retreat to his room. Some things aren't so easy when your heart hurts and wants comfort.

Chapter Thirteen

"YOU'RE A SICK PERSON, DELILAH BELLE MORGAN," I said out loud. "You want the judge to kiss you when Harry is fresh in his grave." I flung the curtains shut so I wouldn't have to look at the offending balcony. "Shoot. You can't get your mind off the sparkle in the judge's eyes when he said good night," I muttered as I tromped to the bathroom to put cold water on my face. "The children are going to put you in a home if you even hint the judge made your toes itch when he kissed you." I spoke to my reflection as I toweled my face dry.

By one a.m. Josephine got all huffy and ordered me to snivel under the covers.

About six a.m. I watched the judge run down the street in his shorts and sleeveless top. Having the judge across the street wasn't going to be easy. I'd even grown attached to his weeny little dog.

And I wondered what Harry's other letters were going to say.

We met the men in the dining room for breakfast. George shoveled down his eggs and gulped his coffee so fast I thought the firing squad was scheduled in two minutes.

"This a hallelujah type church?" he asked Josephine while she pushed a bread crust through an egg yolk.

"Yes, sir. And a praise the Lord one too." She folded her arms across her bosom while her eyes twinkled as she watched George fidget.

Now, I do raise my hands, but I'm not a shouter. Neither was Harry. He often said, "The Good Lord isn't deaf."

George put his watch close to his face and stared at it. The big hand moved toward 8:30. The judge glanced at me like Owen Robertson had in the third grade when he walked me home from school. Not good.

Despite George's glum lips, we loaded the car and left for DeWayne's church. Soon as the engine rumbled Josephine started humming the tune of, "Ain't Gonna Study War No More." Bartles licked George on the tip of his nose. George looked sour.

Bartles took one look at DeWayne's sniffling mother-in-law, abandoned his master and climbed right up into her lap. He doesn't play favorites.

You could feel the thump of the bass guitar before we stepped out of the car at the church. George's face sunk from glum to a tightening of his jaw. George marched after Josephine as if heading toward the French decapitating machine.

The judge smiled and shook hands as if he always went to church in this red-brick building with window sashes that hadn't been licked with paint in twenty years. The building shook with sounds; bass guitar, drums, voices raised in praise. George was distressed. I felt like I'd gone home. George's feet began to wiggle during the first song. It was only an inch or so, but when the tambourines came out his whole body actually began to move.

DeWayne's congregation was lively. I clapped a little then accidentally bumped into the judge. Harry had dubbed the Presbyterians the frozen chosen. I don't think he knew the judge could do Latin American rhythms.

I looked at a woman in the choir. She sashayed around like she was dancing the cake walk and her big purple hat had a movement of its own, as did the red ribbon plunked onto its side. Made me glad to be alive to see her joy.

George was fixated on her too because he bumped me from the other side then raised his hands to clap. I figured Mamie would never forgive me if I converted him from an atheist to a holy roller.

We were settling into worship when a woman

standing in front of us swayed to the music then she went toes up. Her white heels pumped the air as she hit the carpet in front of the altar. George leaned so far forward to get a view he almost fell over the pew in front of us. Two ladies placed a navy velvet blanket over the woman's legs. That's when Preacher DeWayne glided to the podium. He looked at the prone figure in front of him and cleared his throat.

"Lawd, it's mighty fine that you are speaking to our Sista Evalina." DeWayne walked down the two steps from the podium and stood by the woman on the floor. "Slain in the spirit of her sweet Jesus, our sista will need some help when she comes back to us." DeWayne looked straight at a lady at the piano. "Sister Dorcus, please sit right here," he said, patting the front pew, "and aid our sweet Evalina."

George was taking breaths in gallops as DeWayne mounted the podium again. I put a hand on George's arm, and he struck the wooden pew with his knee when he started from surprise.

The whole morning was a surprise for George, I imagine.

Then DeWayne wandered two hours through the story of Enoch, the man who walked with God.

Somewhere in the middle, I thought of Harry as DeWayne talked about God taking Enoch.

Harry was a good man. Young, too. Only sixty-nine when he died. We'd planned to live together a long time. Harry was going to grow his tomatoes, while I taught my grand babies to quilt, sing silly songs, and put words on paper.

Pondering all these things I lost DeWayne at, "So all the days of Enoch were three hundred and sixty-five years."

Thinking about myself wasn't pretty. How could you think about yourself when the one you love was planting tomatoes for Jesus? About that time, it hit me that Harry wouldn't walk Molly down the aisle, and I started to cry.

Now, Enoch leads to Methuselah, and then Lemech, and after Lemech was Noah. Boy howdy. I made my own flood.

I finally gave up all pretense of sophistication and put my hands in front of my face. Every time DeWayne gave a life span of a man, I thought of all the years without Harry. Maybe another thirty. With Meemaw still watering her cucumbers at ninety-six, I could live forty more years. Alone. I straightened my shoulders.

"Get used to it, little girl," I whispered to myself.

After the service the judge flirted with the lady in the purple hat. The longer they talked the more Josephine wandered around talking and getting sassy with the youngins'. George and I stood glad-handing and smiling until our jaws hurt. A woman as round as a cherry waddled up and thumped George on the chest with her pointer finger.

"Heard you want to know what happened at the hotel all them years ago." She jerked her head toward Josephine, who joined us.

George leaned toward her with interest. "I'm all ears."

"No sir, you ain't. You's all thinking, 'what could this old thing possibly have to tell me?'"

"Now, Aunt Claudine, tell your story," Josephine ordered.

Aunt Claudine lifted her chin and stared at George. "I was there that day. Working the shift from two to nine because the night clerk had to go visit his mama at the hospital."

"At the hotel?" George asked.

"That's what I'm telling you. On the morning of the sixteenth, the blonde from the doctor's room and that dark-haired woman, Clarisse, got into a fight. Right in front of me and Joe Spencer, the maintenance man. I was adding more towels in number 234 when the woman in Room 237—that's what I calls the brown-haired lady's room–marches up to Room 240 and raps real smart on it. I seen the doctor head down the stairs not two minutes before, so the blonde answers. That's when Room 237 woman slaps Room 240 woman smack in the face. She didn't say nothing before she hits her either. Just whack."

I tried to sort out the room numbers with hair color. Aunt Claudine waved her hands in the air. "Then Room 240 woman pulls the hair of the other lady, the one with the short hair. They fight like women do, with yelling, and crying, and slamming of doors."

My eyes stretched wide. Maybe as big as the saucers you put under plants.

"Well." George pulled an index card out of his shirt pocket and scribbled something.

"That ain't all," Aunt Claudine trumpeted. "The dark-haired one yelled about her money. Saying they had stolen her twenty thousand dollars and she wanted it back."

"Well, thank you, ma'am." George scribbled notes so fast I thought the ink would fly out of the pen. "Must have been something to behold."

"I almost covered my ears because what they were saying wasn't fit for nobody."

"I can well imagine," added George.

"I had to get ice and Band Aids for the blonde lady in Room 240 on account of the scratches on her face, which were bleeding."

"You the ones interested in the double murder?" We turned to see a man dressed in a deputy sheriff's uniform.

George grinned at his luck, but it wasn't luck. Josephine had a queue going down toward the front of the church.

"Don't know what I can say since it's an ongoing investigation," the deputy said.

George flashed his ID.

The deputy stuck out his chin. "Well, now, I've never met a federal officer." They shook hands, a sort of comrade-in-arms handshake, muscles flexing.

"We looked up the old file of the O'Neal cousins' arrest." The deputy shuffled his feet. "It states there was a blonde woman with the doctor. The police wanted to interview both the doctor and his blonde girlfriend, but they never did. The report says the hotel maid saw the pair of lovers drive off in the red car about four thirty in the afternoon while the O'Neals were talking to the sheriff."

Nothing new. We'd unearthed it all earlier.

"Just a minute, Lester," Aunt Claudine said. The deputy's head jerked when he looked at Aunt Claudine. "I recalls the woman came back that night before I left for home. That'd be about eleven, because Mr. Jeppson stayed at the hospital on account of his mother passing."

"So this woman who came back . . . did she come back alone or with the other woman?" I asked, a little confused.

"Alone. Didn't see the man again, either, come to think on it." Aunt Claudine titled her head.

"But the blonde came back, right?" pressed George.

"Pretty sure it was the blonde, but I didn't see her face or her hair 'cause of the baseball cap she had on. The woman jogged up the stairs, so's all I saw was her backside."

"And the next day? Did you see her?" George kept on it like a terrier with a mole.

"I was busy on the first floor. Started 'bout six back then doing the laundry. Didn't see hide nor hair of any of them."

"Well, I did," piped a voice hidden behind Aunt Claudine. A rabbit of a woman slid around her elbow and ratcheted her head toward George.

"What did you see?" George asked as his eyes grew wide.

"Saw the woman in 240 hauling her bags down to her car."

"Let me get this straight." George's brow puckered

as he spoke. "We're talking about the blonde."

"Hair the color of moonlight," the small woman said. "Styled like a movie star, all high and curly."

George's eyebrows lifted, echoing how I felt. "Miss Claudine, on the sixteenth a woman comes back sometime before eleven, but you don't know who. And you never saw any of the three again?"

"That's right. The next morning, I was shoving things into the washer when the lady from the doctor's room paid the bill and checked out. She was gone by eight."

"And you, Miss... are...?"

"Euphemia," said the small woman.

"Miss Euphemia, you say the blonde woman in Room 240 carried her luggage to her car then disappeared."

"No, sir. She checked out and ate breakfast in the dining room. Didn't leave until close to nine."

"You didn't tell me that," interrupted Aunt Claudine.

"Her having breakfast didn't make no matter. Her leaving was what the man asked about." Miss Euphemia crossed her thin arms real firm.

The deputy scratched his chin. "The brown-haired lady in Room 237 never did pay her bill. She left her clothes then up and disappeared. The car the blonde registered at the desk disappeared too. The day the blonde left was the same day the doc became a phantom. Report said a lady who was not a local went to the post office at nine and mailed a package. Clerk thought it might have something to do with the two men in jail so she called the police. The report stated the postal clerk remembered her face was pretty and that she wore a Cincinnati Bengals baseball cap. Had a package sent to Boyle County."

"Hmm," George said, his eyes almost popping. "Two women, one disappears. Well, actually both do." He bristled like one of Harry's coon dogs catching scent. "One of them sends something to our county."

"No," I said. "Darlene Frogmiejer didn't disappear. She's in the Dominican Republic working as a missionary."

"Who says?" asked George.

I smiled sweetly. "Her family. They get emails and post them all over town."

"We'll see." George whipped out his cell phone. When he connected to someone called the director, George and the Paducah policeman went outside.

"There's a barbecue at a park in the Land Between the Lakes this afternoon." Josephine wrapped a friendly arm around my shoulders. She was trying to manipulate me with her sweet smile into going off to meet strangers. I'd been there before when she cozies up, then wham, you're going door to door with Christmas wreaths made out of pine cones.

"Do you good, Miss Dee Dee, to be sociable." How did she know I fantasized about sitting in my house by myself, not talking to anyone for days—maybe weeks? "Sides, Mr. Harry don't want you moping around, not getting any sleep, eating like a bird. He'd be ashamed of me if I didn't get you movin'."

"It's all right," I said. "I'll go. Looks like George is caught up in something with the police for a while."

"That Mr. George with his flashy government ID's finally getting somewhere," she mumbled.

"I would love barbecue. Beats mac 'n' cheese any old day," I said to rearrange the conversation.

"Don't count on there being no mac 'n' cheese." Josephine smirked. "Geraldine Hotchkiss makes blue ribbon mac 'n' cheese, and from the look she's giving the judge, she'll be sending some home with him."

I grinned. Serve him right to have to run fifty extra miles to wear off the fat grams. Uncharitable, but he was surrounded by women, and it was unseemly in the sanctuary. I bit my tongue by accident. I had become a prude.

That afternoon we had music and barbecue. Best meal I'd had in a month of Sundays. Geraldine's mac 'n' cheese trumped all of the ladies in our congregation. I took one tiny bite. Her potato salad should be sold by the gallon. And the meat wasn't dry rub barbecue, but good, honest, slather on the sauce, ribs and brisket.

DeWayne put a drum set under a white canopy. The judge grabbed a stool beside him and asked for a guitar. Geraldine-of-the-Purple-Hat picked up a mic and began a melodic wail.

"Whoa, Nellie." George's face broke into a grin when things got to stompin'.

We left as the sun was thinking about western horizons. My feet throbbed from all the dancing. Unladylike to rub bare feet around a man not your husband, so I sucked it up, as Molly would say. George sat in the front seat with the dog.

That dog liked a warm lap and a view out the front window.

Chapter Fourteen

WE DROVE TOWARD OUR HOME TOWN on a two-lane road on a levee. The water along the marshes glowed soft orange as the sun eased over the Ohio. The land between the lakes settled in for the night. Clouds of bugs made tornado spirals in the air and pummeled the car with little ticking noises as they flattened against it. The judge turned the radio on to a jazz concert. A good way to end the day—jazz at sunset, and a soporific car ride.

The trunk of the car was packed tight with a borrowed cooler and ice for the mac 'n' cheese, potato salad, and half a sweet-potato pie on the top of the food containers. I thought about using the food to make an engagement party when out of the blue a Hummer sped past us and cut in front. Red brake lights flashed, but I swear there hadn't been any lights on the front when it passed. It sort of snuck up on us from the back then whizzed by.

The judge slammed on his brakes. We hit the big car square in the middle of the bumper. Our heads whipped forward and back as if we were puppets. The car sped ahead then pulled a U-turn, coming back toward us. We were on the side where the flood plain curved sharply left. The judge slowed to negotiate the sweep of the road when the Hummer veered into the driver's side. The impact spun us off the road toward the swampy land on the right.

The whites of Josephine's eyes were as big as Dixie cups. She didn't have time to scream, but she moaned a prayer, "Help, help, help, Lord."

As the front tires hit the embankment, the judge turned the wheel and tromped on the gas. His hand pulled on the emergency brake at the same time. I thought we were going to high center. We skidded on two wheels and did a 180, like kids in the school parking lot on icy days. We ended up heading back onto the gravel and stopped right before a steep drop off.

The judge was some slick driver.

Josephine's fingers wrapped around my arm until I thought it'd fall off. Bartles, who had been encased in George's arms, whimpered. I reached out for him. He leaped over the head rest and landed in my lap. I couldn't find any blood, but he shook like a maple tree in October.

"You ladies all right?" The judge's voice was raw.

"I'm fine," I said, ignoring the pain on my side where I had slammed into the door. I began to examine the puppy's legs one at a time to make sure nothing was broken.

"That fool driver could have gotten us killed." Josephine blew out a puff of air which moved her hair into her eyes.

"I think that was the intention." George sounded gravelly.

I looked in his direction. His hand was plopped onto the side of his head. Red liquid ran between his fingers.

"Call 911," ordered the judge. "The Humvee may be back. Those weren't kids out on a joy ride."

George dialed.

The puppy licked my face, starting with my nose. I squinted and wiped my face.

The judge put the car in motion, heading back the way we'd come. He kept looking in the mirror. Josephine thumped the judge on the shoulder with her hand.

"Hit it, Judge. Them outlaws want to see if we're in the bayou, and if we ain't, they'll come looking." The judge stomped on the gas. "Head straight to the hospital," she ordered. "Mr. George done crunched his head and Miss Dee Dee is shaking like a newborn calf. I ain't too steady myself, come to think on it."

The sun was down, the moon not yet up. Our headlights lay on the road in splinters. It was dark. Three-stories-down-a-coal-mine dark. We flew past the service station by the bridge and were whizzing toward Paducah when car lights penetrated our back window. Not just any lights but lights high up, like the Hummer's. George had rallied the police but there wasn't an oscillating cherry anywhere.

"Get my GPS from the floor by your feet, George, and find the hospital." The judge's voice was as still as untroubled water.

We flew past the low lands, the cat tails, and cane. The high-up lights were gaining. Josephine and I studied the road signs trying to find the blue H rectangle. Bartles crawled up my chest and wrapped his furry body around my neck. It was nice, the dog warming the place where stiffness settled into my shoulders. Josephine looked done in. Her hair, all groomed for church, had sprung around her head like a frayed Brillo. Her eyes said, "I'm scared and there's nothing you can do about it."

I took her hand and squeezed hard and didn't let her fingers escape back to her lap. When the Hummer caught up, George was saying to the police dispatcher, "No tags on the Hummer."

"Duck." The judge's voice rose.

I saw the judge ease down low, his eyes below the steering wheel. I picked Bartles from my neck and bent over him, using my body as a shield and praying the puppy stayed safe in my arms. Bullets riveted the car. One burned over my arm, another made Josephine yelp.

"Lower your window and stay down," George ordered the judge as he fired past the driver's seat toward the dark-windowed car.

The car sped into hyper drive, and we were thrust forward then thumped back into the seat. Bartles shook so hard I thought he'd disintegrate.

Finally, two black and whites with their sirens'

wailing cruised toward us. The Hummer peeled off, paralleled the river, then cut down a side street heading toward the industrial area. One cruiser went on pursuit, the other escorted us to the hospital.

"Josephine's been hit in the back," I said, my voice trembling. I put pressure on a ragged hole beside her ribs. Copious amounts of blood seeped through her clothes and onto my hands.

"If'n they upset that cooler there'll be mac 'n' cheese all over the trunk," she muttered. "I'm fine, Miss Dee Dee. You get your hands offen me so's I can sit up."

She gets bossy when she's in pain. Josephine delivering Savannah wasn't for the faint-hearted. Half-way into transition Josephine said she was done with the baby business and it was time to take her home. I'd out-stubborned her. Now, I kept pushing on her floral church dress wondering what the wound looked like.

When the ER nurses eased her out of my arms the judge growled, "Take the other lady as well. She's hurt too."

"Fiddle dee dee," I said to him. I held his little mutt and stepped out of the car. My knees were wobbly. The judge scooped me up like I weighed nothing and carried me through the big swinging doors.

The emergency room lighting revealed the side of George's face was a stream of red. A slice above his right eyebrow was the shape of a crescent. The judge looked mighty fine, meaning he hadn't been hit.

I squirmed to get down. "No, you don't," he said in my ear. "Your breath is thready."

I let that sink in. "What about Bartles?" I asked, holding tighter to the dog.

"I'll call DeWayne. Have him take Bartles to the vet then ask his mother-in-law if she will take care of him."

People in blue scrub suits started popping up around the three of us. Josephine was carted off first, then George, and finally they put me into a tiny cubical with a flimsy curtain. I felt naked without the puff ball dog in my arms.

Josephine went to surgery. George was concussed and lacerated. I had bruised ribs. The judge had nary a scratch. He checked us into the hotel. Same rooms. My roommate, however, remained in the hospital attached to an IV. The bullet had entered her back on the right side, caressed a rib and exited. The medical prognoses was she had blood loss with damaged tissue but nothing vital had been hit.

"Molly and Cam are sitting tight, keeping Mamie company," the judge reported as he settled me into the room with bags of frozen peas to place on my assorted bruises. "The police want to interview you. I told them not until tomorrow. Tonight, everyone sleeps."

The medication I swallowed made my mind wander. I lay on the clean sheets and thought of Harry. Before we married Harry had said, "You need to know where I've been before you saddle up with me." He placed poems from his military days in my hands. "These hold a young man's dreams. I give them to you because you hold my heart." After reading his poems I put my hand in his and held on tight. He didn't let go until he put his hand in Another's. Thinking about it made me blubber myself to sleep.

I woke at ten a.m. to find the judge sitting on the chair staring at me. I whipped the sheets up to my neck then groaned, not quiet and lady like either, but loud as a stuck hog. The ice bag vegetables were still frozen and placed on parts of me only Harry knew. I squinted my eyes at him because I knew they had been replaced. Frozen vegetable bags thaw in short order.

"I'm wondering what to tell the police who are pacing downstairs. They need to ask you a few questions." He flashed me a smile and rose.

Getting a breath was an undertaking. My whole right side was the color of purple irises. After a shower, I eased into pants and a shirt then attempted the stairs. Everything was sore, my neck, the tips of my fingers and my rear end, which had done nothing but stay fixed to the seat. I was as creaky as Meemaw, and not grateful to know it.

The judge met me in the lobby with two policemen in tow. One was the deputy from church. The deputy's mouth made a small O when he saw me stumbling along on the judge's arm.

"Miss Delilah is a trifle sore." The judge eased me onto a seat in the hotel's restaurant. "They're holding the breakfast menu for you."

"Coffee." The thought of chewing when my scalp ached wasn't appealing.

The judge gave me his courtroom eye, which is worse than my squinty one. "And?" His voice was more order than ask.

"Hmm." I fingered the menu and saw my right hand had a big splatter of bruise growing.

"Coffee all around," he said to the waitress who had materialized from the counter. "The lady will have the eggs Benedict with one egg but two muffins with hollandaise on it and a fruit salad."

"We can only give her two eggs. It says on the menu, two eggs and that's how we do it." The waitress looked at the judge and waited for his protest.

"Fine," he said. "Bring an extra plate."

The police got little information from me. I had only seen the car from the side and hadn't gotten a glimpse of passenger or driver.

The police left when the eggs arrived. The judge slid one egg off onto the second plate and waggled his fork at me.

"Eat up, Delilah, so we can head to the hospital. Josephine is suspicious since she hasn't seen your face. She thinks you're in the morgue." The egg was fine, the sauce, however, didn't hold a candle to the Chicken Coop's. But what can you expect?

"It's about time," Josephine said when we arrived.

"Sending George to keep me company wasn't the best idea. He's been on the phone all morning talking to people in Washington." She sounded proud of him. "No doubt y'all are seein' the town while they got me penned up in this here institution." She shook her head at us. If she hadn't been lying on her right side to avoid the bandages on her back, she would have crossed her arms. "When can I bust outta here?"

"Tomorrow, Josephine," answered the judge. "We will stay until you can travel."

She yawned.

"Anything we can do for you?"

"You just keep Miss Dee Dee safe. I don't want to have to answer to Mr. Harry if anything happens to her." The judge nodded solemnly.

Later in the day a couple of fishermen found the Hummer abandoned near the river. George said it was wiped clean of prints. We left him to his government pals via AT& T.

By the time we liberated Bartles from DeWayne's, I think the dog had gained a couple of pounds. As we walked through town Bartles pulled at the leash, trying to lead. The judge, who never admitted to being hurt, winced. And his legs were stiff as we ambled past the shops and restaurants. The judge kept my arm in his because I was hunched over and breathed through my nose like Meemaw when she climbed the cemetery hill to lay flowers. We didn't go far, just ambled until Bartles did his duty.

We turned the lock on my door and stepped inside. My clothes were turned inside out and thrown on the floor, my makeup bag opened in the bathroom, the tubes and jars scattered on the tiny counter. Even the mattress was flipped onto the floor. I stood like a mannequin, the only thing I moved was my eyes, taking in the mess, then I thumped down onto the box springs still on the bed. "Ah, nuts." I crinkled my brow. Having my orderly life messed with was too much.

The police searched for prints. George hadn't heard a peep. He claimed kettle drums were concussing behind his eyes from his head crack. Inching around the room, holding my ribs and stooped over like a woman in labor, I took my time reordering my belongings. The door between our rooms remained wide open.

"We are not taking any chances," George declared.

The judge left, then returned with a long piece of paper. He spread it out on a bed in his room and scrawled, October fifteenth. "There may be a clue we've overlooked."

Without Harry's journal, I was lost. "Do you remember last Wednesday at five p.m., George?" I asked. The pair of them glanced up at me.

"You need your pain pills, Delilah," said the judge in a tender tone, one you'd address to a granny.

"I'm sitting tight." I plunked down in the chair by the desk. I wasn't about to go to sleep again, their investigation was interesting.

He went through our connecting doors and brought back a pill and glass of water. I went toes up in less than ten minutes.

"I think that does it, George," I heard him say. I blinked. I was on the second twin bed in their room and under a blanket. George's ear was still attached to his phone. The judge stood over his paper and frowned. "Now I need to know where everyone was on the day Clarisse disappeared."

"Me and the blackbirds were in the garden." I attempted to sit up. Moving was a mistake. Breathing seemed okay if the breaths were shallow. "Harry was at the counting house when Clarisse was there, then he was gone all day and had a meeting that night. He got home after eleven."

They looked at me without comprehension.

"Nursery rhyme," I explained. "I gardened every day when the weather permitted, and Harry was on campus Monday through Friday." We were accounted for, even though we weren't suspects.

I'd have to see Harry's journal to put it all in order. The fifteenth was a Monday or Tuesday. Harry had promised to take the boys to the school for baseball try-outs that week. He'd been a first baseman in college and could make a one-armed sweep, tagging out a runner like a major leaguer. In the drama of the day Harry must have forgotten, so I drove Cam, Beau, John, and Paul.

"When did he get home that night?" George asked.

"After I'd tucked the boys in bed. It was after midnight, I guess, not eleven." Pushing up from the bedcovers made me gasp. My right side was on fire.

"More ice," stated the judge. He went to the small refrigerator under the TV stand and brought out a packet of peas. "Here," he said, his eyes skittering left so I wouldn't notice that he thought Harry might be involved with Clarisse's disappearance.

"Harry could be forgetful," I began. "Sometimes he'd have a poem rambling through his brain, so he'd stop in mid-bite and scribble on a napkin. Not a paper one, either."

George didn't give me eye contact.

"Where's your little dog?" I asked, wanting comfort.

The judge slid his gaze my direction. "Asleep on George's foot. We'll have dinner, then discuss this again."

My appetite disappeared.

Chapter Fifteen

A STATE POLICE ESCORT WENT IN front of us from Paducah to our home town like they do at funerals. Josephine took one look at the levee where we had two-wheeled our way to safety and shivered. I held Josephine's hand, glad the bullet hadn't hit anything vital. It had simply done an in-and-out, grazing the ribs. Her problem was blood loss. She was a bit light-headed. I thought of all the questions I wanted to ask Harry.

"In due time, little girl," I heard him say.

We got to Josephine's home as an evening breeze began to cool the after-dinner porch sitters. I don't think George knew this part of town with its crab-grass yards and peeling-paint houses. These were people raised on little and expecting little else.

Josephine had stayed with her mama and daddy to raise her daughter. When her daddy died, Harry paid the mortgage and gave the house to Josephine and her mama. A sweet place that had a porch with Victorian gingerbread on the facing below the roof. I'd painted the house two summers ago with her mama manning a paintbrush chattering alongside of me. Her dementia had been on hold while we worked. Doing something with her hands was helpful.

When we arrived, Josephine's mama was slumped on the metal swing by the door. Miss Vickie put her hand over her eyes and stared at the unfamiliar car.

"Girl?" she called through the screen door. "You've got company."

Josephine's teenage daughter, Savannah, came bursting through the doorway. "Mom, I thought the hospital would keep you longer." Her voice was just above a whisper. The girl bent her long frame and wrapped an arm around her mother's neck before planting a kiss on Josephine's cheek. Then Savannah fiddled with her hands, putting them first in front of her before sliding them into her pockets.

"Oh, Mom," Savannah whispered, looking into Josephine's gray face. The judge escorted Josephine across the porch and into her parlor. Josephine didn't stop. She aimed toward her room and inched down on the bed as if each movement was agony.

Alone, Savannah stood in the bedroom doorway with her arms wrapped around her waist.

I tucked Josephine into bed, clothes and all. The judge placed Josephine's suitcase by the window then turned his back on us, staring out into the side yard. You could hear the happy song of the birds in the honeysuckle and the whoosh of air on the ceiling fan blades.

"You stay and rest," I ordered. "Ladies from the congregation are applying their wisdom to casseroles."

Josephine's mouth puckered. I think she would have said something sassy if her mother hadn't wandered to the bed. "There you go, girl, getting chicken pox." Miss Vickie waggled a bony finger at her daughter. "Don't know what I'm going to do with you while I work. Maybe Miz Lily can hop over to keep you company." Josephine's eyes stretched wide.

Miz Lily had been dead for twenty years.

The judge, George, and I slowly mounted my front steps. Molly and Cam took one look at us and shook their heads in tandem like they'd practiced the mime.

"We're staying until Cam's classes resume," Molly announced.

Arguing would be futile. Once Josephine was up and at 'em I'd decide what to do about their protective detail.

"Your mac 'n' cheese was a big hit with the ladies next door," Cam said with a grin.

"How much did you get rid of?" I asked.

"All of it." Cam's grin widened.

"You're a good man, Cam," said his father, clapping him on the back.

I looked over the lawn to see Mamie standing on her verandah with her face still red from the poison ivy and her eyes hidden behind dark glasses. Her arms were crossed over her ample bosom. It did not look good for George.

"Now, you head to our house if you've a need. After your phone call to her about the local DAR women, you may be bedless." The judge spoke to George while eyeing the lady with the rigid face.

Maylene Frogmiejer poked her nose out of the Salases' screen door. George casually put his brown leather suitcase on his porch. After a few words with Mamie, George vectored toward my yard, a smile on his lips.

A gaggle of women burst out of the Salases' door and clucked around Mamie, resembling the brood Harry wrote about. I smiled, then I chuckled, which hurt.

"Thinking about Harry's 'Ode to the Hens'?" the judge asked, his hand still on my shoulder.

"No. 'The Peckin' Party.'"

At that, Cam and Molly lost all composure and doubled over. Harry's prize-winning poems were about people disguised as occupants of a hen house. Meredith Wilson's song from the "Music Man" had nothing on Harry's satirizing, tenderizing, and shish-ka-bobbing the locals.

George mounted my front steps. "My favorite is the 'Roistering Rooster.'" George's eyes crinkled with suppressed laughter. "I'm not begging a room, Judge. I've given her ten minutes to clear her flock out of my house."

I half-wanted to watch the women fly out of George's coop and half-wanted to crawl upstairs and lie down. But fly they did before I'd made up my mind to retreat. Sunglasses affixed to their noses, Charlene and Maylene skulked down the driveway, eyes glued our direction. Cam made a little chicken noise as they sidled around the trees and climbed into their cars.

"Don't laugh, don't laugh." I put my hand over my mouth to keep the giggles in check.

That left the perpetrator of the ivy fiasco, Mamie; Eleanor, the choir director at the Episcopal church; and Olive Lorraine Patrick. Olive Lorraine's car, last in the line-up, trapped the others. She squared her shoulders, stepped down the limestone walk, and started her engine. The other women made a run for their cars, hunched over as if they suspected we'd lob bombs. I thought we were home free until Olive Lorraine backed out of George's drive and pulled into mine.

"This will be interesting," the judge muttered as Molly brought a tray of ice water to us.

The realtor got out of her car, reached into her passenger seat, and pulled out the little wheeling gizmo they use to measure the outside of a house. Olive Lorraine Patrick didn't become student-body president because she sat on any laurels.

"I was over yesterday but you weren't home," she called to me as she started dragging her machine from the right side of the verandah toward us. "There seems to be a mis-measurement." She looked at her wheel.

Molly put the tray down.

"My turn, Mom," she said, pushing up her shirt sleeves.

"You better stop her, Cam, before the DAR has another revolution on their hands," the judge said.

Cam leapt to his feet and swept Molly into his arms. He kissed her long and slow. Molly was panting when he finished.

"I love it when you're steamed." Cam's face was serious. "Not at me, mind you. But now, sweetheart, we're going to let your mom handle this."

The judge rose and helped me to my feet. We

walked down the stairs with my hand on his arm.

"There is seven to nine feet missing from my inside calculations.   I   can   accurately   estimate measurements," the realtor said proudly. "Do you have a hidden closet near the library?"

"No," I said. "We did have. Harry had it converted."

"Into what? A smoking den?" She snickered.

She of all people knew Harry didn't smoke. They dated through high school and into their college years. Everyone believed they were perfect for one another. Harry the dreamer living with a go-getter-calculator was the town's idea of a heavenly match. Harry had other ideas.

Olive Lorraine Patrick didn't need to find my hidey hole, writing room, sanctuary. The judge scratched his head as if confounded.

"Olive Lorraine," I said quietly. "This is my home. You do not have the right to intrude upon it without an invitation. It is time for you to leave. I will not be selling this house now or in the foreseeable future." I paused, grabbing a shallow bit of air. "I expect you will no longer feel obligated to drop by."

I used my sophisticated Southern accent, the one my New York publisher would recognize. Olive Lorraine's eyes darted from my face to the judge's, then back to mine. Her mouth opened but no words flew my direction. She wheeled her little machine down our walk to her car without saying a word.

"Delilah," the judge said around his twitching lips. "That was marvelous."

"I feel ashamed." I would have run into the house, but I couldn't breathe let alone stand upright and do the 100-yard dash.

Lyle patted my shoulder. "Olive Lorraine would have been a terrible wife for Harry."

"Dad and that pushy woman?" Molly said. "You've got to be kidding."

"No." Lyle shook his head. "From what I heard, the town was set on the match. When your daddy came home with your mother some people turned their back and haven't made a one-eighty yet. But they will, I promise."

Sometimes the judge embarrassed me.

Checking on the garden seemed a good idea. I unearthed my leather gloves and straw hat in the garden room. When I eased down the front steps Sidney's nose was inches from Harry's zucchini. He often searched for produce toward evening.

"Any visitors to report?" I asked him.

"Only a delivery man. I let him put the box in the library since I had mud on my boots."

I made for the library like a courier pigeon during a war. The box on the desk had Harry's name on it. I sat in Harry's chair breathing hard. I had expected destruction from a thief masquerading as a delivery man. What I got was Harry's last book—fifteen leather bound copies, ready for autographs. I sniffed. The book was an aberration. Before Harry died, we'd put together his Christmas poems as private gifts to his family. The verses depicted his wonder at the abiding, unconditional love given from our Creator.

"You all right in here?" the judge asked as he lounged in the doorway.

I drew a finger across the top of the box. "Harry's last book." My voice sounded clogged.

"I see." His blue eyes darkened. He turned on his heels and walked out the front door. I heard his voice and Cam's receding as they walked around the verandah, then I heard them clearly because they stopped outside the turret window.

"Cam, let's head for home," the judge said.

"I'll wait to tell Molly goodnight."

"I'll be up when you get in. We need to talk."

"About what?" Cam said, startled.

"I've put my foot in it regarding Miss Delilah. She says I'm hovering like a mosquito ready to invade."

"She never," declared Molly, joining them.

"Practically," was the judge's answer.

I thought about his complaint, deciding I'd apologize in the morning if I'd offended him. Not that I knew what I'd said.

Night came lazily on as it does in a Kentucky July. Sidney slept in the guest bedroom with a Little Slugger bat by his side. Molly meandered to her old room. No prowlers interrupted my sleep and Josephine was in the kitchen when I came downstairs at seven.

"What in the Sam Hill are you doing here?" I shouted.

"Mama sat up all night rocking in her bentwood chair and singing Lena Horne blues songs. Nobody got a lick of sleep."

"Your mama's Alzheimer's can be a problem. You need rest to recover. I'll have Molly change the sheets in the guest bedroom so you can sleep there," I offered. "And no work. I can't, so *you* can't. And that's the rules."

"Humph," was all she said.

I decided that meant "fine." By nine, when the judge hadn't made an appearance, I looked out the front door to see if he was up. Maybe he had a prowler? Was he sick? Was he wanting me to cross the street and apologize for I didn't know what?

The thump of a basketball on asphalt intruded my thoughts. Cam was shooting hoops in our drive. Attempting to block him was Molly, whose long arms reached skyward like a hold-up victim. No sign of the judge. I would have breathed a sigh of relief, but Josephine came up behind me. I jumped as high as Cam did for his lay-up.

"You flightier than usual, Miss Dee Dee. Won't catch sight of the judge if that's why you're peering out the door like a love-sick puppy."

"Really, Josephine. It's none of my business what the man does."

"Uh-huh."

"He's been sticking to me like chewing gum on a loafer. I expected to find him at daybreak lounging on my verandah sipping coffee.”

“Well, he ain't. Cam said his dad took off for the airport this morning.”

“He did *what*? Who does he think he is? Without a by-your-leave he takes off?”

“You sure are mad, 'cause your nostrils are all pinched.”

“And did he check with the local law enforcement to see if he could go gallivanting about as if he's royalty? Didn’t they tell you not to leave town?”

“Not that I remember. However, I saw the sheriff standing on his doorstep and shaking his hand as I drove in.”

Miffed at the judge disappearing without talking about it, I went out onto the verandah to cool down. As I paced and grew calmer from the jasmine scent, I caught a glimpse of Mamie and George walking hand in hand toward their car. A smile crossed my lips as Josephine opened the front door and joined me.

“I’ve lists upon lists for him to participate in.”

“I'll bet you do,” Josephine said with a tight smile. She wasn't fooling me. She was in pain.

“Are you still taking the medicine we picked up for you?”

“That stuff makes me diddle-brained. With my re-spons-o-bil-it-ies, I've got to be in fightin' form.”

“For what? In all this hoo-haw no one's forgotten you are quite capable. But . . .” I paused like a ham actress. “Now I need you to help by taking care of yourself.”

“That'd be the day,” she huffed.

Molly scooted past us with sweat streaking down her face, her bangs flattened and stringy from the workout.

“Josephine, you're hurt.” I stared at her to make my point.

“Don't worry, Mom,” Molly said from the stair landing. “I'll help to keep her in line.”

Chapter Sixteen

After a quick trip to the garden center I walked toward the front of my house where Cam was parked on my wicker love seat shelling peas. The judge's pup was at his feet.

"Miss Delilah." Cam stood so abruptly he almost dumped the bowl. "May I help you with your things?"

"I'd be obliged, Cam." I nodded toward Bartles. "That pup seems at home."

"I'm letting Molly keep him for a while." Cam sprinted toward my car.

With my potting soil hefted on his shoulder and a large clay pot in his right hand, Cam traipsed to the garden shed. A few minutes later, hopping up the stairs empty handed he grinned. "Dad went to visit Beau."

"Oh?" I pretended to be disinterested in his wanderings.

"He and a friend will then head to Hawaii. Dad said since it was so close, he might as well hop on over."

Dad-rat the judge. There was a wedding to plan. I needed him to keep Cam busy. The men could hang out in their wood shop and fashion something for a wedding gift.

"How'd the sheriff let him leave town if he's on the short list of suspects?"

"Oh, Dad got permission. The FBI claim to be looking elsewhere or, to quote Dad, 'giving me a long leash.'"

"Or rope on which to hang himself," I finished his thought.

Cam held the front door open with his backside. I eased past him. Molly stood on the stair landing in her running shorts and T-shirt. I looked at her and thought about the wedding dress packed away in a fancy gold box.

After a fitting, I stayed in the parlor for three long days taking apart the bodice. As I celebrated the last stitch unstitched, the doorbell chimed. I put down the silk to stand but settled back when I heard the hurried steps of Josephine.

"On your verandah is Mr. Neely Patrick," Josephine announced a minute later. "He's leaning against one of the pillars as if he owns the place." She sniffed with disapproval. "Olive Lorraine is behind him, hanging onto her ginormous purse like a shield."

I put down my sewing. "I'll see them. Why don't you send Molly in here with your world-class lemonade?"

"You should know better than to treat with the enemy," she muttered as she stalked off.

I walked into the foyer. Neely Patrick was a slick-looking man with jet black hair, a deep tan, and a gold chain necklace wreathing his neck wrinkles. He shook my hand but skittered his eyes sideways, so he didn't look me square in the peepers.

"Always be suspicious of someone who can't give you eye contact," Daddy said. "They might be lying, they might be shy. It's good to figure out the difference."

Neely Patrick didn't have a shy bone in his body. Neither did his wife. They were the only married couple I knew who planned separate vacations. Three or four times a year he headed some place tropical and came back sporting skin the color of mahogany. Olive Lorraine preferred health spas or places where she could shop. Apparently, they had recently been on vacation because Neely looked as dark as a polished chestnut while Olive Lorraine had on the latest fashion color, lime green.

"Please come in," I invited. "Molly is bringing refreshments. What may I do for you?" I used my gentrified voice.

Neely raised his eyebrows. "Don't mind if we do." He slid past me, aiming toward Harry's office.

"The parlor is on the left." I took him firmly by the arm and moved him into it.

They sat on the divan. Olive Lorraine tugged at her skirt hem. Collectively their eyes looked at the heap of white silk.

"Is someone planning a wedding?" Olive Lorraine asked.

"Molly and Cam Henderson are engaged," I answered as smooth as the dupioni draped on the chair.

"And you are *making* her dress?" Olive Lorraine couldn't hide her shock.

"Remaking *my* dress. Molly wanted to wear it." I waited.

They lifted their gaze to the painting above the fireplace like a pair of comedians.

"Is that an original Burns?" Neely asked abruptly.

"Yes."

His eyes circled the room then he cleared his throat. "We would like to apologize on behalf of our company for intruding upon you in your time of grief."

"I see." I bit my tongue, making my eyes water as Molly approached with a tray of drinks. She served us, then sat opposite me in the other wing chair.

"We were admiring your painting above the fireplace." Neely motioned toward it.

"Oh, my aunt's painting? We've several I believe." Molly shrugged. "Dad admired them, so she painted a few only for him."

Neely choked on his lemonade. "Your aunt is Suzanne Burns?"

"Yes," Molly said, her expression puzzled.

"Isn't that remarkable," Neely licked his lips. "I believe I heard that somewhere but didn't quite believe it."

"All Mom's siblings are amazing. One's an orthopedic surgeon at John's Hopkins. Of course,

Mom graduated..."

I shook my head firmly. Molly narrowed her eyes and she wasn't smiling.

"I think, sweetheart, the Patricks aren't interested in our family history. They came to apologize." I stood up and walked to the divan. "Thank you for your apology. I accept it and forgive you."

"Ah." Neely hung onto his lemonade glass like a life ring. "Kind of you, I'm sure. Olive mentioned that the painting in Harry's study was remarkable. May I have a little peek before we go?"

"Actually," I said brusquely, "No one enters Harry's study until I can finish resorting after our break in. We want to protect Harry's writings."

I was steamed. They hadn't come to apologize. They'd come to snoop. Molly looked at the ceiling to keep from bursting into laughter.

Olive Lorraine leapt to her feet, while Neely reluctantly stood.

"We have a meeting," Neely explained. Olive Lorraine nodded like a bobble-head doll. Her mouth was puckered shut so she wouldn't say anything. I figured it was on orders from her hubby. They longingly gazed at Harry's office. Our front door was wide, and they stepped out together, as if on parade. I walked onto the verandah and smiled.

"'Bye." I waved.

"Thank you for your kindness, Mrs. Morgan."

They studied the side of the house, the place between Harry's study and the guest bath. The missing nine feet five inches. I walked into the foyer, closed the door, and leaned against it.

I headed to the cemetery where the families of our town had been properly buried. It wasn't simply a local cemetery but a national cemetery for the boys in blue and gray who fought in the summer of 1863 in central

Kentucky. There were Inmans, Jacksons, MacDowells, and of course, Morgans. They'd been here since the beginning. Had fought on both sides during the Civil War and now lay incarcerated in the ground, awaiting the great wake-up day. I didn't want to talk to Harry with Molly around, because I wanted to tell him a thing or two.

The Morgan plot was on the right, front and center. There was a black iron fence around it with fleur-de-lis at the top. It had a fresh coat of paint. After his diagnosis, Harry had announced he intended to spit polish the place before he had to join the ranks. He and Sidney took an afternoon, and then another, and another. Harry came back from their jaunts pale and tired, but he finished before April headed into May.

The afternoon sky was scudded with white fluffy clouds as I eased the van through the cemetery's wrought iron gates. I looked at the lines of tombstones. Harry didn't have a headstone yet. I was dithering about it. What words carved into stone can give the essence of a man? Chiseled into my heart was the truth about Harry.

Sighing, I climbed out of the van and took my bucket of fresh flowers from the backseat. The gate to the Morgan gravesites was swinging. I frowned. I always closed it tight. Harry's grave was in the back of the plot, shaded by a massive tulip poplar. The ground was still scalped clean, the grass mottled with dirt patches. I stepped around the poplar's trunk and gasped. Stuck in the dirt were little plastic animals in pink, blue, yellow, and green. Two little lambs were perched on the headstones of our little boys. A Noah's ark of animals trotted along the mound sheltering Harry's bones. At his feet was a vermillion plastic vase with red plastic tulips, six in all, haphazardly jammed in.

Oh, drat. We had some nut wandering around the cemetery.

Chapter Seventeen

IT WAS PITCH BLACK, AND BY the clock hand, three a.m., when I woke to sirens and pounding on my front door. Cam stood under our porch light in his BVDs looking muscled and embarrassed.

Josephine dashed from her room. "The police are having a reunion over at the judge's." She pointed out the window to the flashing lights.

As Josephine grabbed Cam's arm and pulled him into the house, I put my hands on my hips. "What in the Sam Hill?" There were two oscillating lights flashing across their house. The glow made the dark night striped red and yellow.

"Prowlers. As in more than one. I heard them talking," Cam said. He ran a hand through his tousled hair before Molly threw herself into his arms. "I'm all right, my sweet," he said around her curls. "They were intent on searching Dad's room, so I climbed out the window, tiptoed across the roof, and shimmied down the drainpipe." He smiled at me. "Good thing it's sturdy."

I arched a brow. "You have been doing it since you were six."

His smile changed to a look of shock. "You knew?"

"Of course. Boys need a little exercise. Your daddy didn't think it was harmful to let you sneak around. If you'd tried it in high school that'd be another story."

When the police came to question Cam, we all walked back with him. The darkness cloaked us with its mystery, a phrase I think I'll use in a story if I can scribble it down. George Salas was on the judge's porch when we arrived.

"Sorry about all the noise, Mr. Salas," Cam apologized.

"Not a problem." George patted his holstered gun.

He wore his like they do in movies, a leather holster slung at his hip, butt forward for a quick cross-draw. He walked with us into the house, his eyes studying the windows . . . doors . . . lights . . . the shadows on the stairs. He ambled to the back door and peered at the lock.

"Did you leave this door unlocked, Cam?" he asked.

"No, but the alarm should have sounded when it opened."

"Hmm." George pulled on his left ear, thinking. "They must have had a key and known how to disengage the alarm. Do you hide a key somewhere?"

"No, sir. Dad never forgets his keys."

"How long have you had the alarm system?" the deputy asked.

"It came with the house."

They talked while I studied the décor. It had changed since Clarisse left. Years ago, when the boys were little, I'd been in the house a few times to pick them up. I'd always liked the wainscoting, high ceilings, and ornate cove molding that told the story of the Federal period. I pushed my nose into the living room and was stunned by the beauty of the clean-lined modern furnishings. Thomas Jefferson, meet Frank Lloyd Wright.

The judge's bedroom was ransacked as thoroughly as the Goths pillaged Rome. Picture frame glass was shattered over his carpet, his mattress was bi-folded, his clothes turned inside out and thrown on the floor. Everything in his bathroom was scattered across the counter or tossed in his Jacuzzi tub.

The family photos were ripped in two. Cam found one of his grandparents and teared up. When the police left, Josephine and I set to work putting things right. We piled clothes on the bed.

I waved at the pile. "What can we salvage and what needs dry cleaning?"

I marched into the bathroom to clean the smear of

shaving cream off the mirror.

The thieves had been searching for something. Were they the same people who attacked us in Paducah? If they wanted to be malicious the bathroom lotions would have been poured onto the bedding, the carpet, or his clothes, rather than a smear of white on the mirror. But that didn't explain the fixation on the family pictures.

Somebody hates grandmas?

George suggested we head to my house for breakfast. He ended up rattling around my kitchen with Cam.

The sun was rising when Mamie scuttled over.

"George called and asked me to breakfast," she explained, meek as a kitten. "I've been wrestling with some things since Cam and Molly helped with my poison ivy illness. Maybe I've been un-neighborly." Her face said otherwise because it was pale, and her brows were pinched together. Even though our daughters were best-friends, Mamie rarely came to my house. I'd concluded I was anathema in her DAR circle and nothing I could do would alter that.

"Come and join the party," George said as he strained the crepe batter.

Mamie Salas sat beside Josephine and cleared her throat. "May I have a glass of orange juice, please?"

Molly raised her eyebrows at me. I wanted to shout, "Hallelujah and praise the Lord," but figured it might scare Mamie off. Juice was passed, creamer, then sugar for her coffee. Her face began to loosen. Maybe George had broken down the high walls of rectitude and perfection. George winked at me. The judge would enjoy this.

I chewed on my lip at the thought...the judge was enjoying himself with his "friend" in the tropics.

"George and I are so pleased there is a wedding in the neighborhood," Mamie said, real polite. "Is there anything I can do to help? I'd be happy to address invitations."

"That's on my orange clipboard, Miss Mamie," piped up Josephine. "I's could do with some help with the invites."

I couldn't help but think that the women in our congregation and Mamie Salas working side by side should be a memorable occasion. Mamie getting a glimpse of the sweetest people in town and hearing those women pray for Molly's wedding would be an eye-opener.

We weren't taking any chances on the bridegroom getting injured by invaders, so I told Cam he could sleep in our basement with the puppy.

When he'd looked hopeful, Josephine said, "A floor between you and Miss Molly ain't a bad thing. And don't try any of your smarty maneuvers on me, Mr. Cam. You two can meet on the first floor."

"I'm twenty-four, Josephine." He crossed his arms over his chest.

"And don't I know it! Twenty-four and hormones escaping out your ears."

What with the burgling and wedding, we were fit to be tied. It took three more days of phone calls and running from printers to florists to feel as settled as you can be in chaos.

Still, the judge was in absentia. Cam said, "Dad and his friend were riding horses at a ranch in Hawaii." I didn't know the judge could recognize stirrups from a bridle.

Between pricking my finger with a needle and playing with the puppy, I searched high and low for Harry's journal. Still no enlightenment.

Six weeks before the wedding, Molly finally decided who was going to be in the wedding party. She wanted three bridesmaids.

We went to Lexington to the shop that catered to Miss Kentucky contestants where Molly chose dresses for the bridesmaids.

"Maybe less glitz, Mom," she said as lights glinted off the bodice beads. "I've asked Mr. Maurice to find a dress for you. No suit, Mom. It's not a business meeting."

I wasn't much interested. Shopping was stressful. Getting in and out as fast as a fox in a hen house was the goal. The pastel dress Molly brought me seemed more bridal than motherly.

"This one, Mom. It matches your eyes." The French blue dress with a sweetheart neckline and a floor-length skirt, accentuated my curves.

"Perfect," Molly exclaimed. "We'll take it."

Molly was encased in a jonquil-yellow dress that reminded me of a honey bee when her cell phone croaked like mating frogs.

"Oh, hi, Cam." Molly's smile faded as she listened. "What? . . . You mean, she's still out there somewhere?"

"What? Who? When?" I blurted, hanging onto my Kentucky blue clipboard with both hands. Had they lost the judge's little dog who'd moved into my house and now owned the place?

Molly set her attention on me. "According to preliminary tests, the body in the car might not be Cam's mom."

"Oh." My word sounded deflated.

If it wasn't Clarisse, where was she? And who was the skeleton in the car? Darlene? Or maybe an unknown woman. Perhaps another disgruntled husband had bumped them off instead of the judge. Or . . . my mind went a little haywire . . . our illustrious mayor did the deed, trying to cover up Darlene's indiscretion.

We winged home with only a small drive-thru stop for chicken and slaw. We got enough food for our boarders, which still included Josephine who was sleeping with a rolling pin handy in the boys' old bedroom. She said it was for burglars, but she eyed

Cam with upturned lips when she said it.

Five weeks after his death, Harry was to receive an honor from a prestigious poetry group. I felt lost packing a bag without Harry's tan pants beside my fancy dress. As I exited JFK's baggage area, a blue-suited man stood holding a sign with my name on it. Harry's publisher sending a driver in livery to pick me up made me smile. I felt like bowing he looked so fancy. We drove straight to Max's Manhattan office.

"Delilah," Max stood when I was ushered into his book-strewn room. "I am thankful you came." He kissed my cheek. Max's bushy eyebrows wiggled theatrically as he placed a chair near his desk.

I'd known Max for years before Harry slipped him a book I'd written, and Max insisted on a contract. Thanks to Max, my historical romances became best sellers. Only Max, Harry, and Josephine knew about the books. We were a clandestine club, secretly amused at the success of the Revolutionary War stories.

"I've a letter Harry wanted me to give you."

Max always came to the point. He was from New Jersey. Max scooted a Kleenex box my direction and settled into his chair. He fingered a cigar he always had nearby. No longer allowed to smoke due to a coronary, Max chewed on them when he concentrated. Currently he chomped on the cigar like it was a sea-salted caramel.

I tried to steel myself.

Flunked. Grabbed a wad of Kleenex and smooshed it into my right hand.

Dearest girl,

I don't know that I will miss you when I'm with my Jesus, but I miss you now. You've just left the room to take away my dinner tray and your honey sweet smell went with you. I'm going to ask something hard of you. Something you don't want, nevertheless, I think it is time.

The world needs to know who D.B. Burns is, my love. They need to know that you are a gifted writer, stringing words together with power and grace. You call your stories historical romances. I call them moral tales, set in a time when God's word was honored in our land. They sing to me, little girl. Lyrics with truth are strung along the melodies.

Pray about letting old Max introduce you at the honors ceremony as my wife, lover, friend, and fellow writer.

Lyle has other missives from my heart to yours. Keep your chin up, my love. Life's journey is but a brief one with pleasure and sorrow sitting side by side.

With my heart always in your hands,
Harry

Breathing had become difficult. Not because my bruises throbbed but getting used to breathing without Harry beside me was taking time.

Chapter Eighteen

I WASN'T READY FOR MY UNVEILING, as I'd let Max know in no uncertain terms. At the dinner honoring Harry, Max introduced me as Harry's wife, Delilah Burns Morgan. The ballroom, filled with white-clothed round tables and people in fancy dress, was so large I couldn't see the people sitting at the last tables. Who knew poetry could draw such a crowd?

"Harry was a marine in Vietnam," I said mid-way through my thank you. "I'd like to share the insights of a young Kentucky man who encountered despair for the first time." I read one of Harry's poems, an unpublished one, written from 'Nam. There were tears when I finished, and this time, not mine.

"My husband was a simple man who loved his God, his family, and the soil. He tamed stallions and spoke to presidents. Harry found the core of a person intriguing and could sniff out a phony or a lie as if he had second sight. Before we married, Harry took me to a political debate. We left halfway through, Harry's face all tight with anger. He said both rascals were liars and winding the truth up into knots wasn't entertainment for him." Chuckles rippled throughout the room.

"Harry grabbed words with both hands, holding them close so they wouldn't escape." I took a deep breath before closing. "I was blessed to be loved by Harry," I continued. "Blessed to have memories of him and challenged to carry on with life, knowing he is part of my great cloud of witnesses, as the book of Hebrews states. You have honored him with accolades. I'd like all of us to honor him with our heads bowed." The audience actually bowed. Which was a surprise. "Think of a poem or phrase he shared that made a difference in your life and rejoice."

As I returned to my seat I looked toward the back of the room and saw the silhouette of a tall man. He was walking out the rear doors with a thin blonde on his arm and he moved just like Lyle Henderson. I shook my head. It wasn't the time or place to think about the judge.

There was a breeze, damp with river moisture, as I drove from Lexington toward home. The backroads skirting the Kentucky River eased past the stiff, plain buildings of the Shakers and ran alongside the fences corralling the thoroughbred farms. I had all four windows down, and my thoughts drifted to a convertible sports car. Wind in my hair was decadent. A sports car may be as well.

Life was a new normal at home when I arrived. Normal meaning, Bartles was still in my house, the judge was off rollicking in the tropics, while Cam and Molly were stacking flats of lattice along the carriage house front.

The garden art had come from the Presbyterians. In March their big stone church had an Easter play and Cam talked them into donating their stored lattice for the wedding. The Presbyterians had the largest sanctuary in town. Ours was a wee thing. The lattice could go around it twice. The arbor Molly wanted to stand under was enormous. The curved top would hit the ceiling and bump the fans.

I waved hello, trolleyed my bag inside, and grabbed the mail. One looked like a personal note. Every day I received sympathy cards. I swallowed hard. The envelope was plain vanilla. No return address. On the inside of the card was scrawled in school-boy cursive,

Dearest Delilah,
You haunt my thoughts. I dream of your face when I

lay my head on my lonely pillow. I will call on you real soon to help ease your loneliness.
    Yours forever,
    Earl Inman

I wadded the card into a tight ball and tossed it in the waste basket by Harry's desk. It made me flat out mad. I was separating the ads from the bills and fuming when I heard Molly's footsteps on the verandah.

"Mom," Molly said, wiping her hands onto her jean shorts. "Mrs. Patrick was right. Cam and I measured and there *is* a hidden room by Dad's office."

"It used to be a closet, honey," I said offhanded. "We blocked it off."

"Mom." Molly's hands were on her hips. "What's the big secret? Is there a dead body I don't know about?"

"Of course not. Your dad had a small office made for me. That's where I do the household bills and a few other things."

"You're sure not into show and tell." She laughed.

"It's my . . . well . . . my sanctuary, I guess. I pray there. Do some work."

Molly wrapped her arms around my shoulders and leaned her head against mine. Her hair smelled lilac sweet.

"Then it's none of my business." She released me and walked toward the kitchen.

While in New York I'd thought about Harry's journals. He kept them in order like his tools in the garage or his special writing papers carefully placed in the left-hand drawer of his desk. I'd been distracted by wedding dresses and brunch menus. Time to search again.

I returned to the attic. It held years of our accumulated memories. The trunks gathering dust stared at me from the south corner. The assorted suitcases were stacked chest high. I hadn't noticed that Harry's sea locker was on the top. Last time I'd stored things had been after Christmas when the olive-drab metal was near the bottom.

Harry's locker was filled with his scent. I wiped my eyes on the moth-eaten blue sweater Harry loved. He must have tucked it in because I'd confiscated it in March when he'd tried to wear it when the college president visited. Black journals for the missing decade were lined up on the bottom, waiting to be discovered. All but one. Wedged between volumes eight and nine was a note in Harry's cursive.

I thought you'd get here, little girl. You always were good at ferreting out my surprises. "One if by land and two if by sea, I on the opposite shore shall be." I trust I'm across the Jordan when you read this. Look for a searchlight to unearth the treasure. Take Lyle with you. You'll need his legal expertise and muscle.

Your Harry.

Drat.

Harry was sending me on a scavenger hunt. And I'd have to wait until the wandering judge materialized.

"Mom? Hey, Mom?" I heard Molly call, followed by footsteps on the attic stairs.

"In here," I shouted.

"Oh," she said, spying me on the floor. "Dad's stuff. You okay?"

"Yep." I hugged his sweater tight. "I'll repurpose your dad's sweater by shrinking it and making a pillow."

A wailing baby Sarah, my little granddaughter, was handed to me on Friday morning. Bartles cocked his head, then scurried off to the parlor and dove under the divan. Never thought the judge would have a chicken dog, but babies have been known to make even grown men cower.

"I don't know what to do with her, Miss Delilah," worried my daughter-in-law. "She was fine until I put her in the car."

"Shoo," I said, reaching for the teary baby. "We'll be fine. You and Austin have a nice lunch after his dental appointment."

The baby's little knees were drawn up tight to her tummy. A sure sign of a contrary burp. Walking about always eased my babies' tummies. We went into the kitchen where Molly was slapping together ham and cheese sandwiches.

"Mom, can you put these on a plate and in the fridge while I help Cam?" Molly didn't even look my direction before she dashed out of the screen door toward Cam.

The sandwiches were easy to put on the plate. Fighting my way into a drawer and pulling on the sticky plastic was a no-go with a baby sobbing in my arms. I bent with my knees and put the plate in the fridge. None of the sandwiches hit the floor. I counted that a success.

Sarah wailed like she'd been pinched.

"Well, sugar," I said. "You need a song to take your mind off your problem." I crooned as I hip bounced the baby, "Hush a bye, don't you cry, go to sleep little baby."

"Day will break, you shall have all the pretty little horses," sang a resonant baritone behind me.

I almost dropped Sarah. My heart pounded like a kettle drum in a German opera.

The judge reached over my shoulder to tickle her under the chin.

I turned to see the judge's face. His wide smile was accentuated by a dark tan. His eyes were fixed on Sarah. He lifted her sobbing little body out of my arms, put her over his shoulder and began to rub her back.

"We missed you," popped out of my mouth too fast to suck it back in.

"That's nice."

The judge vigorously rubbed on the back of the squirmy little body. Before I could fling a tea towel over his shoulder, she decorated his Hawaiian shirt with a three-inch-milk-belch.

"You must be feeling better, little one." Ignoring the urp on his shirt, the judge winked at me and began to waltz around the kitchen. Sarah quieted.

The judge turned away, showing Sarah the prism sunlight made through our old window. "What did the doctor say about your bruises?" the judge tossed over his shoulder.

"Josephine got her stitches out last Wednesday." I moved to grab the dishcloth and displaced bread crumbs into the sink. "She is doing well." I sounded prickly.

"And you?" He turned around.

Fortunately, Bartles raced into the kitchen and collided with his shoe. The puppy was so excited he dribbled on the floor. I unrolled a handful of paper towels.

"Well, it's about time. I thought Miss Delilah had you locked away for misbehavior," the judge chided his dog.

I dropped the towels on the spreading puddle. It was easier to step on the pee than crawl around, so I did the pick up the spill stomp. The judge handed me the baby then gathered the dog into his arms. As I walked into the parlor toward my rocking chair, Sarah began to coo.

"You didn't answer my question," the judge said as he trailed after me.

"Well, I haven't exactly spoken to my doctor."

"I leave town for a few days . . ."

"Sixteen to be exact."

"You *did* miss me."

"I think the dog did."

"Right," he said. "You decided to ignore your bruised ribs and carry on. That it?"

"I've been busy."

"What are friends for if they can't stick their noses in?" the judge said as he gazed over my shoulder. My agitated rocking disturbed the baby. I slowed as he spoke, rubbing her little bottom as she lay across my knees.

"I'm perfectly capable of caring for myself."

"Yes," he answered softly. "But you tend to put everyone else first. When you do consider your needs, something else takes precedence. Am I close?"

I acknowledged him with a nod.

"If you're doing well enough to not need a physician that's your call. I'd like to take you to lunch, though. We need to talk about the wedding without interruption."

"Oh. Of course." I would need to gather his yellow-hued clipboard with the schedule on it.

He bent in front of my chair and scooped Sarah out of my arms. Cradling her, the judge searched for a spot where he could lay her down. Josephine walked through the doorway, looked at him, and beckoned for him to follow. Josephine had set up the port-a-crib in the guest bedroom. I figured that was where they were heading, so I dislodged Bartles and traipsed behind.

"You mosey home, Judge, and change your shirt." Josephine's laugh stirred the baby. "Looks like you need to change out of your shorts to look presentable," she said to me, eyeing my white knees. "I'll sit here and keep an eye on things until Molly comes inside."

The judge didn't turn around, just acknowledged her with a wave over his head.

The judge took me to the Country Club. It wasn't a place I frequented. I wore the last of my summer cotton dresses with a tidy white sweater. My cotton dresses were becoming rags. First a zipper had broken and frayed the fabric at the neckline, then a tear appeared in a another one's hemline and couldn't be fixed. Josephine had asked for the dresses for her mother. It should keep Miss Vickie in cleaning rags for years.

Miles Reading opened the car for us when we pulled up at the club's double doors. He grinned when he saw me.

"Well, well, Miss Delilah. You are a sight for sore eyes." Miles bent his lanky body as I got out of the car, then he gave me a sideways church hug. The kind shared between men and women who aren't married to one another. "Heard there's a wedding comin' on." Miles's grin lit up his face like a holiday sparkler.

"We're uniting our families," announced the judge. "I hope you are planning to attend."

"Wouldn't miss it, Judge. You have to promise it will be as exciting as your Kentucky Derby parties, though."

"I'll attend to it." The judge and Miles being friends was not a surprise. The judge had friends from all parts of the social register.

"I'd avoid the beef if I was you." Miles rubbed the back of his thinning gray hair. "Looks scrawny." Miles drove away in the judge's fancy car searching for a parking place amid the golfers' SUVs.

"I like you in your librarian get up," the judge said when we walked into the dining room overlooking the eighteenth hole.

"This old thing?" I smiled, thinking a librarian's wardrobe a sight better than the get-up Harry had picked for my Washington Street hike.

I let the judge order the meal, reckoning he'd know the menu. We had mixed green salad, fresh-caught catfish, roasted potatoes, and vegetables. I nibbled at the potatoes since they were mostly starch and looked longingly at the warm garlic bread in the basket on the table. Doing sit-ups were so troublesome with my body whacked up I'd flat out stopped. The treadmill was gathering dust too.

Lyle leaned toward me. "What do I need to know about the wedding?"

"Molly has lists. We need to cooperate."

"I wonder where she got that idea?"

I didn't dignify his comment with an answer.

"Color-coded on clipboards?" he laughed.

"Yours is chicken yellow for avoiding the chaos for sixteen days." He kept on laughing, which made Ellie Irene Snodgrass at the next table whip her head around and join him in his contagious laugh.

"Well, I'm here for the duration. I'm to cut out miniature horse shoes, get the lattice painted, secure lattice in the church, make the festivities exciting enough for Miles, and keep the groom from escaping."

"I don't think Cam is going to desert his bride." I smooshed the butter into my potatoes with my fork. "Is that why you never re-married? You think it's imprisonment?"

"Finding the right woman has proven a challenge."

"You've been engaged once or twice."

"Actually, three times." The judge surveyed me as if deciding if he should continue. "There were issues."

"Picky, are we?"

"Perhaps." He eased back in his chair. "Josephine was right. You don't like being bossed around."

"I was the middle child."

"That explains all." He stuck his tongue in his right cheek and gazed at me.

Smiling was my best option.

"Add to your clipboard a bachelor party called a Thunderstorm, September eighth at 6:30 p.m.," he said. "It's for the groom and his friends. A shower is not something men needed. We'll hand out tools and advice to Cam while feasting on barbeque. Barbeque beats tea cakes any day."

"What do you need me to bake?"

"This is a guy thing. We don't bake."

Chapter Nineteen

I SPIED GEORGE SITTING ON MY verandah when we pulled into my drive. He was hunched over like an irritated bulldog, drumming his fingers on my rattan armchair. "Mamie's got a gaggle of her friends over. I thought I'd catch you up on my investigations."

"Anything more than our conversation last week?" The judge settled on the love seat.

"Plenty. The twenty-thousand dollars has been identified as the money you gave Clarisse. It took some work, but it was a new shipment and consecutive bills. The money will be transferred to your account."

Lyle slapped George on the back. "That's terrific."

George shook his head. "Not so fast. I don't have the DNA results in from the lab, although the blonde woman at the hotel could be the body in the car. Found out via the Paducah deputy, that a woman bought a blonde wig on the sixteenth. Could be Clarisse used it as a disguise." He was ticking off his points on his fingers. "Dental records are next on the agenda. I suspect their teeth are scattered on the lake bed. Fish and waves tend to do that." George cocked his head toward me.

I'm not squeamish but I winced at the thought of the deterioration. "One woman didn't return to the hotel to collect her things."

George's eyes flashed. "It turns out it was Clarisse's room. She may be another victim or on the lam."

I sat down. "Oh, dear."

George skewed Lyle with a quick glance. "Judge, where did you go after Clarisse left?"

"I met with a client. When I heard from the investigator, I took off from my meeting and headed for Paducah. That was in the late afternoon."

"Did you meet your client in Perryville?"

"Actually, near Fort Knox. Last week I called his office in Washington. He will confirm with the FBI that we met that day. My client kept calendars over the years in case some noisy reporter invented a bogus story to forestall his political ambitions."

"Feel good to be off the hook?" George asked.

"I'm still not cleared. They disappeared on the sixteenth, remember? I only have an alibi through four p.m."

"Lawyers bill by the minute, don't they? Finding out your schedule shouldn't be that difficult," George put his hands behind his head and linked his fingers.

"I've had Janice search through my billing records to verify my appointments, but I was gone the nights of the fifteenth and sixteenth."

"Can't remember that far back or did you get snockered to ease the pain?" George asked.

"Possibly. Maybe I don't want to remember."

"If I was trying to cover up a murder, I'd have things so tightly battened down no special agent could punch a hole in my story," I said.

George coughed into his hand.

I wanted to believe the judge, but he was making it difficult. "You must come up with something pronto. How many people go to jail because they didn't have an alibi, just motive, opportunity, and evidence?"

Molly wandered in the garden with a wicker basket. As she gathered Harry's lettuces and tomatoes, she looked like a throwback to the nineteen-forties in her jean shorts and two red pig tails on either side of her head.

"George?" she asked when her basket overflowed. "Do you think Miss Mamie could use any vegetables?"

"What a kind thought, Molly. Why don't you ask her?" Molly lifted her chin and marched with her face westward, her eyes fixed on the Salases' front porch.

I retrieved Harry's note from the study. Lyle and George read it together.

"Harry loved scavenger hunts," Lyle explained to George. "Around Halloween he'd get the local merchants to join in a fund-raiser for the hospital. Rhyming clues or objects were in their shop windows. People paid a hundred dollars per person for the privilege of participating. The final clue brought them back here. The Morgans hosted hot drinks, appetizers, and desserts."

"I never heard of it." George scrunched his lips together in thought. "For years I was out of town on assignment during the fall. Mamie probably knew I wouldn't be around."

"I think Mamie had other plans with her friends that night," Lyle tactfully stated.

Josephine brought out a tray of sweet tea and water. We sat comfortably on the verandah watching Cam stack paint cans in front of the carriage house.

The Salases' front door burst open and Molly came marching through it, her face flushed with anger.

"Honey, are you okay?" I asked.

"No," she shouted over her shoulder. She ran toward Cam and flung herself into his arms. I rose from my seat. The judge waved me back.

"They'll settle whatever it is."

The front door slammed. Mamie marched to my yard, her face as red as Molly's. On her arm was Molly's vegetable basket. In Mamie's wake tomatoes rolled, zucchini squatted, and a few cucumbers flipped onto the grass.

George eased out of the wicker chaise and went to stand on the stairs, an eyebrow lifted as if forming a question mark.

Mamie's housekeeper, Esther Freeland, opened the Salases' door and wafted her apron as she shooed three women out of the house. Charlene, Olive Lorraine, and Lydia Hamilton collectively started to argue with Esther. Esther crossed her arms and directed them down the steps as if they were naughty poultry.

"George," Mamie huffed. "Where's Molly?"

George pointed to my tree-lined drive, and Mamie headed toward Cam and Molly.

The mayor's wife, the realtor, and the spouse of an English professor stood with their mouths all going at once. Esther, with legs akimbo, barred the door. Judging from her expression, no one would gain entry.

"My, my," Josephine said. "Something is amiss over at your house, Mr. George."

We looked from the gathering at the Salases', to the three huddled by the pale lattice. Molly and Mamie hugged, then Mamie turned her head toward her house, put her hands on her hips and glared.

"Think I'll mosey over and help my son," offered the judge, digging in his pocket for his linen. "Please stay here, Delilah. George should keep an eye on his guests."

"Mamie," shouted Charlene over the fence. "We need to get our purses and notebooks."

George moseyed through the gate between our homes.

"Anything I can do to help?" he asked. "My wife is occupied."

"Mamie told us to leave and we were not given time to gather our things," Charlene whined.

"That right, Esther?"

"That's right, Mr. George. I'll fetch them."

"No, you won't," shouted Lydia Hamilton. "You might steal something."

Esther took a step back. Josephine and I gasped. Olive Lorraine shrunk in her shoulders and sidled toward her Cadillac.

"As a former government official, I shall deliver your possessions post-haste." George spoke words clipped with displeasure. Josephine settled into George's vacated lounge and put her feet up with a disgruntled thump.

"Esther Freeland's the most honest person in our county." Josephine spoke so loudly it carried to the sidewalk. "The Salvation Army has her count their Christmas collections."

Tiny Mamie placed Molly's head on her shoulder and patted my daughter's back then raised her head. Mamie blew her nose on the handkerchief the judge offered. The judge put a hand on Mamie's back and whispered in her ear. Mamie's lips curved into a smile. His eyes lifted to mine and he winked.

"From the look of things," muttered Josephine, "Miss Mamie is going to lose heading up the Christmas Committee."

When things calmed down and everyone was sheltered on my verandah, Molly leaned against a white pillar. "Mom, when I walked into the Salases', Esther put her finger to her lips. I tiptoed through the hall to the dining room thinking we would surprise Mrs. Salas with the produce. I got as far as the front hall table when I heard Mrs. Higgenbottom say, 'Wouldn't it be fun to find a way to interfere with the Morgan wedding? Something clever, like the caterers not bringing the right food. They would be the laughingstock of the community.'" Molly's voice cracked with tension.

"Oh, honey." I got up and reached out to her. "No one wants their children to see the world's ugliness."

Molly kissed my cheek then continued. "Mrs. Patrick added, 'We need to find out what Harry is hiding in that secret room. Neely thinks it might be a gallery filled with Suzanne Burns paintings.' Miss Mamie said it was time for them to leave in so stern a voice I jumped. So, Esther mouthed to me, 'You better go.'"

Mamie looked at her hands, then rubbed a thumb and index finger together.

"I thought they were my friends." Mamie's voice throbbed with tension. "To ask me to hurt Molly was wicked. I said as much to Charlene. She looked at me as if I had lost my mind." Mamie took a drink of sweet tea before she continued. "Charlene said that the humiliation of a fiasco instead of a wedding would make—and I quote—'Delilah Morgan crawl back to Dog Patch where she belongs.'" I stood up. My knees were shaking, so I grabbed the edge of the table. I knew what I was about to do would change everything for me.

Mamie turned to face me. "I couldn't be part of hurting you, Delilah." She reached for George's hand and hung on tight. "You've done nothing except bathe them in kindness. Because Harry wrote a few poems you became their enemy? I don't understand." The deep lines on either side of her lips softened.

Bartles squirreled around my feet. "No. They attacked me because I didn't care to play their games."

"Thank God for that," declared the judge. "Charlene Higgenbottom and her colleagues do not run this town. Privilege is earned."

"We see the power hungry all the time in Washington," George stated.

"Seeking power almost cost me my soul." The judge's voice had ragged places around the vowels. "After Clarisse left, I was still a hot-dog trial lawyer. I hungered for success, money, a wife to complete me. It was an empty dream."

"What did you do?" George straightened in his seat and leaned forward.

"Changed everything. Relinquished my life, really. Gave it to Someone more reliable than I. And chose to love my boys." The judge smiled to himself then asked politely if I'd pass the sweet tea.

George shook his head as if puzzled.

After dinner, we sat on the verandah and watched the sky. The night colors grew to hazy blue with a heap of dark clouds off to the east where lightning played hide and seek. Our garden's cardinal zoomed in and out of the shade trees between the Salases' house and ours.

"I love watching a cardinal's dip-and-soar flying pattern," I said. "A family nests in the large chestnut tree in the back. Harry and I would sit and study the fledglings, enjoy the evening air and one another." I didn't mention that cardinals mate for life.

The judge took one look at me and lifted Bartles into my lap. "To keep you warm in the evening breeze." He backed into his seat by the railing.

Cam and Molly trotted off to shoot hoops.

Their laughter rolled over the road, settling on us like a blessing.

The Salases sat close on the wicker love seat, the most contrary, lumpy seat in the house. Mamie stared into George's eyes as if she didn't recognize him. With his eyes opened wide as garage doors, George looked gobsmacked.

"Night's late." George rose. The slow sunset turned the clouds a hot shade of pink before changing to carmine.

"'Night, George. Mamie." The judge dipped his head.

George walked home faster than I'd seen him travel in days. Mamie loped alongside him. I was thinking of couples when an idea zinged in. Wonder how I can fix Lyle Henderson up with Mademoiselle Bousquet? A small dinner party, perhaps? But the more I thought about her in his arms the less inclined I was to participate in the event.

"The coast is clear." The judge interrupted my conniving.

"What?" I said.

"We need to follow Harry's verbal treasure map. Any ideas?"

"Well . . . yes." I had decided to sneak into Harry's library after everyone left, even though Harry wanted me to include the judge.

"Care to share?" He crossed his arms and looked steadily at me.

"The Longfellow quote refers to Harry's lighthouses." I took a deep breath and let it out slow. "His collection is in the library. In May he wanted them placed just so. Even had them all numbered with a chart drawn so I wouldn't scramble their order when I dusted."

"Come on then." The judge reached a hand out to the dog, tucking him along an arm before he pulled me up beside him. "Yes, I do want to kiss you, but I won't." He seemed to read my thoughts.

Wished he would have. I wanted to know if the first one was a fluke. I needed to make certain his lips making me tingle was only an aberration.

"Harry began collecting lighthouses on our honeymoon when we went to the Outer Banks for ten days."

The judge still held my hand when we entered Harry's office. Harry had sturdy, work-calloused hands. They were broad and surrounded mine like a glove. The judge's felt unfamiliar.

We squatted in front of the bookcase with the lighthouses. Only two had working lights. Harry had been proud of those little beams and turned them on during holidays to flash around the room. It was still too bright in the room to determine if the beams pointed to anything.

"We'll have to wait until dark." I stood.

"Good idea." He turned from his study of Harry's collection and gave me the look he must give victims about to testify. "About that kiss. I don't ever want to hurt you, Delilah. I'll try my best not to." He was standing tall and looking into my face. Small flecks of gold glinted in the blue of his eyes. He reached up to touch my cheek. His fingertip rubbed across my cheekbone and my legs turned watery.

"Risking to love means you can get hurt, Di."

The dog did his circle dance—chasing his tail and looking for a place to settle. He chose to jump onto the tapestry chair by the window. I watched him for a minute.

"Judge," I whispered. "When Harry was dying . . . my heart broke into little pieces. I've bits scattered all around. I only have a sliver left." I cupped an empty hand and held it up.

"I know," he said, raising my palm to his lips and gently kissing it. "I can see it's barely enough to keep you alive."

"Excuse us," said Molly as she stepped into the room. "Do you have something to tell us?"

"No." The judge's voice was almost a whisper. "Your mother was explaining how tender her heart is since your father died."

"Oh, I thought it might be something Dad mentioned." Molly waved her hand in the air as if warding off bugs. Her gaze took in both of us. She smiled. Cam ran a finger along her spine thinking I wouldn't notice.

"Dad?" Cam was hesitant. "What are you up to?"

"Still searching for Harry's journal," he said.

"Can we help?"

"We're at an impasse. Have to wait until the light fades."

Cam smiled and winked. "Then we'll just sit in the parlor and play a board game while you two work in the study."

Chapter Twenty

LIGHTNING BUGS FLITTED AROUND THE SHADY side of the garden, letting us know it had finally grown dark enough to turn on the two lighthouses. Placed halfway up the right bookcase by the fireplace, the lighthouse from Charleston harbor and the one collected from Nantucket shone their searchlights out of tiny apertures. They crossed at a painting mounted on the wall between the east facing windows. The oil was one of my sister's. The landscape was not of horses or chickens, but of Harry's family farm.

The painting was new. Suzanne finished it for Christmas after she heard Harry was dying. The painting was designed so your gaze swept up the maples lining the drive to the house the Morgans built more than a century and a half ago.

The lights crossed and illumined the house's name, Rosehill, on the bottom left corner of the picture. The judge felt along the back of the painting. I shook my head. That was too easy. Harry was subtle. Well, sneaky. Rosehill either directed me to the family book about the farm or the book on floribundas that Harry gave me for Christmas.

"Let's try my new rose book." I drew the volume from the bookshelf and handed it to the judge. Tipping the book upside down he fanned the pages with his thumb while I searched the shelf on either side of it for a message. Nothing.

The judge read aloud the inscription Harry had written on the title page.

To my love who creates beauty wherever she walks. May your creative seeds flourish in your hiding place.

With abiding affection, Harry.

Harry added the second sentence between the salutation and his signature.

The judge lifted quizzical eyebrows. My heart pounded. If I opened the door to my sanctuary what would he think of me for hiding my writing from the world? In the hidden space were my treasures—the pictures Harry sketched of the children, Harry's poems written in his own hand, my books.

"Give me a minute." I plopped into Harry's leather writing chair.

"Are you in pain, Delilah?" The judge brushed my shoulder with a fingertip.

"In a way. Harry wants me to tell you something."

"And you don't want to?"

"Yes. No. I don't know."

"Well, that's definitive."

"I mean, this will change what you think of me."

"We'll worry about that later, shall we? What is it?"

I got up and went to the door. Molly sat on Cam's lap in front of the game table. There was a chess set before them. I don't think they noticed the board.

"Judge." My voice shook. "I'm not who you think I am." I didn't want to explain that I wasn't a poor little housewife but the supporter of Harry's writing and our family. How could I explain that in keeping my writing secret I was, in a way, selfish, and lying? I didn't want a lie perfuming my life with its odious scent.

Lines grew between his eyebrows. I wrung my hands again. He reached out and took my hands in his, then rubbed his thumb over the back of my right hand.

"Follow me," I invited. Bartles lifted his head from his paws and studied us.

I went to the bookshelf to the right of the fireplace and pulled out a book next to a bust of Beethoven. The bookshelf slid behind another bookcase, exposing my office. A light automatically came on over my desk.

"The missing nine feet, I presume?"

"Nine feet, five inches. Harry made this space for my office. I do the household accounts here, and I er-well, I write a little."

"Do you think I didn't know you were D.B. Burns, Delilah? I was a military lawyer. I couldn't let the boys hang out with a felon, now could I?"

"But you never said." My mind slipped from investigating to something else. "Say, were you really in Hawaii or were you in New York?"

"Why do you ask?"

"Don't go lawyerly on me, Lyle Henderson. Were you in New York for Harry's literary award ceremony?"

"You spoke eloquently."

"So, you and your friend Charlie just dropped by?"

"No. Charlie, a male classmate from my Naval Academy days, and I went to Hawaii together. I escorted an old friend to the banquet."

I took a deep breath. "We'd better look for the clue."

"She's married, Delilah."

"Well, then you should be ashamed." I put my hands on my hips, embarrassed for him. "One doesn't cavort with married women unless they are your own wife," I said with sass.

The judge began to laugh. "Serves me right," he finally sputtered. "I'd promise to never try to pull a fast one on you again, but you're fun to tease, so don't hold me to it."

My right foot wanted to tap I was so impatient for him to get on with it.

"She's my cousin, and her husband is deployed to the Middle East. I promised to take her to a show on her birthday. I did. You were the icing on the cake. She was an English major and loves Harry's poems."

"Oh." The puppy thumped his way across the oak flooring in Harry's library and stood beside his master. "I'm sorry I jumped every which a way."

"Think nothing of it. Now, what's next?"

"Something about roses."

The mat under my computer mouse was decorated with faded roses. I lifted the mat and felt under it. There was another slim piece of writing paper.

My hands were shaking. "You read it," I said, handing it to the judge.

He handed it back. "It is for you to read." His lips were arrow straight. I didn't argue.

"Well, little girl and Lyle, I hope."

As soon as I saw his opening, I knew the judge needed to hear this too, so I started over and read it out loud.

"You're on the right path. It should lead you to my Old Kentucky Home where the sun shines bright and the meadows are in bloom. No, you don't have to leave the property. I'm too tired right now to drive out to the farm. But somewhere there is a reminder of summer's scent in the bluegrass. I shall miss that and the spring when I set out my garden. I've seen your sketches and the dreams of the new landscape, Delilah. It will be beautiful for your wedding. You are right to plow under and replant. One can't hang on to the past. You must grab at the future with both hands.
Love to you both,
Harry."

"Harry can't arrange a marriage for us." I was white-lightning mad.

"I agree."

That let out the air I'd gathered for my next statement.

"I don't believe in arranged marriages," he said.

"Me either. The only people getting married are our kids."

I was so relieved I flung out my arms and brushed against the file on my desk. Out flew my brochures and ticket info for Paris. The judge retrieved the one that landed on his toe. There for all God's children to see was the Eiffel Tower.

"Planning on a vacation, Delilah?"

"Not 'til after the wedding."

"Good. The mother-of-the bride running off to Paris before the nuptials would set tongues wagging."

He peered through my other papers, my tour book on France and the dog-eared pages of a guest farm in Provence. He gathered my stray papers, then the brochures, and struck his hand with them. Not a word came out of his mouth.

"I'm not certain what Harry meant by this line." I pointed to the missive he left. "The scent of summer in the bluegrass is a mystery to me. We've got a horse barn, onion grass, and cow pasture all perfuming the air around here."

"I think Harry means the scent of your roses. He's been aiming us that direction."

"Wow, Mom. This is way cool." My daughter's vocabulary needed more Shakespeare. "No wonder you wanted to keep this private." She stood in the doorway with Cam. Their cheeks were flushed, their eyes luminous.

"What are you two doing?" Cam asked.

"Following a series of clues Harry left." The judge waved the latest note. "He is sending us on a treasure hunt, but we don't know what we're looking for."

"I think whatever it is, resides in Harry's beat up red tool box." I grabbed at the letter in the judge's hand, so he couldn't share it with the kids. Remembering Harry's last months made Molly cry. He was too fast for me. He held it high and lifted it over my head to Cam's outstretched fingers.

Molly slithered around us and stood in front of my bookcases. The ones chuck-a-block with my novels. She plucked one off a shelf. It had recently arrived and wasn't yet on the market. "Hey, you must like Burns' writing, you have so many. I don't think I've seen this one. Is it new?"

The judge ushered Cam out of my hidey hole and into Harry's library. They put the letter on Harry's desk and leaned over so they could read. I needed to keep an eye on the judge. He might go haring off and find the next clue without me.

"About the books." I licked my lips. "I've been planning to tell all of you. But with your daddy's health going to heck and gone I couldn't find the right moment."

"D.B. Burns," she said thoughtfully. "You must think me an idiot, Mom."

The judge looked up from the desk where he leaned and winked.

"Your daddy and I wrote most evenings. Your daddy slipped my stories to Max and one thing led to another."

"Do we have to take a blood oath to keep this quiet?" Molly looked as if she might try it.

"No. I'll tell at my convenience. Not before your wedding, though. When this fudge hits the fan, I'll be mighty busy with publicity and talking to fans."

Molly hugged the book to her chest. "I'm so proud of you, Mom." She kissed my cheek. "Hey, is this another door?" Molly asked, looking at the west side of the room.

She began to palpate the bookcase. Her fingers probed to find a hidden catch.

"See the 1730s framed map of the Mohawk Valley mounted by the second shelf?" I touched the brass oval label at the bottom of the frame. The bookshelf slid open exposing the guest bedroom hallway.

"That was slick." Her curiosity drove her into the hall. She looked for a way to seal the door closed.

"You won't find it." I grinned.

"Give me a minute. I'm good at hide and seek."

"Precisely why your mother kept it from you," the judge rumbled from my office behind us. "It would be difficult for her to write with kids zooming through her space." The judge stood beside my desk, his palm resting on the travel brochures. After a minute, Cam and the judge sauntered into the hall. All three of my treasury initiates scrutinized the wall. The judge genuflected on the floor, his nose on the edge of the eight-foot French mirror that had hidden the entrance.

"There must be a way to close the door," Cam said.

The door was voice activated as well as having a door button for emergencies. My voice only. Harry insisted, saying he'd respect my privacy, because I allowed him to fiddle with poems and earn diddly-squat for his effort.

"Okay," the judge said. "We're defeated by your ingenuity. Where and how do you open this door?"

"Samson." The word was no sooner out of my mouth then the door began to slide into place.

"I suppose to open it, I say Delilah?" The judge pivoted and looked at me.

"Nope. You don't say anything. It only responds to my voice. Josephine got trapped in there once when she decided to dust. It took me an hour to find her. The room is soundproof with no phone. That's when we installed the buttons to open and close the doors."

"So how does it open?" Cam asked.

"Top secret," I said. "You have to be a code breaker."

"Navajo?" The judge's dimples indented when he smiled.

I glanced around, missing something. We had left the puppy in the hidden room. "Stay here." I held up one hand to keep them from following me.

I opened the library side and Bartles came trotting out. No keepsakes left for me to clean up, either. Maybe we were gaining on the housebreaking.

Chapter Twenty-One

IN THE MORNING I PEERED AROUND my roses and meandered through the vegetables, my mind on Harry's hints of scents and bluegrass. The hunt through Harry's workshop produced half-finished round-to-its. The judge and I hadn't found his, either.

"What's gotten you so upset you're snooping around in Mr. Harry's paint thinners?" Sidney asked, when he thrust open the door and poked in his head. "Were you here last week? Everything was messed with around my workbench. My mama's house key is missing too."

I shook my head. Did Sidney misplace the key or had someone been snooping in our workshop? Too many break-ins to overlook this. I chewed on my lip at the thought. "Looking for a note Harry might have left. Did he say anything about a gift for the judge, or a message for me?"

Sidney had a mobile face, one that can't hide a thought. His muscles screwed up so tight with concentration that I thought his lips would be permanently canted left.

"Cain't say he did. Cain't say he didn't. Let me think on it. I suppose you mean those round thangies he used to put on the judge's doorstep?"

"Yes."

"Mr. Harry said he didn't figure he'd make it out to the shop to finish it, so's he gave it to me to do." Sidney shook his head as if clearing it from summer's dust. "You added a little wormy thing." Sidney took off his baseball cap and flopped it between his hands. "Wal', he had me put one in his office when he took to that hospital bed in there."

"Where'd he put it?" I spoke with eagerness.

Sidney tucked in his chin.

"Cain't say I know," he said in a stressed voice. He scratched the back of his head. "I recollect it was on a Wednesday, because you were off shopping for groceries. The thang was gone next time I visited."

"When was that?"

"Saturday. I come in to give him a gander at the tomatoes I'd picked. He was right proud to have them for his dinner."

Sidney's remark sent me scurrying to Harry's library. Nothing seemed out of place. No shiny round objects gleaming on the bookshelves, desk, or table tops. Mystifying.

I would have settled down to do the bills, but the judge's puppy came trotting in. Picking up Bartles I stood in the middle of the room and peered from wall to wall wondering where the round-to-it had been stashed.

The judge's footsteps bounded across the wooden verandah then skidded to a stop. "Mornin' Molly," he said. I could see him bowing his head to her. "This is a beautiful day the Lord has given us."

"Yes," answered my daughter. "I sent Bartles in to scout for Mom. I figured you'd want to speak with her."

"No," he said slowly. "It is you I've come to see. We'll let Bartles play with your mama while we investigate my idea about that dratted lattice. It is too wobbly and needs a stouter frame."

I had a sinking feeling and plunked down in Harry's writing chair. Maybe I'd been too obstinate, and he was about to head out of town again. The puppy settled in my lap. The sunlight streamed in the window. I closed my eyes. When I opened them the sun was straight up. Looking around, I noticed spiders had danced from one pleat in my curtains to another. I tiptoed into the kitchen. Josephine was in the garden giving orders to Sidney. The frown on Sidney's face didn't promise harmony.

With the coast clear, I slipped into the laundry room and hitched the step ladder onto my left shoulder. I passed the formal dining room and trod into the foyer. There were no voices on the verandah.

Placing the ladder by the front window, I grabbed the spray. A fragment of an old dress turned out to be handy whapping down the cobwebs where the ceiling met wall in the front bay. Footsteps entered the foyer as I massaged the wide wooden rod on the north side.

I tried to scramble down and act innocent as a lamb, but the dingy fabric caught on something. I climbed to the top step and attempted to free the bit of dusting fabric.

"Good heavens, Delilah! That ladder is as unstable as a kite in the wind." At the sound of his master's voice, Bartles ice-skated across the wood floor and skidded into the library. The judge raised his eyebrows at me and his dog, who was scraping his pant leg with his paws.

"Cleaning," I muttered, as I fought to free the cloth from the hook. Something skittered down the folds of the velvet curtain and hit the floor with a thump.

The judge pursed his lips as he helped me down from my perch. I sighed with relief when he turned mute, since he regularly chewed out felons with his erudite vocabulary that made hair catch on fire. He bent to hunt for the fallen article along the curtain hem.

"Well, well, well." He chuckled. "A round-to-it, with a letter attached. Harry must have put it up by lasso."

He flipped the metal ring in his hand then bent to examine it. The circlet was embossed silver and looked like a spoon from my mother-in-law's silver. The judge folded himself into Harry's chair the way thin men do. A crisp, white envelope was attached by hook to the ring. Judge Henderson took out a glasses case from his breast pocket and put on tortoise shell reading glasses.

"Addressed to me," he added softly. "Finally."

I sat on the edge of Harry's desk top. The judge read, his eyes moist, his mouth soft. Harry's letter was three pages. When he finished, the judge removed his glasses, put them into his dark blue case, and placed them in his pocket. By running a fingernail along each edge, he tri-folded the letter and tucked it into the envelope. His blue eyes were half-closed. "Di, I'm sorry, but this is rather personal. I think sharing it with you is inappropriate." Then, without another word he rose, scooped up his dog, and ambled out Harry's library door.

I waited for him to return. He didn't. I carted the ladder to the bookshelves by the fireplace and was setting it up when Cam cleared his throat.

"I've been sent to remove you," he said apologetically. "Dad said it's time I learned to dust because when Molly is birthing babies, I'd better know how to be domestic."

"Do you want instructions?" I asked.

"Think I can handle it."

I left to unruffle my feathers. Whatever Harry had written was for the judge's eyes only. I tried to find peace in that.

The next two weeks were a blur until I drove into Lexington to run errands and had an impromptu lunch with the judge.

During lunch the judge handed me another letter from Harry. My hands shook when I took it. To sit with the judge over a plate of rare roast beef, with tiny roasted-vegetables and fresh horseradish, feeling as if Harry sat with us, was peculiar. I looked at the judge. He continued to cut his meat, focused on the business at hand.

It was not the letter I expected.

Dear Heart,

I trust that you are planning Molly's wedding. I regret that I will only be with you in spirit. Your daddy will make a fine substitute as father-of-the-bride. Do watch out for Lyle's emotions. Cam is his first child to wed and you know how it affected me. I got a little cranky, thinking I needed more time to teach the groom a thing or six about life. Cam is a good man, honorable like his father. Men read other men, you know.

Watching the Henderson boys grow up was a treat for me. I trust Cam with Molly. He will protect her.

Do celebrate, my love. Rejoice. I have nothing left to give to you but my hopes for your future. I do not wish you happiness, which is fleeting. I pray for joy, however God plans it.

With abiding love,
Harry

The judge looked at me without lifting his head. The bright blue of his eyes seemed hazy, as if a moist cloud had descended. He reached into his pocket for his ever-present tear absorber as I took his fingers in mine.

"I'm fine. I keep hearing Harry's voice when I read his letters. Remembering his rumbly voice makes me feel wrapped up in a knitted blanket. I miss him, Judge. There is a burning right here."

I touched the bodice above my heart with our hands together. I hadn't meant to. He blinked. A long and lazy smile curved his lips.

The heat rose in my face. I dropped his hand hard on the table. His smile broadened, lighting up his eyes so the gold bits flashed as if they were recently polished.

We didn't speak for a while. I pushed the paper into his hand to let him read. Bluegrass music filled the air as did my breaths. Which were faster than normal.

To be friends was enough. I hoped, fingers crossed, that he felt the same.

"I cherish our friendship," he said into the silence.

"Yes." I settled my eyes on my plate.

Chapter Twenty-Two

W‌HEN THE JUDGE AND CAM WEREN'T slathering paint on the lattice, the judge spent time at his home. Every few hours one of the Hendersons marched around the drying lattice and stared. With a paintbrush in his hand, I only saw the judge at a distance until early Thursday morning when he was standing in my foyer studying the wallpaper.

"Admiring your shooting skills, Delilah. Mighty fine hole you plugged in this wall." He chuckled then turned around and removed his glasses. "Do you have any left-over wallpaper we could use for patching?"

"Of course. I save six-inch scraps." It helps to grow up poor, you learn to rethink things.

We trooped up the stairs and into the hallway leading to the addition. The judge opened the hall closet door and took a step back. Everything was in baskets, labeled, and color coded.

"Cam better not leave his underwear on the floor," muttered the judge.

"I've a cure for that."

"Really?" His voice dripped sarcasm.

"Put them in the freezer. All of them. Next time he has to dash to the hospital he'll think twice about tossing his underclothes about."

"Worked on Harry, did it?" The judge wrapped an arm around his left side keeping the laughter jailed.

"Harry was a Marine. He folded his things into a four-inch space and asked me to do the same. You must too, because you were in the Navy."

"Well . . ." he hesitated. "I do tend to be tidy."

"I've noticed."

I left the judge to examine the wallpaper seams so I could garden in the cool of the morning. He was gone when I returned and found Josephine up to her elbows in soap. She hollered at me to get to the grocery and take our list. I think she needs a hearing test—I was not two-feet away when she trumpeted.

Grocery shopping was on another whole level of stress than wedding shopping.

Steering the cart one-handed, I set about comparing prices on eggs when Maureen Thackeray marched up and started to cry. Maureen was a Girl Scout leader. Each year she dressed out the deer she killed bow-hunting. I didn't expect her to start bawling in Kroger. I patted her arm.

"I miss him so much," she sobbed. "Your Harry always would come in the fall and talk to the girls about farming and poetry." Maureen sniffed then leaned her square-frame on my shoulder. I patted the wavy hair on top of her head.

"He'd bring his vegetables and usually his"—she sobbed out the word—"Silkies." Maureen's wailing was drawing a crowd around the yogurt case. "Sweetest little chickens I've ever seen." She hung onto my neck, crying like no tomorrow.

"Well, Miss Delilah," said the judge into my ear. "You have an interesting effect on the citizens of our fair city." The judge gently removed Maureen's arms from her stranglehold. She turned to him and began to hiccup.

"Sorry, Your Honor, *hic*. The whole dern-*hic*-town misses Harry-*hic*-Morgan. Oh, but I don't need to tell you-*hic*. You were like this." She wrapped her right middle finger around her index finger with a final hiccup. "Two cords knitted together."

"Yes," agreed the judge. "Harry and I were close." He stepped away from her and nodded to the assembled housewives, retirees, and clerks. "Mrs. Morgan, I need your assistance in the produce aisle. If you will excuse us." He took me by the arm.

"I'm having trouble picking out ripe avocados," he said loud enough for the audience. "Does that happen often?" he whispered, grabbing his cart.

"Every time I'm in public."

We passed the chips and salsa display. "So you comfort them and are left feeling hollow?"

You could see in the judge's eyes his own anguish. It was arrogant of me to think I was the only one bereaved.

"They tackle you too?" I said so quietly only he could hear.

"One of the reasons I'm on an extended vacation."

"I'm so sorry."

"Don't go patting my back and cooing sympathy. I'm a tough character." He was back to his lawyerly deception. I didn't buy it.

"Good morning, Charlene," Lyle Henderson drawled.

I sucked in my breath and leaned way over my cart trying to be invisible.

"There hasn't been an opportunity to explain the confusion at the Salases'," she said in a sticky-sweet voice. "Since I bumped into you, I'd like to clarify a few things."

"Ah," said the judge. His tall frame hid me from view as I tried to get smaller.

"It was nothing. Really, nothing." Charlene Higgenbottom's placating voice wouldn't sell coffee to a caffeine addict.

"Oh?" said my linebacker.

I left my cart and crept behind a display of canned milk stacked in the aisle.

"Actually, we were joking about the wedding. You know how it is when ladies talk."

"Yes." His one word was tart.

"Careful," piped up another voice. The voice was Maylene's with her distinctive drawl. "Salt and Pepper are here somewhere."

"And who would that be?" asked the judge, his

voice suddenly gruff.

"Well, just a little joke we have," muttered Charlene.

"Do you mean Miss Delilah and Josephine?" the judge pressed.

"Like I said, a simple misunderstanding. I'm off to get the remainder of my list."

The judge's shoulders tensed as if he was ready for combat. "You were saying?" he continued, inching his cart forward into the dried-nuts space.

I thought he was going to pursue her down the row of cake mixes.

Charlene was silent.

"I didn't think you were prejudiced, Mrs. Higgenbottom. I see my discernment was in error."

"Well, I, we . . . I think you misunderstood me."

"No. I did not." The judge's voice was razor-sharp. "I rarely misunderstand you, Mrs. Higgenbottom." He drew out her name as if written by the finger on the walls of Babylon.

The sound of Charlene's retreat was a clatter of metal, a huffy "well I never," and the crisp stutter of high heels on tile.

I grabbed onto my cart and studied the bottom row of five-pound flour bags. Josephine pegged them rightly. Spitting cobra, sneaky rattler, pit viper all fit.

"Did Harry know of their animosity toward you?" the judge asked gently.

"I don't think so. Josephine and I did know about the nicknames. *We* made it a joke. Sometimes I was salty, sometimes she was, depending on what flavor we wanted in our verbal stew."

He stepped toward me, his face troubled. If he clutched me to his chest or patted my back I'd melt, because I'd been a first-class coward. Instead he drew a finger across my cheek. Which was worse.

"We called ourselves the 'Spice Girls,'" I said. I reached for his hand and rubbed the back of it with my thumb. It always worked to calm the kids.

His forehead rumpled and eyes squinted. "Lupita asked for next Wednesday afternoon off so she could join the 'Spice Girls' for lunch and shopping. They include her in their wicked judgments?"

"Well . . . yes."

He wriggled loose and crossed his arms. "Who else?"

I didn't evade his stony-eyed stare. The nicknames extended all the way to the judge's secretary at the courthouse. "Janice."

"I might have known," he said in a sinking voice.

"We rather liked the names. I would prefer mine to be cinnamon, but they hadn't the imagination."

"Lupita?" he asked with a controlled rumble.

"Nutmeg. She likes it. Janice is Ginger in case you need to know. The only reason they don't like her, is because she is my friend."

"Ah."

While his understanding deepened, I filled my cart. In time, perhaps he'd know that we prayed for them. Didn't matter what he thought of me, but he adored his Lupita and her family. She shrugged off their insults with her magical-black eyes doing a forgiveness rumba.

I pulled my list out of my pocket. "I've got to get some other things."

"Just in case I'm needed, I'll follow you."

"I don't see why you should."

"For one thing, you're breathing too rapidly, which tells me pushing the cart is causing pain. For the other, any more emotional outbursts from Harry's fans and you'll need a handkerchief." He pulled one out, wafting it my direction.

Molly had a run to Lexington early on Friday. Early in the morning I snuck upstairs like a thief in the night and was at my quilt frame before eight. With my

French tapes on my iPod, I was *voulez-vous*-ing when there was a hand on my shoulder. I almost leaped over my frame. I pulled out my earphones as I whipped around.

"Morning, Miss Delilah," said the judge. "Up late last night, I believe." His little dog fought his way through the wad of quilt pooling on the floor then flopped down for a nap.

"What?" My voice was tight.

"These days getting my eight hours sleep is elusive," he explained. "I saw your light in the window about one."

"I'm working on a wedding present."

"I see. Quite lovely. Wedding Ring Quilt is appropriate." He bent toward my stitches. "I imagine you haven't eaten." His question was spoken around a smile. His tongue roamed around inside his cheek. "Let me find out if Josephine would include me for breakfast." With that pronouncement, he headed for the stairs. I blew a tense breath up my forehead.

"That does it." I leaped to my feet. "I declare, you are the most irritating man."

"Yes," he agreed. "I can be. You must find my behavior difficult." His eyes narrowed. "You, Miss Delilah, are as much a pebble in my shoe as I am in yours. What in heaven's name was Harry thinking?" he exclaimed as he erupted from the room.

We met in the kitchen and ate Josephine's scrambled eggs and bacon in silence. Part of me wanted to acquiesce to Harry's wishes because I was growing fond of Lyle, the other part wanted to dig in my heels.

"I'm sorry," I finally eked out. "I'm opinionated."

"You are too fatigued to support Molly. At present, she needs your attention."

"I can't sleep anyway so I might as well work."

"Find another room if you can't sleep in Harry's bed."

The man had no idea what ran through my head

when I entered our bedroom. I couldn't turn fizzing thoughts on and off like a water faucet.

"Don't neglect your sweet daughter, Di," he urged, his tone turning gentle. "The kids deserve our best."

I bleakly nodded. Compromise was a good option to this conflict.

"How many stitches-to-the-inch do you quilt?" came out of nowhere. "I'll make a few phone calls to find someone with the same number."

"You can't hire someone to do a wedding quilt," I sputtered. "It's for family to do." Harry didn't have any idea that the number of stitches-per-inch was the sign of a master quilter. Lyle knowing was startling.

The judge gave me a slight smile. "While you sleep, I'll round up the artisans."

"I'm up," I said firmly.

"But not for long, I hope. You've circles around your circles. Last thing we need is for you to get sick. Josephine is creating a quiet place for you." He smiled then waved me away as if shooing a fly out of the pantry.

Josephine's step echoed on the stairs. "All set up in the bedroom like you requested, Mr. Judge." She was using her sugary voice. Her lips curled mischievously as she glanced at me. "Miss Dee Dee needs more sleep. Sidney said she's been out in the gardens stirring up dirt. He reckons it must have been at sunrise."

Weeding took my mind off my astringent life. I huffily paced down the dark-wood floor when I heard Josephine say, "Here's the phone numbers you wanted. Hope she don't find out you're messin' with her schedule."

The judge laughed.

If he wasn't going to stick with his assigned wedding duties, I'd let Molly handle him. He seemed putty in her hands. I was on the stair landing when the front bell jangled. I hopped down the three steps and flung open the mahogany door to Earl Inman. He had a scraggly bunch of flowers in his hand. They looked like they'd come from our garden. He thrust them at me. I stood stock still, blinking. I was too old for this nonsense.

"Didn't know you were up to receiving visitors, Di," said the judge behind me.

Startled to again be called Di, I raised my eyebrows. *Di? Where did that come from?*

"Have you been ill, Miss Delilah?" Earl Inman asked. "It must be the reason you haven't responded to my invitations." The judge growled in the back of his throat.

"I heard about your accident, but I didn't know you were still suffering."

That was the only good thing to come out of the blame Paducah fiasco. Maybe it'd scare off Inman.

"Nice of you to come to commiserate," said the judge, stepping in front of me. "The lady, however, is heading upstairs to rest. Perhaps another time?"

I retreated and battled with my pillow on John's old bed. The sheets were cool. I didn't wake until the judge shook my shoulder.

"Seems we've found the cure to your insomnia. Lunch is served."

With that he sauntered out the door and disappeared for home.

Chapter Twenty-Three

For the first time, Lyle and Cam joined us in our little, wood-sided church. Our pastor pushed up his glasses when we entered the sanctuary. We had ceiling fans in our church, not AC. The hot air circulated, wafting dust when George and Mamie walked down the aisle and sat in front of where the judge and I were sitting. Made me think anything could happen.

Cows fly.

Charlene Higgenbottom halt her vendetta.

The preacher gets up his nerve to speak to Josephine about his feelings.

Church still felt foreign without Harry's hand in mine. I'd steeled myself to it during the months he suffered. The day felt odd, though, as if there was a fog between the Lord and me. So, we had a conversation about it during the offering.

"What's the matter, Delilah?" the judge asked as we walked out of the sanctuary and into the sweltering August noon.

"I feel as if I'm halfway between here and someplace I don't recognize."

A half-hour after we left the church, the sheriff found us sipping miso soup and waiting for the bento boxes we'd ordered.

The sheriff sat abruptly. "Need to speak with you, Lyle. Last Friday the city council had their meeting at the Coop. Our mayor flamboozeled them into having a town gathering at the park near the college. His soiree is scheduled for the same day as the wedding."

"I don't see how that will affect our day," I said.

"No one thought much of it until BethAnn told Carter and Carter put two and two together. The mayor plans to block off the streets leading to your house, Miss Delilah."

Molly reached for my hand.

Josephine had expected Charlene to try something. She'd wagged a finger my direction. "Sitting around waiting for Charlene to strike ain't wise. It's like watching a water moccasin taking aim. You's got to outsmart her."

"That all?" asked the judge. He didn't seem concerned. I breathed out slowly.

"No, sir. Seems every rental chair and table is needed for *their* event. The mayor got those nodding heads to sign a decree. All rentals for Friday and Saturday are canceled. Tents too. Not a tent to be had in the whole blame town."

"I have a contract with Charlie Kent." I smiled at them both. "He's an honest man. He wouldn't break his word."

"Charlie called me on Saturday," the judge stated. His voice held little emotion. "He told me he had no choice. Seems the city council made it an enforceable ordinance with a hefty fine. Charlie's sending back your money." The judge studied my face. "Because you had a deposit, I told him breach of contract was a suit waiting to happen. Charlie said he'd rustle up more chairs and tables."

The judge kept his eyes on my face as he spoke. "I felt you had no need to know of Higgenbottom's shenanigans, Delilah. This is in the category of a small annoyance. Please let me handle this."

"Oh, Lyle," I choked out.

"I'd appreciate you keeping me posted on the drama at the courthouse, Sam."

"No problem, Judge Henderson. Seems our mayor is set on canceling any friendly votes in the future."

Bellows left us to our meal, but I didn't have an appetite. What was it Josephine had said about heaping coals of fire on your enemy? According to her African ancestors the act was a way of blessing. If someone ran out of fire to use for heat, coals were placed in a bundle for them to carry home. In many cultures it was carried on their heads. To bring peace to an enemy was to provide for them. How could I bless the Higgenbottoms on Molly's wedding day and not resent it?

"Di, can you eat?" the judge asked.

"Di?" I said.

He shrugged. "Thought I'd try a nickname. Dee Dee is too fifties, Delilah sounds too formal. Di is more hip."

"Oh," I mouthed. "Sorry, I'm distracted by nefarious behavior and odd conversations."

As we drove closer to the house, we saw police lights flashing out front.

"Not again," I muttered.

George and Mamie were standing on the verandah with Sheriff Bellows. Three police vehicles were parked in the pad to the right of my house. The judge eased into his drive and walked me across the street, his hand on my back for reassurance.

"I won't faint if you're afraid I might," I whispered.

"Wasn't something I feared. Thought you might go in search of your ammo, though."

I was laughing as we walked across the yard.

"Not particularly funny, Mrs. Morgan," piped up the Sheriff.

"I shouldn't tell jokes," said the judge.

"While you were at church, Miss Delilah, your house was broken into," George waved toward my door. "Those cameras installed by the verandah and in the house were a good idea, Lyle. No damage done to the house that I could see."

Mamie wrapped her arms around me, shaking. "I've never been assaulted before. It was horrid. The people who robbed you came out of your house so fast they rammed into us. It was as if we were bowling pins knocked over."

I led her over to my wicker rocker and put her gently into it. The front door was wide-open and letting the cool air escape. I closed it with more slam than necessary.

"George has refused an ambulance. Look at that gash." Mamie waved her hand George's direction.

"They turned off the alarm and entered with a key," George said. "Mamie and I surprised the masked intruders when we came to check on your dog. One pushed my Mamie against that urn." George pointed to the sturdy metal urn I had jasmine in. He squatted beside Mamie, slid a protective arm around her shoulders, and gave her a squeeze.

"The second one took a bash at me with that." George nodded to the silver bowl award I had picked up in New York. Blood dripped onto my verandah.

"Don't know how long they had access. Miss Delilah, I need you to check and see what they took. Then, talk to my men," Sheriff Bellows said. "They are camping out in Harry's office. They didn't dust for fingerprints. Too expensive these days after the mayor's budget cuts."

"Right." The judge reached out, picked up George's injured hand and shook his head. "Needs attention."

George gave a dismissive shrug then took Mamie home to get a Band-Aid for his wounds. I released the dog from captivity, then set up a search for Sidney, whose worn pickup sat in my driveway. Bartles led the party. His tail wagged with joy at being free to sniff and water every bush he wished. Bartles put his nose to the ground like my daddy's hound dog, Rex.

Cam headed to the rose garden, peering around the shrubbery before charging toward the old tree house at the back of the property. Molly aimed for the fruit trees. The judge grabbed my hand and dragged me behind him.

"Afraid I'll do something stupid?"

"Stupid, we don't say stupid." He quoted little Austin, which made me laugh.

No Sidney behind Harry's pickup, or the riding mower, or the phalanx of bicycles. The carriage house, where the cars were parked, was empty.

As we emerged into the hotter air, Cam shouted. "There's a trapped critter in the garden shed."

It wasn't a critter—he'd unearthed Sidney. The poor man was trussed up near the galvanized watering cans and had a cut above his right eyebrow. He'd wriggled so vigorously to get free that he'd smashed two red clay pots into fragments. Even with a duct tape gag you could tell Sidney was fuming. His arms were behind his back, pulled away from him, and inched toward the ceiling. His shoulders must throb from the angle. The judge knelt behind him and untied the ropes binding Sidney's hands together. Cam ripped off the duct tape sealing Sidney's mouth. He gave a high-pitched yelp, putting his fingers onto his tormented lips. I wrung my hands.

"They had a gun, Miss Delilah," Sidney sputtered. "I stuck my hands up high like they said, but the short man hit me anyway." Sidney sniffed his displeasure.

Sidney's philosophy of life came from 1950's shoot-'em-ups. "When a man was unarmed and compliant, the honorable thang for a man to do is leave him be," he'd argued with Josephine not long ago.

"They swiped my keys so they could get in your house." His eyes scrunched up tight. "Next thing I knew I was wedged in here and tied with Mr. Harry's pulley ropes."

That explained Sidney's complaint from last week. The housebreakers must have tried before when they trashed the workbench and stole his mother's keys thinking they were mine. We were ushering Sidney in to give the police a report when my feet clapped to a halt beside the Bourbon roses. They reminded me of the perfume Harry'd purchased for my May birthday, the one with roses on the label. I casually mentioned the gift to the judge. His mobile eyebrows lifted.

"Lead the way, Delilah. I'm assuming it's more rose clues? We'll tackle the boys in blue later."

The four of us deposited Sidney in the arms of the

law and headed to the master suite. Bartles found a cozy spot in a sunbeam while we stood in front of the faux-marble counter. The judge read Harry's note aloud. He picked up the curvy bottle. It was the perfume I usually wore. A soft smile flitted briefly on his lips then the judge ran a thumbnail around the label where the pink roses curled around the calligraphic letters. A corner was loose.

"Got any tweezers, Delilah?"

I fished in my makeup drawer and handed him my tweezers. The judge fiddled at the edge of the label with a delicacy a surgeon might envy. A pink slip of paper emerged in the tiny jaws of the tweezers. The note was a quarter of an inch in width and no bigger than the span of my little finger.

"*Lo how a rose ere bloomin'*," read the judge.

"Nuts," I shouted. "I should have known. He is too clever by half."

"What?" three voices shouted back. I looked up at the ceiling.

"Oh," I said slowly, "let's talk to the detectives in the library. When they're gone, we'll call George and Mamie so they can participate."

"Mom!"

"Like to be mysterious, Delilah?" The judge's voice rumbled with amusement.

"Er-ma'am, maybe a hint?" Cam couldn't contain his excitement.

I shook my head firmly.

I let them go ahead of me and zeroed in on my office from the hall entry. The string I'd placed along the sliding door crack was undisturbed. In their hunt through Harry's office, the intruders hadn't discovered my hiding place. I slipped out, coming into the library through the foyer.

"Everything all right, Di?" asked the judge, alluding to my absence.

"Fine and dandy," I said. Harry's office, however, wasn't. Books lay haphazardly on the floor, two of

Harry's desk drawers had been opened and papers strewn across the top of his desk.

We kept the police and Sidney in the dark about the existence of the hidden space. Our silence seemed safer. The patrolmen were out of the house by three, saying they now had to report an assault. "Because this is the second break-in here, we expect to be regular visitors to this address on the Avenue," the sergeant added as he closed the front door.

"We'll need shovels," I said when they were out of ear-shot.

"Cam, why don't you call on George and Mamie? Molly, phone Josephine. If we're going to find treasure, might as well have a party," said the judge.

My sentiments exactly. I smiled at him. The two of us could start over. *Being a team on the hunt for treasure will perhaps change the way we interact.*

Harry and I had been as easy together as ice cream sliding down a throat. Sweet and natural, with different flavors when the occasion demanded. It took a little time. Harry teaching me the things I needed to know about the marriage bed and all. Not that he had much experience in the matter. Seems he and Olive Lorraine kissed a little and held hands.

I must have smiled at the memory because the judge cocked one eyebrow. I put my "no trespassing" expression on. He brought his lips together and nodded.

"I'm heading back to the roses, Miss Dee Dee," said Sidney, emerging from the study.

"You need to go home, Sidney. I can tell by the way your eyebrows are knitted together that you've a headache. Come back tomorrow if you feel like it."

"Nope. I've a job to do, headache or no. Those robbers ain't going to get the best of me. I've roses to weed around and then I'm mowing." Sidney marched down the long hall to the kitchen and eased the door shut as if it was made of eggshells.

The judge paced. I went in search of glasses and lemonade.

He cleared his throat. "It's time we got a few things straight, Di. First, I'm going to be around a while. Get used to it. We need this wedding to be as hitch free as we can, and our villains seem intent on causing trouble." He smelled of spicy aftershave. I took a whiff out of the lemonade pitcher so I could focus.

"So," he said, ticking off points on a finger. "Tomorrow afternoon your mama, daddy, and Meemaw arrive to help with the wedding. I believe your mama quilts twelve-stitches-to-the-inch. Next, you shouldn't go anywhere without an escort. Finally, I'm confiscating all your revolvers. Last thing I need is for you to be shot by your own weapon."

"A slight mishap. The guns stay. Only *I* know where they're hidden." I crossed my arms. "You're being too pushy, Lyle. And remember, you're the one who said I should call you on that."

"Our nefarious friends had time to search through your house. I guess they know where you hide your pea-shooters."

Footsteps on the back steps told me to close my mouth and await further developments.

"Cam came over and invited us for an archeological dig," George said as he entered. Mamie stood behind him while his eyes swept the hall. "What are we waiting for?"

"Josephine," I said.

Josephine arrived in her Sunday best dress, turquoise straw hat with the peacock feathers, and a smile as broad as the Mississippi. She looked eager to join the hunt.

There were three shovels in the tool shed. The men carried them over their shoulders. Sidney was at the side of the house plucking out the onion grass and whistling off key when we came around the building.

He jumped to his feet. It may take some time before he was content again to massage the dirt and not look over his shoulder.

"Where are the roses Harry had you plant last spring?" I asked.

"I'll show you, Miss Delilah," he said.

Sidney halted by the Betty Boop roses, a Valentine's gift from Harry. "Funny thang about these here shrubs." Sidney waved his hand. "I planted them on a Saturday. When I come on Monday to water, I found the dirt I'd tamped down was all heaped up like a vole had been chasing its tail underground. I mentioned it to Mr. Harry. He said, 'I'll see that nothing else disturbs Miss Delilah's new flowers. Suits her, don't you think, with the curly black stamens and red and yellow petals?' Then he up and laughed."

"Where was the soil disturbed?" Cam asked.

"Cain't rightly recall. I planted seven new ones on account of Mr. Harry, who said seven was a complete number. You know, seven days for creation, seven years of plenty, and seven of drought."

"What did Dad mean?" Molly asked.

Josephine moved to Molly and took my daughter's slim fingers in her work-worn ones. "Honey, your daddy meant his life was complete and he had run his course. He was at peace knowing heaven was a breath away."

"We'll have to dig around," Cam said.

The judge and Cam rolled up their sleeves. Cam forced the blade of his #2 shovel deep into my specially concocted soil. He dislodged rich, loamy dirt, but no treasure.

The judge tried the next bush, but no tick of blade on metal. They alternated places until all the Betty Boop landscape was ruffled.

"Hmm." Sidney scratched at his thin tufts of hair. "Maybe it's that new bush he had me plant as a surprise. The one by the arbor."

"What color is it?" Molly asked.

"Mr. Harry called it, 'Delilah's rose,' but that's not its name."

Sidney loped in front of us heading toward the tall, metal-arbor frothing with pink and cream roses. This might be another of Harry's jokes, having us do calisthenics in the yard. One tap on the ground to the west of the pink bourbon rose bush and the shovel tinked.

"Pay dirt," exclaimed Sidney.

Cam got on his knees and scraped away the soil from Harry's banged up metal tackle box. The lid wasn't locked. However, it took a bit of finagling to get it to open. A small silver key was taped to the inside of the lid and a letter tied in pink ribbon was beneath it. With solemnity, the judge handed it to me. The note was written on Harry's distinctive, fine-linen writing paper, the kind he ordered from a company in New England. My hands trembled.

What did he want to say that was so important?

Chapter Twenty-Four

DEAREST,

THIS IS MY CONFESSION. I have a few things I need to write that couldn't be spoken. First. I've pushed you toward Lyle. Forgive me if it was offensive. I know this world can harm a tender-hearted woman and few men I know are qualified to protect her. Lyle was my choice. Perhaps not yours. Although he only occasionally shared our table with his boys, you have not been friends, just acquaintances. Thank you for not looking past this old man to one who was younger, handsomer, kinder in many ways.

I wandered over to the wrought iron table and chairs on the patio between the Salases' and our house. I plunked down onto the seat. The other participants in the treasure hunt followed.

Second. I've mentioned I want the world to know you are D.B. Burns. You will object. I've asked Max to set it in motion. By Christmas he will have your picture in the New York Times. It is a promise I wrangled from him. Dearest, if I'm pushing you too hard on this, I ask that you forgive me. You deserve to be recognized for your work. I hope you will allow Max to keep his word.

Max will have to rethink Harry's little assignment. I'll be in France, unavailable for public scrutiny.

The last thing I have to tell you is that I lied to you.

I dropped the letter. It bounced over the bricks and got caught in a tuft of Irish moss growing across the patio. The judge tightened his jaw as he gathered the paper to hand it back to me.

It is the only thing between us, and it weighs on my heart. I followed Clarisse that day in October, sweetheart.

I felt a sharp pain in my chest. Harry hadn't trusted me. I could barely breathe I was so hurt. I should have known he'd gone after her. He always came home for lunch. Said eating lunch out was a waste of money and time. He banked on the fact that Josephine had a convenient hearing loss when the kids were at school, and Harry and I needed a bit of 'private time.' Usually we talked about our day, but occasionally, Harry would grab my hand and head up to our room.

I parked across the street from the doctor's office and I watched Clarisse with Doc Timmons. They ran out of the building laughing and holding onto one another as if they'd won the confounded lottery. They headed toward the sixty-five with Doc Timmons driving Clarisse's shiny Corvette. I wasn't far behind. In the diner he met up with Darlene Frogmiejer. Darlene showed up in her little blue VW bug and parked next to the Corvette. I watched as Clarisse went to the lady's room, then Darlene sauntered in and grabbed a hold of the doctor.
They tossed Clarisse's suitcase out of the Vette then they screeched out of the parking lot with both cars, side by side like a drag race. I found Clarisse storming around the linoleum in front of the diner's register fishing in her wallet to pay the bill. Clarisse only had her alligator purse with her grocery money, because the doctor had taken all her money from the bank. I called you from the diner and lied. Said I was going to be late.
I offered to take Clarisse home. I said, "Lyle is a forgiving man and things can be worked out." She'd have none of it. 'I'll kill that S.O.B.,' Clarisse shouted in front of the other diners. 'He stole my car,' the blankety-

blank.' Well you get the drift. You never did like swearing so I'll just leave it at that. She was mighty irritated. Clarisse ordered me to take her to Paducah where she said the doc would be. I left her at the quilt museum. Haven't seen her since, but I've heard from her. About a week after she took off, an envelope came in the mail. In the envelope was a note and a key. A storage unit key. She included a thousand dollars to pay for it until she returned.

Clarisse wrote, "Tell no one and hold on to the key until I ask for it." I've had it in my desk all these years. Not said a word. Last April, when I knew my days were shortening, I took myself off to find it.

Old Frazier took over the place twelve years ago and told me the rental bill had been paid regularly. With the key in my hand he shrugged and let me in. I looked into the nine by twelve space and decided the antiques and other things in it couldn't be hers. Clarisse must have been hiding the items for the doctor. I transferred the smallest items into our safety deposit boxes. Didn't think you'd look inside them for a long while, being occupied with managing life without me.

If you haven't peeked yet, now is the time. Take Lyle with you. You shouldn't see this by yourself. Call Special Agent Madison from the FBI. Someone in law enforcement should be present, and Madison is trustworthy.

I reckon Clarisse is dead since the things weren't claimed by her and the thousand dollars would have been used up long ago. Who was paying the bill, all these years?

Whatever you do, my dearest wife, know you are in my prayers as I write this.

Harry.

"I'd read it aloud, but maybe summarizing will be easier." I didn't want to tell them Harry had kept a secret, but how else would I explain? "Harry received a key and letter in the mail from Clarisse about a week after she left."

Eyebrows in the group went skyward they were so surprised.

"She instructed him to keep the key until she asked for it. So, he did. When Harry was dying, he figured with Clarisse silent for eighteen years, she was dead. He needed to find out what was in the storage unit before I found the key and went hunting."

Molly leaned against Cam, her brow furrowed. The judge mulled over my shortened version—his steady blue eyes on mine.

"Tomorrow the judge, and at Harry's request, his friend, Special Agent Madison, and I will meet at the bank where Harry transferred some items he found."

"Good," said the judge. "Now if you don't mind, I'd like to read the letter at my leisure." He held out his hand. I didn't want anyone to know that Harry had lied to me. The lie was like a physical blow. I slowly folded the letter.

"Perhaps a trade?" he asked, sensing my reluctance. "My round-to-it letter for this one?"

Our fingers touched as I handed over the linen paper. The judge's were warm. Mine still shook. He rubbed his brow as he backed away, pushing at the worry furrows that gathered above his eyebrows.

"Come, Bartles," he called, jogging toward the house. "We both need some exercise."

George and Mamie walked home through the garden gate, fingers intertwined. Cam and Molly waved goodbye to Josephine and hunted for a basketball. I went to the cemetery and unhappily wandered around the Morgans' fenced-off rectangle of graves. The judge would read the letter and conclude that I was off the matrimonial merry-go-round, because even Harry couldn't trust me. Which suited me fine, I reckoned. At least that was what I said to Harry while I was confiscating the Star Wars plastic figurines the resident nut left on top of his grave. I fingered a Han Solo look-a-like. Those toys might be worth something.

I decided I'd donate the lot to the Salvation Army to resell.

"Well, Harry," I said into the late afternoon air. "You sure made a mess of things. Lying to me about Clarisse is the least of your problems. I've got your friend the judge salivating on my doorstep, and some certifiable character trashing your grave. I've not even mentioned the intruders and feeding lemonade to the entire police department. Seems to me, Harry, you should have thought things over more carefully before you decided to skedaddle."

That was about as close as I would come to whining to the Lord about timing. I hadn't even mentioned the monkeying with the wedding that Charlene was up to.

Harry probably knew all about it.

"Finished?" asked a familiar baritone.

"Really, Judge." I planted my hands on my hips. "Can't a woman have a little peace and quiet?"

"I realize I'm intruding." The judge stepped from the shadow of the chestnut tree and sauntered my way. His characteristic smile was in place, but his eyes were sad as he glanced past Harry's grave and rested his gaze on the headstones of our twins.

"I came to give Harry a piece of my mind. It wasn't fair of him to push us together." Lyle shrugged.

I cleared my throat. "It isn't that I don't like you. You're a fine man. It's . . . well, I'm still reeling from Harry's death. Making any real decision about my future isn't wise." I sounded like an old-maid librarian.

"I concur. Best to keep all options open."

He moved in front of me. The lowering sun hit the gray along his temples. I was moved to tears. He handed me another handkerchief, this one without initials. He half-closed his eyes, but he was studying me as if I were a bug under a microscope. I kicked at a tuft of new growth onion grass that was inching toward Harry's feet and blew my nose.

"Here." He handed me the small envelope that had

hung behind the curtain. "Read it at your leisure. Harry isn't the only one who had secrets, Delilah. I've kept a few myself."

If there had been a bench I'd have sat down and read the whole three pages. Not having a seat gave me an idea about Harry's grave marker. A bench seat would suit me fine. Then we could sit and chat without me standing around looking lost.

"Thank you," I spoke into the stir of evening wind. "I'll read it when I get home."

He nodded.

We stood for some time without speaking, listening to the sounds of evening tiptoeing onto the land. A breeze came and stirred the August-green maple leaves, then a call of a cardinal seeking its mate broke the silence. The feeling of being still and comfortable together stole over me. I shook my head.

"I know," he said softly. "You and I are content in the silence."

Harry and I sat before many a winter fire, listening to the crackle of the wood. I'd knit, he'd write or read, then we'd go to bed without saying a word. One moment I was sitting on the couch, he in his easy chair, the next we were on our feet reaching for one another's hands.

The last time we'd been that close was in June, three weeks before he died. It had been a cool day, not reaching past seventy-seven, humidity low. Harry had been comfortable. We were alone in the library, Harry in his hospital bed, I reading a book. I looked at him, kicked off my shoes, and climbed in beside him. He smelled fresh like a baby. Harry was fastidious about his hygiene even toward the end when others helped him. I put my head on his shoulder, in the place where it fit perfectly, and slept. We were saying our goodbye.

Glancing sideways at the judge I caught him

grimly staring at the buzz cut of new grass on Harry's grave. Whatever I said would be inappropriate. I reached for his hand.

"I'll see you tomorrow." I took his strong fingers in my left palm. "When we go to the bank." With that I left him to yell at Harry for the pickle he'd put us in.

I took my time traveling home. Stopped at the grocery and got bouquets for the dining room table and the bedrooms where Meemaw, Daddy and Mama were to sleep. I chose a tub of ice cream for Cam who'd cleaned us out the night before. The letter sat on the passenger seat like an exclamation point, daring me to look. When I finally got home and did, it was more troubling than a room full of whispers.

Well, old friend, here is the last missive I'll write to you. It has taken a lifetime to store up these words. You have been a true friend. You recall fifteen years ago when I asked if you were interested in my wife? Thank you for admitting you were growing fond of her and wouldn't let it grow any further. You didn't, Lyle. You remained faithful to our friendship, ignoring your heart.

Now that you've had a closer acquaintance, I would guess fondness has turned to love and you're finding yourself in a dilemma. My fault entirely. Delilah has a mind and will of her own and will most likely not cotton to my interference. I could suggest she go to a nunnery after my demise, but I'm sure you can guess how that would go over.

You have my blessing, Lyle, if Delilah is amenable to your suit.

That is the most important thing I have to say. The other is a legal matter. Delilah finds herself rich, alone, and prey for the unscrupulous. Whatever happens between you two, I do expect you to see to her care. Financially she is quite competent to manage things, it is her tenderness that worries me. Some in this town have been mightily unfriendly to her. I don't imagine that will change with my demise. See that she is guarded from the gossip that fixes itself upon the bereaved.

There is a little matter of an incident eighteen years ago when I gave a promise and kept something hidden. I recently discovered a cache of property I was entrusted with. If I don't give it to the police, will it cause Delilah harm? Is possession nine-tenths of the law or is that just an old wives' expression?

I rejoice that Cam and Molly will marry. Celebrate. The Henderson and Morgan clans joining will improve the gene pool. Enjoy our grandchildren. You will make a wonderful grandfather, graced with wisdom, patience, and tenderness.

Perhaps it is wishful thinking that you and Delilah might marry. I want Delilah cared for and decided you were the man. I will choose to trust in God and not my own plans, but it is hard going.

With friendship and phileo love,
Harry

At least Harry wasn't handing me over on a silver platter like a roasted pig with an apple in its mouth. However, Judge Lyle Henderson was not an option. I could only handle one man at a time. At present Harry held the high ground.

I was not about to surrender it to another.

Chapter Twenty-Five

AT EIGHT FORTY-FIVE MONDAY MORNING, THE judge arrived for our jaunt to the bank. He was in a conservative, light-gray suit. I added a splash of color to the day with a pink and orange floral dress that swung past my knees. Showing my thighs as a grandmother could get me arrested.

Madison pulled into the parking lot of the bank as we stepped out of the judge's BMW. It was a breezy morning. I had to grab the hem of my dress as I rose from the car, so it wouldn't rise with me.

The bank's vice president waited by her office door looking as fresh as a bouquet of daisies in her white summer heels. Since the V.P. and I were numbers people and she attended our church, we had an affinity. Not a lot of women liked to chase numbers around a page.

It was a quick journey into the vault where the shiny lockers of deposit boxes were imprisoned. On a narrow metal table Harry's large unopened box was laid to rest by the bank officer. Another large box was eased down next to it.

Standing in the muffled room reminded me of a morgue and the widow Harrington who brought her deceased cat in and placed it in a box she had lined with satin. Being a hot Kentucky summer, the bank began to reek within two days. The place was a furor of consternation. They evacuated the bank and brought in the sheriff's dog. Harry and I had been depositing his first check from Max the day the bank was held up by scent.

We joined the crowd congregating in the oven outside, craning their necks to see what Buster the bloodhound could discover. Since that occurrence, you had to sign a certificate stating that you have not placed a dead animal in your safety deposit receptacle. I took a deep breath. Madison dismissed the vice president. She stepped out of the room, but lingered by the clerks, eyes fixed our way. Madison eased the heavy door partly shut.

"You have the honors, Miss Delilah." He'd taken over the event as soon as he stepped in the bank.

There should have been a squeak as I opened the box. Sound effects would add to the suspense. The large metal rectangle was filled with lumpy linen type bags. Perhaps a dozen large ones were stacked on the bottom, small ones toward the top. No markings on the bags.

I picked up a small one. The linen bag was surprisingly heavy. Untying the drawstring, I let the contents scatter over the metal table. The tink, clink of rocks on metal echoed in the room. Not just any rocks, mind you, but perfectly cut diamonds gleamed in the overhead light.

We sucked in our breath. I thought about running my hands through the sparkling stones, but I'd probably drop a few and be scrambling undignified around the floor to retrieve them.

"Do you think all the bags have diamonds?" I asked.

"Only way to find out is to open them." Madison gestured at the table. "Mrs. Morgan, Harry's treasure is yours, as it is in your deposit box and legally in your possession being Harry's widow."

No one had mentioned to Madison that Clarisse gave Harry the diamonds. I looked at the judge waiting for him to speak. He winked at me.

"Is it like the Richardson versus Donnelly case you had twelve years ago?" I asked.

"Perhaps." The judge nodded.

"The verdict was, Donnelly kept the painting since he had possession. Didn't he also produce a hand-written note from his aunt saying she gave it to him?" I asked. "Richardson claimed he was the intended recipient because money was owed to him by said aunt. Have I got that right?"

"So far, so good." The judge lounged in the stiff metal chair. "Richardson can have claims against the estate of the deceased aunt, but Donnelly was not the executor and not responsible to settle the debts."

"Ah," I commented.

"I thought you were knitting when Harry and I discussed cases."

"I was." Why anyone thinks a woman can't knit, purl, use a cable needle, and carry on a conversation at the same time was beyond me.

"Shall we get on with this?" Madison glanced at his cell phone to check on the time.

I rubbed the back of my neck which was getting tense. "We should get paper and pen to record what we find."

The judge started taking pictures with his cell phone while I spread out the stones from the first bag. Madison exited the vault and returned with a legal pad and two pens. He and the judge sat beside me writing down the approximate size of each stone. I separated the gems by shape as the judge took more pictures. We counted one-hundred-and-five rocks in the first bag. If each large diamond was worth two-thousand dollars, that was $210,000 dollars in that bag alone. I didn't know the 4 C's of each diamond, however if there were twelve bags of "loot," then I was looking at three million dollars and change.

Who did this treasure belong to?

The judge let out a low whistle when I opened the second bag. The diamonds were larger. Maybe the rocks were put in the bags according to the carats. These stones were larger than the sapphire Harry had given me as an engagement ring. That one was two carats. Were these stolen? Did they have tiny numbers lasered into them? My hands were clammy.

It took us three hours to make a list of the stones. Coffee was delivered about ten, donuts arrived at eleven. The judge and Madison ate through the pastries while I kept separating the stones. We took bathroom breaks, always having two people in the room if one left. When finished with the counting and picture taking, I put all the bags back in the boxes and closed them with a clink. The judge walked to the door and asked Candy to bring her key to lock the boxes into their niches. As we were sliding the loot into place Madison disappeared to make a private phone call.

If he thought he was going to put these in police custody he had another think coming. I wanted to be certain that the stones didn't disappear like drugs that somehow had legs.

"Would you care to join me for lunch, Miss Delilah?" the judge asked as we stepped out of the vault. Squinting at the bright sunlight I dug in my purse for sunglasses. I planned on walking home through the campus to clear my mind which was distracted with whos, whys, and what-nows.

"Mrs. Morgan needs to pay the sheriff a visit." Madison's eyes swung from the judge to me. "She needs to sign papers about the break-in yesterday."

"After the judge and I dine, perhaps Sheriff Bellows can stop by the house," I suggested. "There is so much to do two weeks before a wedding. I just don't know how I'll manage." I flapped my hand helplessly. "I've guests arriving this afternoon, meals to prepare, fittings. I'm on my last nerve, I must admit."

The judge turned away, his eyes dancing with laughter.

"You owe me." Madison muttered as he walked out.

"Whatever for?" I took the judge's arm.

"Probably because we took up so much of his time."

"You're not a very good liar."

"I'm not trying to be. Madison thought you would refuse my offer, so he gave you a little nudge my direction." My hand fluttered off his arm. The judge recaptured my hand then placed his right one on top like a wood clamp.

"I'm not going anywhere," I said.

"Only Harry and Clarisse knew about the diamonds."

"And probably the not-so-good-doctor. I'd guess they were more of his secret stash. Did he have Clarisse get the box? He must have known the Chicago drug lords wanted his hide. Why trust Clarisse if he was going to double-cross her for another woman? Or was Darlene a last-minute plan?"

"Did the doctor have a duplicate key to the storage unit? Maybe for his wife?"

"Maybe. Judging from the things the Feds unearthed in the storage units they found, the doctor hid everything he couldn't nail down. Which means," he said softly, "that he planned on coming back. Is that why he and Darlene argued about sticking around Paducah instead of heading out of the country? I'd wager the doctor planned to head back to town, grab his diamonds and whatever else he stashed, then vanish. His killer stole the safety-deposit key."

Which meant Clarisse or someone faking her name.

"Well, at least he accomplished his vanishing goal. He's dead, so he isn't one of our midnight visitors. I'm wondering who else knew about his greed? His office manager? Partner?"

"A definite possibility."

We crossed in front of the college coffee shop as we headed toward The Coop. Seemed appropriate to celebrate the diamond cache with Carter's fried chicken.

"Josephine has been alerted to our absence from her luncheon table." The judge tossed me a smile.

He was certainly cocky, thinking I'd agree to lunch.

"I didn't know how long the counting would take,

or if the police wanted in on the action." The judge was a little hesitant as he pushed open The Coop's glass door. "I thought it best that Josephine not wait lunch for us, since Cam and Molly had afternoon appointments."

"Oh," I mumbled. I was so judgmental. "The kids are seeing their doctors today. I made a couple of other phone calls. Things are on track for the wedding." I smiled with relief.

"As I live and breathe." Carter slipped from behind the counter. "My favorite lady. Where'd you pick up this feller, Miss Delilah?" His normally jovial tone was a little louder today. "Seems to look familiar, but the man I'm thinking of dresses in sissy robes and has a sour expression most of the time. This here gent seems to be a foreigner on vacation."

Everyone laughed. Carter seated us at Harry's table by the far wall. "Since I canceled the city council meetings in the back room," he continued loudly, "the Rotary, Lions Club, and Elks have all pestered me about using the place. Those clubs give scholarships, glasses for the poor, and provide grab bars for the elderly instead of persecuting their neighbors." Carter sniffed his disapproval then backed away, letting BethAnn and her order book take his place.

"I want to celebrate with Carter's fried chicken," I told her. "But don't tell Josephine. She thinks hers is the only chicken fit to eat."

"The usual?" she asked the judge, her eyes wide with interest.

"Let's brook tradition," he said. "The French dip. Instead of fries, I'll have green salad with French dressing. I'm in a *joie de vivre* mood."

I was fingering the small deposit key and slid it across the table while BethAnn took his order.

"You know what this means, don't you?" I asked when we were alone. He raised an eyebrow. I leaned forward. "Clarisse is dead, or she would have come back for the diamonds. The doctor and some unknown woman are dead. So, who is left that knows about the key? The doctor's widow?" I tapped on it. "Who's to say she didn't follow him to Paducah and pull the trigger?"

"Perhaps." He leaned toward me until our foreheads were nearly touching. "Could the Paducah pair who went to prison have seen Harry with Clarisse and connected us to the diamonds?"

"Interesting theory. Things don't add up, though. The destruction of my family photos tells me the attack was personal. There is no association with my break-ins if it is the Chicago Irish gang."

"I forgot about the personal destruction in your bedroom."

"Did you also miss that someone named Darlene has been sending letters requesting aid for orphans, hospitals, food for the hungry, and goats to give to a poor family? They've been posted on every church bulletin board for years. If Darlene is the body in the car, someone took her identity. Who else was having an affair with our resident Romeo?"

I bounced that idea around. "Darlene wasn't the missionary type. And what kind of ninny would send donations to someone without checking for accountability? Foolish when the person hasn't been seen in eighteen years."

The judge leaned back when BethAnn delivered our water. She carefully positioned the sweating glass above his knife. He smiled his thanks and took a sip. The ice clinked. BethAnn walked toward the counter.

"Quite a racket someone has going. They must have been living it up in the Caribbean, collecting from the naive and laughing at all of us." The judge tilted his head as he shook it.

"Do you think the con artist is the one who shot George and tried to run us off the road?"

"No. That doesn't usually fit the MO of a con. The risks they take are minimal. Running us off the road was dangerous." A shadow thrust itself across the table top.

My hand slapped down on top of the key as if I were playing Slap Jack. I kept my palm flat on the table.

"Neely, Olive Lorraine," the judge said in a formal tone. He rose from his seat and towered over the Patricks.

"I want to apologize again to Mrs. Morgan for disturbing her the other day, and for my wife's behavior at the Salases'. I think we've straightened out that little misunderstanding, haven't we, my dear?"

Neely Patrick's hand was clomped onto his wife's wrist. Her hand was white from lack of blood flow. Two Merlot-colored circles sat on Olive Lorraine's cheeks.

"Yes, Neely. Molly overreacted. We were only joking." Her voice was on autopilot. Olive Lorraine didn't look at me, not once. Her eyes were on the judge.

"Saw you two leaving from the bank." Neely had ignored Olive Lorraine's lie. "Some estate business I'm certain." He smiled wolfishly, waiting for us to enlighten him. BethAnn slid our plates of food past Neely's watchful eyes and eased them down in front of us. "Always do like Carter's cooking. Reminds me of my mama's back on the farm."

Neely Patrick hailed from Chicago, the inner city, not a farm. Harry had found out that tidbit when Neely came to town courting Olive Lorraine. Neely's brother had blown in the week of the wedding and camped out at the Super 8. Harry had asked a few questions. After a couple of beers, Jack Patrick was a bubbling brook of information, giving details about Neely's life in Chicago and his rowdy friends. Olive Lorraine, however, wouldn't hear a negative word about O'Neal Sebastian Patrick. Harry had skipped the wedding.

"Carter's excellent food is why Mrs. Morgan and I are here discussing the details of the wedding." The judge's voice was clipped. "Do excuse us as we finish tidying up a few details."

The judge gave a courtly nod and sat down. The Patricks had the good sense to sidle off. The key went into the pocket of my dress.

The bell above the door tinkled. The judge asked me to wave at the people who had come in. I whipped my head to see. It was the sheriff and Madison, who looked our way, then sat at the counter. When I turned my companion had a bite of chicken between his teeth and the offending piece of filched thigh clutched in his hand.

I burst out laughing and had to hold my side because it still caused a problem. "You could have asked," I managed around my laughter.

"I'd rather seek forgiveness than permission."

He laughed with me.

"Your eyes are lit up like a hot July morning while your dimples are dancing in and out," the judge said. "Nice to see. First time I saw you laugh you were raking up leaves with the kids. I came over to collect my boys and you were in the middle of the pile, cascading leaves over the children."

He swallowed as the memory kicked up. "That was our first autumn in town. It was the week after you stood on our doorstep with a welcome dinner in a basket and an apple pie. I recall Clarisse didn't invite you in. We spoke heatedly about it. She announced that according to the DAR ladies the Morgans were to be left to themselves. A shunning, as it were. Had to do with Harry and his letters to the editor about politics and your being from Owsley County."

He lifted my hand to his lips and kissed the back of my knuckles. You could have knocked me down with a feather. It wasn't the information that caused my shock. I was used to the cold shoulder, but there was a tingling that went from my hand down to my middle.

"Don't get up, Lyle," Madison said as he took up

residence beside us. He waved the judge back to his seat. "Does Harry have paperwork showing where he purchased the stones? I suspect Harry wanted me in on this discovery because he has hot loot. The thieves found out and that is the reason behind all the break-ins. Harry was as honest as they come, so I'm a bit confused." Madison lifted an eyebrow, waiting for me to comment. "So far, no one can recollect a jewel heist of this magnitude. If there was paper work to prove ownership, we'd be in better shape."

Madison was right to be confused, but I didn't want to say anything until I'd had time to pray. I didn't feel good about exposing Harry's letter about Clarisse, but I didn't want to lie, either. Harry had hidden the diamonds intending for me to find them. Why?

The judge and I slid over on the red leatherette seats. The seat fabric protested with the sound of squeegee on glass. Bellows sat beside me, Special Agent Madison with the judge.

Bellows hunched over a cup of coffee he'd carried with him from the counter. "We're guessing that Harry's death brought the thieves to your door. Whether they were looking for the dia . . . er . . . things Harry left, we don't know."

"Sometimes criminals target widows for a quick haul," the judge said.

"Could be that, but it doesn't explain the break-ins at your home, Judge."

"No." The judge stroked his chin. "Seems that you've more investigating to do. I think George's covert friends should be guarding Miss Delilah. Perhaps he has a few retired friends a little bored with the Washington scene. Would tomorrow suit, Miss Delilah?"

I jerked my head upright like I'd been hit by lightning. I had been distracted by an internal argument. Should I admit the diamonds were likely Clarisse's? Imagining Harry's intentions got me addled, and I couldn't formulate words at the moment.

"I'll have the security people report to you, Sam, so we don't end up with our guards in the county jail."

They all laughed.

I didn't. I knew why they hadn't risked the conversation about armed guards. "You may think I'll blow a gasket. After all, I am on my last nerve and it is about tore up." I crossed my arms and looked slowly over the three men. "Give me a minute to re-plan my life to I can squeeze in security guards, extra food, and figure out how to accommodate all the people you are thrusting into it." I narrowed my eyes.

"You do that," the judge shot back. "And George can accommodate his friends."

Madison slid to his feet. "I'll keep you posted, Lyle," he said. "Sheriff?" Bellows rose then ducked his head my direction.

I leaned across the table when they were out of earshot. "You and George might have asked."

"You might have said no."

"I might have."

"Exactly."

Carter's fried chicken sat like a lump in my stomach. I pushed around the heap of mashed potatoes until the judge dipped his last crust of bread in the *au jus*.

Chapter Twenty-Six

AS WE LEFT, I SQUARED MY shoulders. "You and George calling big-deal-special-agents to guard me is ridiculous."

"Hush, Di," he hissed back.

The only people who heard were the Patricks. They were ahead of us as we eased around the tables. Neely Patrick swiveled his head giving us the lizard look, the one with the big googly eyes you see on the TV animal shows. Then a smile slid over his face.

Olive Lorraine's face was pinched tight. Funny to think on it, but I've never seen Olive Lorraine laugh. She didn't do much with merriment except snort through her nose once or twice. She held joy in. The thought made me sad. Was she so disappointed when Harry married me that she'd strangled her emotions?

The judge kept me moving, not stopping to greet old friends or chat with Carter. The judge would have marched me straight to his car if I hadn't wiggled loose.

"I'm heading home on my own power, thank you very much."

The judge drove home in his little car. I tromped the hot August streets and felt the humidity curling my hair. I was angry as all get out about "security guards." Although, I must admit, using Sidney hadn't been a red-hot idea. His lips still appeared swollen this morning. He'd also been uppity when Josephine had taken him coffee.

Things did not make sense. Why come after the diamonds when Harry was dead? Why not when he was alive? Harry knew where to find the key quickly. My walk home was quiet.

"You'd better enjoy the peace," I spoke aloud. I ticked off the events invading my life. Security arriving-courtesy of the judge and George. A bridal shower tomorrow given by the ladies at our church. Wednesday the final trip to Lexington with the bridesmaids. Thursday the bridesmaids' shower, complete with racy underwear.

The judge was parked on my verandah wearing a big smirk when I got home. He looked mighty comfortable in his shorts and flowered Hawaiian shirt. His dog was lapping at a bowl of water.

"Just got off the phone with the governor. He agreed to the request for chairs, tents, wooden dance floor, the works. The mayor didn't get as far as Frankfort in his tying up operation." The judge lifted his ever-present glass of lemonade to salute. "The tables will be arriving on Friday morning before the wedding. Your friend the governor said he intends to enjoy the ambiance of fine linen and silver and is sending that as well. The governor also mentioned he doesn't care for the way things are being handled in our fair city. An escort will be provided for all the wedding guests to get to the reception." The judge settled into his chair as if he owned the verandah. He managed a self-deprecating shrug.

I sat lightly in the chair opposite the judge. The one closest to the jasmine scent. A frilly pink rose sat on the table between us. I picked it up. The rose was from the bush near his front door. "Thank you."

"My pleasure." His baritone gave a friendly rumble. He didn't lift his eyes to look my direction, just kept rubbing his dog's ears and tummy. "About the guards. I realize it offends you, but your daddy bringing his shotgun might not be beneficial."

"Er . . . you didn't mention the break-ins to Daddy, did you?"

"I'm not a fool, Di," he said. "Your fears would be amusing if they weren't a breath away from reality. I've heard about his gun, Minerva, for years."

Of course he had. The judge and Harry had been tight as ticks. Minerva would be one guest too many.

"I'm hot. How about another glass of lemonade?" He was fanning himself with his right hand.

I wasn't letting him out of my sight. No, sir. Even though he had prevented a wedding disaster by contacting the governor, I was not happy with him. My fault entirely. I was touchy these days what with one thing and another.

"Josephine!" My voice was so loud it was impolite.

Josephine pushed open the door and let the screen bang shut.

"You rang, madam, or was that a holler?" Josephine looked put out. Everyone was on edge.

"I hollered." I wasn't apologetic. The judge cocked one eyebrow. "His Honor would like another lemonade."

"Seems to me you have a pair of legs, and I'm plumb wore out. That dratted alarm has been going off all morning. I've been running up and down them stairs trying to find the short in the system. The cops keep showing up to check on things. And if that weren't enough, I burned my coconut cake when Sidney said he was sure someone was sneaking around the side yard."

She crossed her arms. A sure sign of trouble. "There wasn't anyone, of course. His wild imagination is conjuring ghosts. I am not hustling my bustle any more today, thank you very much."

"The judge and I will find the lemonade."

"You'll have to make it. His Honor polished off the last drop."

"You up to showing me your culinary expertise?" I asked the judge, overly polite.

"I'll opt for water. Can't have enough on a hot day." He rose as he spoke and deposited Bartles into Josephine's arms. "Josephine, take my chair and put your feet up. We'll be back with water in a jiffy."

I thought looking up the root of jiffy would be fun as Cam squealed to a stop in our driveway. We turned that direction. I could see Molly's silhouette beside him. Her head was down as if she was studying something in her lap. The trees lining our drive played hide and seek with the light. Cam's hand reached for her face and tipped it toward his. Molly jerked her head away, opened her door, then ran like a wounded gazelle toward the verandah.

It wasn't their first fight, but the way Cam dashed after her had me alarmed. I put the rose bud on the table and began to rise. The judge's hand reached for mine.

"Let them be, Di," he whispered.

Cam veered around the magnolia and stopped in front of Molly. Neither noticed their audience on the verandah.

"We can call the wedding off," Molly sputtered. "I'll talk to Mom. She'll understand."

"Well, I sure don't." Cam balled his fists.

Peering through the lilac bush, I saw Cam put his hands on Molly's shoulders. He gave her a gentle shake then pulled her into him.

"Whatever made you think I'm marrying you to have children? I'm marrying you because I love you." His voice broke.

"I might not be able to have any," Molly sobbed. "I've a tipped uterus and infrequent periods."

Molly's head descended into Cam's chest. She was crying so hard they were both rocking. The fear in Molly's voice fluttered against my heart. Molly had names for all twelve kids she imagined would race through her house.

I must have signaled that to the judge because his arms tightened so I wouldn't throw myself into their business and ruin Cam's opportunity.

"I heard him," Cam said. He cupped her face in his hands. "He could be wrong. I pray he is. If not, we'll adopt."

"Oh, Cam." Molly couldn't continue.

They began to move away from the tree and toward the car.

"We'll learn about this together," he said, kissing the tears glistening on her cheeks.

"Cam, where are we going?" Molly's words drifted to us.

"To a place where we can hold each other and talk. Just talk, Mol, I promise."

They drove away never realizing that they had been overheard. The judge eased his hold on me. We went into the house together, lost in our pain for the children.

I stood in front of the sliding doors that hid Harry's library while the judge went to get water. My hand fingered the carved brass handholds that opened the sliders. The wooden doors opened at my touch. I took one step and caught movement to my right. I figured Bartles had escaped his master and was hunting me down. The figure in my periphery, however, seemed larger than the wee dog of the judge.

Like some slow-motion-replay I turned to face the barrel of a six-shooter with a strange thing on the end. A silencer, probably. I didn't look up, only stared at the dark metal oval pointing at my chest.

Funny what you think of in straightened circumstances. I wanted the judge to seek cover. Next, don't get blood on Harry's prize silk carpet.

"Where's the key, Mrs. Morgan?" said a voice from the past.

She was now a red-head, eyes watery blue, skin a remarkably deep tan, lips puffed up with silicone. But I recognized the hardness of the mouth. I'd looked at that face when walking the kids to school, watching them play soccer, and while riding my bicycle to the park with the kiddie trailer behind. Clarisse hadn't changed for the better on her eighteen-year sabbatical, but I wasn't going to offer that bit of insight.

I didn't telegraph the key's whereabouts by reaching into my pocket. I stood my ground, hoping George's spy cameras worked day and night.

"What key?" I asked, playing confused.

"The storage unit key, that's what key. And don't play ignorant. Harry didn't keep anything from you."

"We don't have a storage unit."

"Harry kept the key to my unit for me."

"Harry isn't here. And why are you pointing a gun at me? I'd give you the key if Harry said it was okay."

"I know Harry's dead, you ninny. He was custodian of my things. I want them back."

"Where is the storage unit? Maybe we can go there and they'll let you open it?"

"Highly unlikely, Delilah," the judge said from the doorway. "Hello, Clarisse, I've been expecting you."

He hadn't said diddly about knowing she was alive. I glanced his way. He was holding two glasses of ice water. Bartles skidded along the freshly waxed wood. With deliberation, the judge walked to Harry's desk and put the glasses on top of the dark leather blotter Harry received from Max. I wanted to say, "Don't, they might leave a stain," but there was the omnipresent gun, and who knew how stable Clarisse was these days?

"I shouldn't have destroyed our wedding picture. Then you wouldn't have suspected me."

"That was one clue. The other was the search. You went to all my secret places, the end table in the living room, my hidden desk drawer, and the back of my dresser where I tape documents."

"Got to say one thing for you, Lyle. You are predictable. Everything was where I expected it. And yes, I thought Harry might have given it to you." Her lips curled into a smirk. "Did you miss me?"

He kept his eyes on the gun aimed at me.

"At first, yes. I had a lot of repenting to do. But after Beau's birthday came and went without a word from you, I didn't miss you at all. Hated you for a bit."

"I never wanted the kids."

"So, that was a lie? I never knew." His voice was peaceable as if he were conversing with a stranger. "I loved you then, Clarisse."

"The problem with our marriage was your mistress."

I gasped.

"Shocked you, Delilah?" She waved the gun a bit. "Oh, he had one all right." Clarisse walked to the bookshelves and picked up a brass statue named Justice, the one you see in the Supreme Court. "You loved the law so much you'd forsake everything to serve her."

"I learned to put her in her place, Clarisse."

"Lucky for your wife, then. But there isn't a wife, is there, Lyle." She laughed suddenly. It wasn't a nice sound, more like a backfire from an old car. "I heard you pined away for me."

She dropped the statue in the wrong place. "You could have been the toast of Washington D.C, but no, not you. The height of your career turned out to be a small-town judge in a backwards state. Can't believe you choose this"—she stretched out her arms—"over power in Washington."

"No, you've got that wrong. I chose to give my life to Someone other than justice. He directed me to love *my* boys to manhood." His voice rose when he said "my boys."

Clarisse extended her hand. "The key, Lyle. I haven't much time."

"Perhaps it's in Harry's desk." The judge started to move around me toward Harry's drawers then stopped.

"What happened in Paducah, Clarisse?" he asked as he turned to face me. "Stay behind me," he mouthed.

"Paducah eighteen years ago?"

"Let's start with that while Delilah and I check Harry's desk. She knows where Harry stored things." His lips formed, "Where is your gun?"

I smiled at him and inclined my head toward the place where Harry usually sat. The gun was tucked under the knee hole of his desk. It wasn't loaded, but Clarisse wouldn't know that. "It's not loaded," I mouthed. He nodded and patted my hand as if comforting a fractious child.

"Really, Lyle. Do leave the grieving widow alone, she can handle herself, and fetch me the key."

Clarisse's voice cleavered the moment.

"Put everything on the desk top so I can see what you find." From the coldness in her eyes I didn't think we were going to make it out of the room alive.

Lyle kept between Clarisse's steady gun and me. I tapped on a small button an inch below the drawer slide. It opened a wide center drawer. There was a release button to push. I pulled the drawer out. It was 1880's solid mahogany and heavy. I handed it to Lyle, feeling the pull on my ribs. As he dumped the contents onto the desk top. I retrieved Harry's Smith and Wesson revolver from its hiding place, keeping it hidden behind the cushion on Harry's chair seat.

Clarisse stepped closer.

Lyle spread out the drawer's contents, papers, pens, note cards, and address book. "Paducah?" Lyle pressed.

Clarisse slowly smiled. "Harry caught up with me right before Eddyville. Did he tell you?"

I nodded.

Clarisse snorted. "Just like him, reporting to his keeper. Couldn't get him interested in anything outside of his family. Man was a bore."

Shows what Clarisse knew. Harry was intense and private, but creative in the areas that counted. Not something I'd offer for her amusement.

"I told Harry to leave me in that little river town and he did. He drove off toward his fireplace and little wife." Her lips curled into a sneer.

I knelt on the floor and eyeballed her over the desk top before turning the lock on the third drawer on the left side of Harry's desk. It was where he kept the bullets.

"I gave him an opportunity most men didn't refuse. You never did, Lyle." Her sneer expanded to her eyes.

My hand sought the A file where the ammo was stashed.

"I settled in a flea-bitten hotel near the river and caught up with Dwight. He was with the youngest Frogmiejer sister, Darlene. The platinum blonde. She fancied herself a femme fatale." Clarisse snorted through her nose.

Clarisse looked at the things accumulating on the desk top, then moved closer. I plopped files out of the drawers and let the judge flip through them. Hoped it would keep her eyes busy while I loaded the gun.

"About Darlene," Lyle said. "Why was she in Paducah?"

"They planned to disappear. When I slapped Darlene, she admitted she was escaping from a mediocre life, Dwight from the law. Darlene followed us from his office. They met up at a restaurant where Little Miss Bluegrass and Dwight stole my car and money."

Still angry after all these years, Clarisse paced from the silk carpet to the curved window wall that faced the verandah. With her eyes averted I stuffed two bullets into their chambers. By now, Josephine should realize things weren't normal.

"Dwight was charming and a prolific lover," said Clarisse. "He appealed to women. Maybe he had a third lover. Or would it be fourth, if we counted his wife?" She seemed amused at the thought. "I don't think he could keep up with all of us. Most likely that's Darlene's body at the state ME's lab. Who else could it be?"

"When did they go missing?" Lyle continued spreading the pile of Harry's flotsam out to the corners of the desk.

"I don't know. I didn't see her again after I demanded my twenty thousand. Darlene said I'd only get my money back over her dead body."

Clarisse didn't have a nice smile. I thrust two more bullets into Harry's break-in deterrent and tucked the gun between my knees where she couldn't see. She inched closer, a step out of range for Lyle to grab her.

"Two men arrived in Paducah about noon of the sixteenth. They caused such a ruckus I could hear it above the television in my room. Dwight was afraid of them. He ran from this pathetic little town because he heard they were looking for him. The goons from Chicago must have followed the doctor and are the ones who clocked them. In their trial the police said they found my money on those two when they were arrested."

"It must have been difficult living without alimony or the money I gave you." The judge sounded pensive.

She needed money to disappear. How had she managed? Did she take Darlene's blue Volkswagen and sell it? It had vanished too. Funny that Clarisse never sought to get the twenty-thousand dollars back from the police or get more from the judge. Had she taken a bag or two of the diamonds from the storage unit before going to the bank to loot the judge's box?

The judge turned to face her, covering me neatly as I fumbled to finish loading the gun. The revolver hit my leg and slid onto the rug. I palpated around until I'd snagged it, then rose to my knees.

The untidiness of the heap of objects on Harry's clean desk top was making my hands itch. I put back the A to G files in the bottom drawer and the H through M files in the second drawer from the top. Harry liked things bottom to top. He claimed it made creativity flow better to have the unexpected jump out at you. I was fishing out the N through S when I heard the slight squeal of the door leading to the back hall. Josephine had to be warned. Clarisse wouldn't hesitate to plug a hole in her, seeing that Clarisse never liked Josephine. Of course, Clarisse wouldn't think twice about shooting me, either.

"I managed to survive," Clarisse said. "Didn't think it was safe to stay where the doctor could be tracked. I met someone who gave me a lift to Miami." That was another lie. I saw the tip of her tongue flick out and lick her upper lip. It was the third time she'd done it, signaling she'd told a tale.

"But you never contacted me for a settlement when I divorced you."

"I heard about that. How can you divorce me when I didn't sign any papers?"

"Desertion." He said the word in a flat voice.

"I had other means than my meager little allowance from you. I didn't need you or your money." I couldn't see her face, but her voice was smug. I shivered at the naked derision.

"It's reasonable to assume Harry placed the key in a more secure spot," the judge changed the subject as he took a step toward Clarisse.

"Don't," she ordered. "I won't hesitate to shoot if you get too close."

"All right." He put his hands in the air, palms facing her. "I'm curious. During all those years away, why didn't you contact your parents? You could ignore me and the boys, but your father was most grieved."

"Do shut up, Lyle." She was so mad I thought she'd spit. "I don't really care how Daddy felt. Daddy and his patriotic blood couldn't wait to have a son-in-law who was a career Navy lawyer. How I hated all the maneuverings I had to do to get you into bed."

I lifted my head up as I put another pile of files on the desk. The judge's neck muscles were rigid. I sat back on my heels. Harry must have known that the judge was trapped in an unhappy marriage. Was Harry attempting to make up for Lyle's lousy wife by saying, "Here's mine, she's a good old girl?"

I felt like a used car with a billboard above saying kick the tires, check the oil, twiddle with the knobs on the radio. I was about to throw the key at Clarisse to get her out of here, but my stubborn button wasn't about to give her the satisfaction, and my mind said I needed to buy time.

The judge turned toward me and winked. He was

smiling like he'd planned all along for her motor mouth to go into overdrive.

Josephine peered in the window. Her mouth opened in shock, then she turned away and disappeared.

"No key here, Clarisse," he said as he flipped through the last set of folders. "Is there another office where Harry kept his personal things, Delilah?"

"His college office. Nothing's been moved. They might make it a memorial." That was a reach. "I haven't cleaned out his things. Maybe he had the key there." I tried to sound puzzled.

So far, I'd told the truth. If I go to meet my maker in the next few minutes, I didn't intend to have a lie poisoning my lips. A robin crashed against the window by the front of the house. They did that as the sunlight struck the glass toward mid-afternoon. "What's that?" Clarisse spit out.

She twisted to the right. When she did, her gun hand hit the leather chair where Harry had composed the chicken poems. She grabbed the gun with both hands. There was no doubt that when she got the key, we were mincemeat.

I rose and circled behind the judge, my weapon still out of her sight in my right hand. The judge shook his head at me. I narrowed my eyes but kept moving. I'd never fired at a living thing. I'd let others in the family bring home the bacon, so I was mighty uncomfortable shooting at Clarisse.

"Open the doors, Lyle, and invite Josephine in." Clarisse waved the gun for emphasis. "I could use more leverage."

I reached the judge's side, the gun behind me. He took a step away then deliberately moved in front of me. A car pulled into the drive—you could hear the tires on the asphalt. Clarisse tilted her head, listening.

Please, please, please, Lord, don't let it be the kids.

The judge sheltered me as Clarisse smirked. "Lyle, Lyle, no use trying to protect little Miss Hootenanny."

As she moved sideways to get a bead on me, Lyle jumped toward her to grab the gun. She fired. He spun when the bullet pierced his chest and exited his back. I reached up to steady him, slipping the gun into my skirt pocket before he leaned into me.

"Oh, Lyle," I whispered. My heart raced so fast it throbbed in my ears. I felt sick.

"Second time you've called me Lyle," he said as blood spread across his blue Hawaiian shirt making the white temple flower turn crimson. His eyes widened and he tried to form more words. I lowered him onto the rug and pressed to staunch the red flow.

"How disappointing," said Clarisse. "I was aiming at Delilah. You got in my way, Lyle. Just like always."

Chapter Twenty-Seven

"MAYBE YOU SHOULD JUST SIT ON me, Di," the judge said sarcastically.

"Well, I'm trying to stem blood loss from two holes, so don't get cheeky."

Clarisse moved from the window to where Lyle lay and stood behind me.

Funny. The air around her was cold like an icy breeze.

"Delilah," Clarisse said, her voice as cutting as a Ginsu knife. "Lyle can fend for himself. Take me to Harry's office on campus."

I didn't move, just focused on Lyle and the blood oozing onto my fingers.

"Get up!"

"You can't leave a wounded man dying on the floor." I raised my voice.

"Yes, I can. Especially Lyle. Watch out, Delilah, he's so sharp he'll lacerate you."

"I'm used to intelligent men," I retorted, remaining on my knees and leaning into Lyle.

Clarisse's fingers grabbed my hair and yanked. My head swung upward with her pull.

"Ouch." I reached to protect my hair and released the pressure on Lyle's wound.

"I said up! Now get moving."

She shoved me in the back. I staggered and nearly fell on top of him. I put Lyle's hands firmly on a blood-soaked frangipani. My hands dripped with bluish-red blood. Could it be arterial? If so, I'd need to dash back to Lyle. We hadn't much time.

"I'll have to wash. If I show up with this mess someone will be suspicious."

"Go, then," she ordered, waving her gun at my back. "Where's your cell phone, Lyle? Think I'll just keep it so you can't phone the sheriff."

Clarisse kept an eye on me as she knelt and felt his shirt where blood was soaking into the cotton. Lyle groaned as she reached into his pants pocket and fished out his phone.

We left the library and headed through the foyer to a guest bath tucked under the stairs. She lounged in the doorway while I massaged my hands. I exited in a hurry leaving a circle of red under each fingernail.

"You know, Harry might have put the key in my office. It makes more sense since he didn't get around much in the last couple of months."

"Show me."

I led her to the mirrored wall and twisted a small curlicue at eye height. The mirror slid away exposing my desk, bookshelves, and comfy chair.

"Well, well, well. There *is* a hidden space in this house."

Clarisse shoved me hard and strode in. She passed me, aiming for the desk. I was a step behind her.

"Where?"

"Most likely Harry hid it among the roses. That was his signal to me."

The desk and bookshelves had a garden of roses staring at her. Clarisse pushed things around, scattering my papers onto the floor. I heard footsteps in the foyer, then voices in the library. I smiled in relief. Lyle would get help. I was barely inside the door when Clarisse leaned over the desk rummaging through my notes in search of the key. I jumped into the hall, said Samson, and watched the door close her in.

I ran to the library, anxious to report my capture. Neely Patrick stood near Lyle, pointing a gun at Lyle's head. I froze at the doorway. Well, that didn't make any sense. I eased out of the entrance. The fifth floor board from the library squealed like a hog caught on a barbwire fence. Neely's eyes jerked my way. I fingered the gun in my pocket as Neely took two steps toward me.

"Where's Clarisse?" he asked.

I shook my head.

"Gone," Lyle croaked.

Moving fast toward Lyle, Neely's foot slipped on the puddle of blood. Neely turned sideways, catching himself on Harry's desk.

I may not be an experienced hunter, but I got the shot off, burning a nice hole in my skirt pocket where the gun was hidden. The bullet nailed Neely in the behind. Left cheek. The impact flattened the man. One minute, Neely was on his feet, the next, he was on his stomach grabbing his buttocks. Neely dropped his gun as he massaged the spot. The gun spun toward me. A shirtless George dashed in as I bent to pick it up.

"You could have waited for me, Miss Delilah," George said, huffing from his exertion. "Josephine burst into my siesta yelling about a ghost reappearing, then she called the police, still hollering."

I thrust both guns toward George. "No time for chit chat. Lyle is wounded. Call an ambulance." I jumped over Neely, who was rolling on the floor like an ornery cat with a sticker in its fur. The words Neely spewed had never been spoken in my presence. Neely swore at Lyle, at me, and at Clarisse.

"I locked Clarisse in my office," I said as I knelt by Lyle. "She's armed, George, and she shot Lyle." George stuck one gun in his waistband and looked around for my office door. "By the bookshelves, right of the fireplace," I said. "By the by, Neely, Clarisse said that you shot Doctor Timmons back in Paducah."

That was an out and out fib. The fishing line I tossed toward him was a meager two-pound test, perhaps not enough heft for a big fish like Neely Patrick, but my statement sent Neely off in another direction with his vocabulary.

Lyle had neglected his pressure duty. I reapplied my hands to his wound. "Leave you alone for two minutes and what do I find? More blood than they have in the blood bank is saturating your luau shirt, plus a man prostrated on my floor saying words that his mama should have applied Ivory soap to."

"You gonna cry, Delilah?" Lyle asked, his mouth crimping with pain.

"Probably."

"The handkerchiefs are in my right pants pocket if you've a need."

"When they're wheeling you away to the hospital, I'll think about shedding tears. Right now I've got to keep you alive. We've a wedding in less than two weeks, for pity sake."

My tears were raining over his shirt front. I don't think he noticed. His color was gray and his breaths getting shorter.

"Miss Dee Dee," Josephine said from the doorway. "The ambulance just cruised in. I'll direct while you keep the judge occupied."

The flashing lights and blaring sirens I chose to ignore. I kept my eyes on Lyle.

We breathed together.

He took a hiatus from oxygen.

I yelled at him to "take a deep breath, gosh darn it!"

"Miss Delilah, I never . . . thought . . . I'd hear . . . swear."

"It's allowed," I responded. "Meemaw says it."

"Ah," he gasped.

Bellows arrived with his gun drawn and a deputy at his side. The EMS people came in at a trot, Josephine yelling at them from behind. "Move it or the judge is go'n *die*."

Shoveled to a corner while they worked, I could see them cutting away his shirt, examining the wound, turning him slightly to see his back. I hadn't seen the entry wound before. It was a nice tidy hole, not like the exit wound, which was ragged. I wiped my tears with my fingers. Without a word Josephine pulled out hand-wipes and cleaned my face, and then the blood from my hands.

The EMS poked a line into Lyle's right arm and put him on a cart.

"Now, you go off with the judge. Don't take no brain surgeon to see what's between you two," Josephine ordered.

I grabbed Lyle's hand as the EMS stepped onto the grass. Lyle's fingers were cool. The crew moved fast. I trotted to keep up. I didn't let go of his hand until he was hoisted into the ambulance. The door was slammed shut with a metallic clank which is how my heart felt. I watched them speed down the drive. I'd forgotten my car keys. I ran to the house to get my purse. Before I'd landed on the stairs George grabbed me.

"Is there some way to get into your office, Delilah? Josephine says she doesn't know how."

"Clarisse might come out shooting, George."

"Okay. We'll let the sheriff take care of it. But you still need to open the door for him."

I could open the space from either side, but I wanted her to see Lyle's blood pooling on the rug. I spit out my secret word and Clarisse exited into the library looking all innocent, her pistol nowhere to be seen.

"Delilah accidentally locked me in her office. Just because Lyle and I had a slight argument, she felt obliged to intervene."

My mouth gaped open. "She shot Lyle while aiming for me." I glared at her, wanting to realign her nose.

Bellows studied my stance, stepped between us, and produced handcuffs.

I glanced around the room and started for the door. "I need to find my purse."

George drove me to the hospital declaring I wasn't fit to drive. The Hawaiian shirt he'd grabbed looked garish in the bright sunlight.

Lyle was doped to the eyeballs when I saw him in

the surgery area waiting a freshly scrubbed operating room. "Well, ish about time you showed up, Delilah," he said, spying me. His breaths sounded congested, as though he breathed through a thick blob of mucus. My knees got wobbly. I sat on a hard metal chair near his head. "Took off . . . .my pants. I've . . . no handkerchief."

I wiped my eyes with tissue a nurse handed me. They clapped a mask over Lyle's mouth to give him oxygen. A nurse in blue scrubs lowered his head, another removed the pillow.

"We'll get time to talk when you're not buzzed," I said to him as they wheeled his bed out the door.

When I arrived in the waiting lounge Madison and George huddled by the sweet tea and coffee urn. They looked up. Special Agent Madison was the first to recover.

"Mrs. Morgan," he began. "I'm sorry we couldn't prevent this."

I shook my head slowly.

"Miss Delilah," George interrupted. "Mamie's bringing Josephine. Cam and Molly are on their way. Any news from the doctor?"

"I haven't seen anyone but the nurses." My entire face felt heavy. "The surgeon was scrubbing, I was told." I blew my nose into the shred of tissue left.

Bellows dashed into the waiting room. "I hate to trouble you, Miss Delilah. I need to ask you several questions. You understand."

I knew what I had to do, and it wasn't filling out a police report. "Would you please give me ten minutes?"

"Of course," Bellows replied. "Come talk to me when you're ready."

I headed for the hospital chapel. The sanctuary was a softly lit cubby tucked near the surgery wing. Cam found me there. We prayed, Cam sounding like the little boy I remembered sitting at my table and thanking God for everything from the mashed potatoes to the meatloaf. His humility as he prayed brought my tears again.

When we finished, I headed for the bathroom and washed my face with a paper towel. The rough paper disintegrated into thin brown strips. My neck muscles were so tense they felt like wood when rubbed. Facing away from the mirror, I did neck rolls, shoulder lifts, and stretched my arms to relieve the stress.

When I returned to the waiting room, Josephine had arrived and sat with her white purse smack in the middle of her lap, Mamie beside her. A large paper bag was at Mamie's feet.

"That Miss Clarisse done cursed you up one side and down t'other," Josephine said. "I had to fumigate the room after the police handcuffed her and led her out. Cain't say much about that Neely Patrick, neither. Why, you'd think it was the judge's fault he got hisself arrested."

Mamie didn't say a word. However, she stared at me with her eyes all big and sorrowful. George poured sweet tea into a Styrofoam cup and presented it to her. George's flaming red Hawaiian shirt Lyle found on Maui seemed odd amid the somber colors of the hospital.

Seconds inched by. I helped Sheriff Bellows fill in his police report. Molly and Cam walked the floor. One hour gone.

"All they have to do is plug a couple of holes. Plumbers could caulk them faster," I complained to the air. One hour became two.

Josephine was talking so much she'd told Mamie the history of the family, how Cam and Molly grew up together, and how Harry and I met. This wasn't news. Mamie had observed us for years. Her daughter Alexa was Molly's bosom friend.

Josephine was not someone who talked excessively. I took her out into the hall and gave her a big hug. "You're spouting off like Moby Dick."

"Don't think I know him." Josephine bunched her lips into a pout.

"Josephine. God has a plan we're not yet familiar with. I do trust Him, even if I'm praying begging prayers."

"You keep that up, Miss Dee Dee. What you got going here is true love. It's sort of off-again on-again like a faucet with you, though. The water is gurgling in you and just waiting to pour out. For the judge, caring has been simmering for years. You done ruined him for any other woman, Miss Dee Dee, make no mistake."

My words of encouragement dried up. Was it obvious that I couldn't rein in my heart, first with Harry, then with Lyle? I hadn't meant to grow fond of the man. I intended to only be friends. But when Clarisse shot him, I knew there was no going backward with my feelings. In fact, my feelings had taken a giant leap forward like a load of emotions on a catapult flung into space. I hoped they'd land safely.

"It might be wise to call the reverend. Let him know what has happened so he can come."

Josephine's face looked like thunder at my suggestion. "You trying to set me up, Miss Dee Dee?"

"No. I think the church should pray, and frankly at the moment, I need spiritual counsel."

"Likely story," Josephine huffed. However, she pulled out her cell phone and punched in the numbers.

I reentered the room with a heavy step. Chairs lined up against walls and gray carpet underfoot. Mamie and Molly had their heads together and were whispering.

"Sure," Molly said, rising to her feet. "Mom, the Salases are making a food run. What do you want?"

The last thing on my mind was my stomach. The amount of blood all over the library pressed on me. Didn't think that much could pour out and someone still live. Perhaps he didn't, and they were stalling in there, afraid to fess up.

I dashed to the bathroom and promptly launched

Carter's chicken into the toilet.

Two hours and forty-three minutes after they rolled Lyle into the O.R., a pair of surgeons entered the waiting room and took off their masks so we could identify them. There was a splash of blood on their green scrubs. Their eyes looked grim.

"The bullet caught a bleeder," one said into the waiting faces. "We had to remove a section of lung, but we stopped the hemorrhage. He'll be in the ICU for a few days. Give him an hour or so in recovery and then you can head up."

Daddy, Mama, and Meemaw arrived after surgery and declared they were taking over the house. I let them.

The ICU was lit so your zits stood at attention. One of us at a time sat beside Lyle. I kept the night vigil so Cam could deal with family matters. The nurses gave me a kit with soap, toothbrush, and paste.

I sat beside Lyle's bed and worried about his shallow breathing. And then I had a wrestling match with the Lord. "She got what she deserved. If Lyle doesn't live then I'll hold it against her forever," I told Him. Into the silence came, "Is it forgiveness if you give it begrudgingly?" That quiet voice shook me up one side and down the other. "My Son forgave those who killed Him," I also heard. I cried, and stormed, and forgave Clarisse, but it had gone down hard, and I wasn't sure but what I'd have to do it again.

The cup of tea I drank in the middle of the night gurgled around in my stomach as I watched Lyle breathe. Cam arrived at six a.m., and we traded places. I walked home in the cool morning while the dew glistened on the leaves of the giant magnolia on the corner of Secretariat Way and Main Street. Any Christian charity I may have had was lost again on Clarisse. At the present moment I wanted to land face first on my bed and not move for a week.

When I arrived home, I tiptoed into the foyer and peered into the parlor, finding Daddy perusing the newspaper. The library doors still had yellow "do not cross" signs draped over sawhorses.

"Mornin', Daddy."

"Hey, there. Your bed's waiting. I suppose you're heading back in a few hours."

"Yes."

"I think it wise to rest, Delilah. If you want to hover a little, I'm sure he'd appreciate it, but I think you need to take care just now."

Only one day had passed after Lyle was punctured by a bullet when Special Agent Madison met Cam and me in the hospital cafeteria. He reported that Clarisse was as vocal as an African grey parrot. So many words aimed at the doctor, the hoods from Chicago, and Neely Patrick, their cousin. Clarisse included Harry in her litany of accusations. Madison said, "She claimed that Harry was holding something for her and before he died he asked her to come pick it up."

I listened half asleep over a cup of coffee.

"I asked her what she came to collect."

I wiggled in my seat. "And what did she say?"

"A key to my storage unit," he answered, as though he were Clarisse. "She said she had a few family heirlooms and letters in it."

Special Agent Madison took a sip from his coffee. "I said to her, 'Funny you didn't make your claim a few years ago.' Clarisse Henderson had the audacity to mention she'd forgotten about it until she read in *Time* magazine that Harry had died. A contradiction from her first statement. When I asked her for the number of the storage unit so I could open it to examine the contents, she made a stink about her rights and demanded a lawyer."

I was beyond caring. Watching Lyle breathe through a nasty tube and having to hold his son Beau while he cried over his father made me rancorous. I didn't have any compassion left for Clarisse, and I knew I'd have to forgive her all over again, which didn't set well. Even the reverend's counsel hadn't removed my anger. No one had the right to take another's life. And Clarisse hadn't blinked.

The FBI was going to examine the missionary letters posted at Maylene's Beauty Shop. Although Clarisse hadn't copped to sending them, that made the most sense. That, and the body in the car being Darlene.

Neely was down the hall from Lyle, according to Madison, and was singing like a 40's big band singer. "The tune Neely sings goes: 'She done me wrong.'" Madison grinned. "Patrick said he had nothing to do with the murders of the doc and his companion. He said his cousins were collecting a debt and were sent to dissuade Dr. Timmons from leaving the country." Madison chuckled. "Neely said the doctor needed to explain to their boss where the loan money had gone."

Madison leaned in close to Cam. "Neely is proving to be a pain in the butt." At that they both grinned while I coughed into my napkin. "He complains about lying on his stomach, about the food, the pain, his wife's inattentions. Got to say this for Olive Lorraine, she's holding her ungrateful husband's hand as he whines. Olive has made every excuse except insanity for his behavior."

Madison was regaling us on Neely's confession when Olive Lorraine slunk into the cafeteria. She stood at the counter with her head low and eyes looking at her fingernails.

I glanced at Olive Lorraine as she took a seat at a table for six. Her hands throttled the coffee mug like it was her errant spouse.

"According to my incarcerated female, Clarisse, she and Neely have been lovers for years. Sorry, Cam,"

Madison said.

"No need," Cam replied. "Dad didn't deserve the way she treated him. I think the whole town knows what a good man he is." Cam's voice caught at the end.

I reached for his knotted fist.

"Clarisse bragged that her affair with Neely started when she first came to town. While Olive went to business meetings, Neely met Clarisse in a hot spot for singles," Madison said. "Can't imagine leaving my wife behind while I traipsed off."

Madison took a slurp of coffee then glanced in Olive's direction. Olive Lorraine drooped over her coffee as if her spine was jelly. Madison sat back and finished his drink. Cam closed his eyes. He looked tired and lost. Kids shouldn't have to bear the burden of their parents' follies.

"You know," Special Agent Madison said, "the O'Neals, those two thugs from Chicago who were after the doctor, have been out of prison for four months. Their parole officers report they are showing up on schedule. No one in Paducah claims to have seen them around the time of your attack, Miss Delilah. They may not be legit, but it seems the O'Neals were not involved with shooting up your car."

Who shot the car didn't interest me. We had Lyle looking pathetic against the white sheets so who cared who shot at us a month ago.

"I'll keep at it, Miss Delilah," Madison stated, "but I'd put my money on the lady. A little more heat on Neely and we'll know."

With the tube down his throat, Lyle couldn't protest the indignities a patient endures. Which was fortunate for the staff, because when he finally decided to join the living, his eyes said he was mighty disgruntled about laying like a beached whale plugged into noisy machines. They took out the plastic airway before he was coherent.

Right before the sun gets pushy in the east, I felt a hand on my head. I wiped at the drool around my mouth.

"Are you sniffling into my clean sheets?" He pretended to be shocked.

I fumbled for his hand. With all his tubes it was difficult. My hand crabbing across the blanket was suddenly encased with his. My fingers were cold, his warm.

"This must be the morning after surgery," he said slowly.

"You've been playing Rip Van Winkle."

"What day is this?" His words were slurred.

"Does it matter?"

"If I miss Cam's 'Thunderstorm,' I'll be more than peeved."

"You'll make it. This is your fourth day enjoying the nurses' hospitality. You'll soon be home to sit in your lounge chair and eat hors d'oeuvres."

"Manly men will have BBQ," he said.

Beau arrived. I got up to leave.

Lyle wouldn't let go. "Promise me you'll come back." His voice croaked the words.

"She's been living here, Dad," Beau said.

On Saturday, Lyle said, "Time for me to go home. I'm feeling fit and won't stand another minute of forced idleness."

He was still bossy and not even sliding into recovery. I laughed at him.

The doctor rubbed his chin, looking thoughtful. "No. Not possible. Your attempt at dying has us cautious. You'll have to put up with our slow response to your courteous request."

Reverend Daniel came to the hospital on Sunday

afternoon.

"I'll replay my sermon," he offered.

Lyle switched off the baseball game he was watching.

"I think we should include Harry in the wedding proceedings." His eyes glanced down at a paper beside him. It was written in his precise penmanship. I took a shaky breath. "So, after your father walks Molly down the aisle perhaps Reverend Daniel could say Harry and you give the bride away."

I had no words.

Lyle's kindness did that to me.

"While you were at church the boys went to see their mother." The judge veered in another direction. There was a dramatic pause. "It didn't go well."

Lyle looked at his notes. "My informant says, 'Cam stood over her like an interrogator. He told her she was the worst mother he'd ever heard of.'" Lyle raised his eyes and glanced outside, as if trying to spit out the next words. "On weeknights while I was working late, Clarisse drove to another county, parked the boys in a car, and went into bars." Suddenly looking lost, Lyle swiped a hand through his hair.

No wonder the boys never complained about the pots of soup I made.

The reverend turned toward me. "I believe an issue with the band is straightened out."

"What now?" Lyle released a tense breath.

"Miss Charlene was checking around to find the band you were using." Reverend Daniel shook his head. "She tried to hire your band for the day. Miles Redding overheard her plotting at a country club gathering. His cousin plays bass guitar for the Wilderness Boys. Between the band and Miles, they've come up with a way to handle the poaching situation."

"Well, Miss Delilah," the judge said, "thanks to Miles, I've one less skirmish."

That announcement was my cue to leave. I called Josephine from the hospital lobby.

"You about to come home and rest?"

"Are you at my house? On Sunday, Josephine, you're supposed to be sitting on your porch with your Mama."

"No time for that nonsense, I've people to feed."

I cut her off. "Josephine, I'm calling about your cousin with the Wilderness Boys. Doesn't he play the sax?"

"Yes, ma'am. And a sweeter sound I've never heard."

"Did he mention anything about the band's arrangements for the wedding and the mayor's meet and greet?"

"Oh, ho!" she said. "Seems they're going to send another band to play for the mayor. They're giving them the list of funeral music as we speak. Should be enlightening."

"Josephine. It was my plan to bless the mayor's gathering with a little surprise. Why make enemies when you can make peace?"

"Oh, you're not involved in this, Miss Dee Dee. We're just behaving biblically."

Josephine was up to her neck in no good.

Chapter Twenty-Eight

I HEADED FOR THE CEMETERY. I was prepared with a paper bag for the offerings I'd probably find on the grave. I came over the hillside to the Morgan encampment and spied Olive Lorraine standing by Harry's freshly mowed plot. I could hear her voice over the distant sound of the cemetery's mower.

"You were right, Harry, I've been a fool. Neely is a skunk, plain and simple. All those years ago, you tried to protect me. I plunged right ahead and married Neely, thinking I'd show you after we broke up and you married Delilah. I've been wrong about so many things and been beastly to Delilah." Olive Lorraine buried her face in her hands and wept. Not tidy for the camera tears, but big sobs with shudders.

My feet walked toward her while my mind said, "Don't." I wrapped my arms about her shaky body and held her. She jerked with surprise.

"You," she exclaimed. "I've tried to—I wanted—I've been cruel."

"I know."

"How can you forgive me?"

"I've been forgiven a time or two."

She seemed to accept that. "Do you come here often?"

"Usually I talk to Harry at home, but home's a little crowded these days."

"What are these things?" She pointed to the tiny stuffed animals placed in a row on top of Harry's grave.

"The signs of an obsession."

She nodded once then kissed my cheek and started to walk away. "That FBI agent questioned me yesterday." She turned to look me in the eyes. "I had to unearth appointment books from my office and check on dates, but it seems Neely was gone at the time of the doc's murder. My note says he was at a meeting in St. Louis. It was a long time ago, but the meeting was held the weekend before not mid-week. Neely told them that he wasn't in Paducah all those years ago, but he was there recently when, Clarisse pointed a gun at the judge's borrowed car and fired." Olive Lorraine shrugged with defeat. "I've lots of questions," she muttered as she headed toward her car.

I stared down at the grave not knowing what to say to Harry. He knew it all anyway, so I collected the critters and sat under the tree. I'd been running on empty and fell asleep. I awoke to Josephine staring down at me while the animals still occupied my lap.

"Think you're invincible don't you."

I wiped my tired eyes.

"I've been thinking that you might be here, so I called. Those graveyard people said you were sitting under a tree, doing nothing. I reckoned I'd come to join you and let your mama and mine wrastle in the kitchen."

"Thanks." I reached for her hand so I could rise.

"Oh, no you don't. I'm going to plunk down here and have a nice chat with Mr. Harry. You been telling him about the judge and all?"

"I figure he knows all about the judge getting shot."

"That he do, Miss Dee Dee. That he do. And he knows about your target practice on Mr. Real Estate's rear end."

While Lyle lounged at the hospital the police had wadded the yellow tape, and in their wake left white fingerprint dust and a trail of coffee cups. As soon as the police left, Josephine rolled up the rug.

"That Clarisse woman thinks she's something. To shoot up the judge, and on Mr. Harry's good carpet is criminal," she huffed. "If I weren't a lady, I'd say some mighty impolite words about that Jezebel. And make no mistake about it, Miss Dee Dee." She spoke loudly when she caught me listening. "She's not a lady."

The judge came home on Monday about noon. Cam's 'Thunderstorm' was set for Wednesday night. I hoped the judge survived the ministrations of his boys and Lupita, who all hovered.

Cam and Molly's simple wedding had turned into a catered affair and a congregation that would fill the church to the rafters and cram my yard for the reception. Enough food for a football stadium had been arranged. I heard shuffling on the verandah as I checked off my clipboard items. And here it was past nine o'clock.

The police still had my gun in their custody, so I grabbed a large book and my fireplace poker and went to see who was at my door.

"You going to hit me with your thesaurus, Di?" the judge laughed when he saw my arm cocked like a javelin thrower.

"What are you doing here? Shouldn't you be in bed?"

"I'm taking my slow-motion constitutional and visiting a neighbor."

For once Bartles didn't head my direction but hung by his master's ankle. Lyle winced in his descent to the wicker love seat. He breathed slowly. I'd seen him conquering the hospital hallways pushing his IV stand but crossing the road and hiking up my drive turned into a mountain for him.

"Things seem to be on schedule," I said.

"By Saturday night the kids will be married, no matter what happens. I'll be thankful for that." He let the dog hop onto his lap.

"You mean Clarisse and her legal mess might

make things difficult?" I asked.

"She is in a bind, isn't she?" He shook his head. "Clarisse's lawyered up, although she's not getting bail because she shot a court officer." The dog rolled onto his back, begging for a tummy rub. "I went to speak with her today."

I was so surprised I plopped down in the chair opposite him.

"I told her I forgave her. For everything. She seemed to think my comment was a get-out-of-jail-free card. When I said I had no power to change her present location she flew into a rage in the sheriff's office and had to be restrained. Blames everyone but herself for the choices she's made." He drew a finger along his upper lip. "Sad, really."

"I didn't like forgiving her, Lyle."

"I don't imagine you did. If you'd been lying near death, I'd not been so free to extend it."

Lightning bugs zoomed in and out of the shrubbery. Their air dance made Bartles leap off Lyle's lap attempting a mid-air capture. The puppy fell flat onto the decking. We laughed, but Lyle's voice was frail with fatigue.

"I'd like to walk you home."

"I'd be obliged," he said.

We walked with baby steps, I held the dog's leash so Bartles didn't pull the judge across the asphalt and rip out something vital, like stitches. I secured Bartles behind the judge's front screen door so he didn't prance back to my house behind me. Our good night started friendly.

"Thank you for walking your decrepit neighbor home, Miss Di."

"My pleasure," I said, extending my hand for him to shake.

He took it, pulled me toward him, and kissed me firm on the lips. It was one of those kisses that made you want to say, "What took you so long?" He leaned into me. Even wounded I could feel his firm chest muscles under my cheek. I staggered against his door jamb. A car passed by. I rolled my eyes at him, knowing our lips connecting would be news in five seconds.

"Go. Go now," he said sudden as a bugle call.

I attempted to skirt around him to get down the three steps to his grass.

"I didn't mean that." He snagged my arm and pulled me tight against his chest. "Yes, yes, I did," he said with anguish. He thrust me away with a groan of pain. Lyle leaned against the door, like a beat-up cowboy. "Night, Di," he said in a fading voice. "I'll see you at the rehearsal dinner."

"That's three days from now on Friday," I whispered with disappointment.

"My schedule is full. That's the next time I'm available."

The light melded with gray shadows along my drive as I dashed home.

I wept a bit. And not for Harry. Selfishly, I wept for myself. I didn't have time to get emotional, but Lyle Henderson stirred something that was best to lie dormant until it was respectful to consider dating.

A deluge of thunder and lightning blew out the power about eleven. I wrote generators on the clipboard list after I found the flashlights.

The fuss that went on in the days before the rehearsal dinner was monumental. Gifts poured in. We had to keep track of who and what. Decorating the church took all day Wednesday. Thursday was nail and pedicure day. A large truck arrived on Friday morning before our set-up team. The crew began to unload deflated blow-up bouncy castles. Daddy met the men disgorging the bright-colored monsters, then mumbled something about knowing why he'd brought Minerva.

The trucker's paperwork gave my address with an order for eight bouncy structures to be blown up and left. It wasn't my handwriting, but someone was trying to sabotage Molly's wedding. George came over, shaking his head and led me to the porch, suggesting I sit.

"They had the wrong address. A simple mix up." He patted my hand. His jaw was clenched, so I knew better.

"Since the blow-up entertainments are paid for, take them to the park to leave for the children," I said.

"I've a little something else in mind, Delilah." The castles were hauled off with George leading them down the street in his SUV.

Molly spent part of her last free day decorating the garden. She had tall, wrought iron candle holders centered in Harry's elevated vegetable beds. When Molly was satisfied with her creations, she directed Sidney and the florist to put them all away under lock and key. "After the bouncy castles, I will not take any chances."

George returned after lunch. His laughter carried over the fence. Finally, he and Mamie trotted over. "I've left a little surprise for someone." George stifled his laughter. "My recipients weren't home, so I had the crew blow them up before they headed back to Lexington."

I didn't have to ask who. With George's gift the feud between ourselves and the Higgenbottoms was building.

"It was an underhanded, dirty, low-down trick for the Higgenbottoms to pull," Mamie said.

"That doesn't mean we have to treat them the same way," I said. "Phone the men, George. They can take it all down before the mayor gets home from decorating the park."

"Can't. The company was paid to leave it through Sunday. I told them to return first thing Monday morning."

Mamie nodded her head, but her face lit up with an isn't-this-fun grin. "Why don't we have attendants collect money and let people play in them? We could donate the money to charity."

"Done," George said. "I'll have notices or something catchy festooned around town."

Mamie and George strolled off. As parents of the maid of honor, they were invited to dinner at the country club. The Salases would be late if they spent hours plastering signs around town.

I ran a brush through my long hair, slipped into my heels, and grabbed my purse. It was time to head for the church. I drove with the windows down to capture the sweet summer breeze that hovers after a rain.

The rehearsal took one-hour-and-two minutes. Daddy and I headed home to get Mama and Meemaw for the rehearsal dinner and neared the Salases' house.

George ran toward the edge of his yard and waved his arms. I pulled into his drive. "Best to pick your folks up here," he said. "We've a little side-show going on in your driveway. I've sent Mamie over to alert the ladies."

I stepped out of my van and spied Charlene Higgenbottom's Lexus parked with its tail in my driveway and a very large man standing by the front of her car. I could hear her screech all the way to the middle of the Salases' yard. The man looked ex-Navy SEAL from his military stance.

"I got home and found little children running through my yard with popsicles and cotton candy," she yelled. "They're littering. Dropping wrappers in my hybrid petunias."

My guard was unmoved.

I got back in my car and cranked up the volume of KLOV so that it would drown out the hissy fit performed in my yard. But I kept my eyes glued that direction, because, as much as I'd wanted to try to bless the Higgenbottoms, this was too good to miss.

Charlene flapped her arms and stomped her feet as if she were attacked by army ants. As Mama walked down my verandah steps, she took one look at the scene and grabbed Meemaw's arm. Not to steady Meemaw, but to keep her from the fray. They piled into my car. I stepped on the gas. We made it out to the street before Sheriff Bellows arrived with his flashers on. George could handle the law.

However, George evaded the confrontation by peeling out behind me.

I had imagined George's signs to be small, but silver and maroon banners announcing the Bouncy Castle event, were strung up on the ice cream parlor, the Art Museum, the corner bank, the Fire Station, Inman's furniture store, the jewelers, a coffee shop, and The Coop.

"How long is the night's carnival?" I asked as we walked into the Country Club.

George dropped his head and I could barely hear his reply. "Seemed reasonable that for tonight, Saturday, and Sunday, the Charity Jumpy Castle Carnival would be held from ten to ten."

"Olive Lorraine Patrick volunteered to find helpers to man the stations for safety," Mamie chimed in.

We were standing at the entrance to the country club's banquet room when Sheriff Bellows brushed past us and waylaid Lyle. The pair moved aside and held a quiet conversation.

Eventually the judge stepped away from Bellows. Lyle drew his sons apart from the gathering. My heart sank. Was Clarisse going to ruin the festivities?

When Lyle was finished speaking with his sons, he strode toward the sheriff. "Go ahead, Sam." Lyle clapped Bellows on the shoulder as if to say, 'you're on.' We clumped together, eyes on the law.

Sheriff Bellows cleared his throat and waved his hand in the air. "They've done conclusive DNA tests on the murder victims found near Paducah," he said loud enough for his audience to hear. "Not unexpected, Dr. Timmons was the male victim. Turns out Darlene Frogmiejer was the second. A few witnesses have come forward and stated that Darlene and the doctor had been seeing each other for a couple of years, even though she was only eighteen when she died."

The sheriff turned to contemplate Lyle. The judge nodded. "We've sworn affidavits stating that Clarisse Henderson sent letters from a phony mission organization duping hundreds of thousands of dollars from good-hearted folk. Since mail fraud is a federal offense, the Feds are taking up that investigation from here." Bellows cleared his throat again. "Some boys fishing near Paducah found a military issue handgun down by their swimming hole. Looks like forensics can tie it to the murders. Navy ever issue you one, Lyle?"

I stared at the judge. Never assume things are tidied up when dead bodies are involved.

"Yes," he answered tersely.

"It been missing?"

"For eighteen years."

"So, you reported it, right?"

"I did. On the twenty-fourth of October, when I checked my safe." Judge Henderson ran a hand through his perfect hair.

Bellows nodded his head as if he already knew the answer. "I wanted you to know before it became public." As if announcing it in the country club in front of fifty people wasn't public. Bellows stalked off as if a heavy weight were on his shoulders.

The judge took a slow breath. "Shall we get back to the evening's entertainment?" He paused, as if gauging the room's emotional temperature, then let out a breath. "I'm happy to have you join my family on this joyous occasion. You will find place cards at your table. I have broken with tradition and mixed families. We're old friends here, and this evening should build on those alliances. In memory of Harry, every course will have chicken or a product of chicken in it."

I was settling Meemaw into her chair when Lyle took my arm and led me to his table. He'd no reason to bump off the doctor and Darlene. It had to be either Clarisse or the thugs. Where did Neely Patrick fit in? I shook my head, then watched for signs that Lyle was tiring while cutting up a chicken breast.

"You think I'm so feeble I'm about to give way, Miss Delilah?" he asked.

I can't hide a thing from the man. "You do look a bit peaky."

"So, I should look peaky."

I didn't think about Charlene and the insanity surrounding her house for more than fifty seconds at a time.

After dessert had been served, Lyle unveiled his wedding gift to the bride and groom, a walnut hope chest with dove-tail sides and a French polish finish that was smooth to the touch. When Molly unwrapped the Wedding Ring Quilt and read the signatures of the Burns women, she gave a strangled sob. The quilt was placed in acid-free-paper inside Lyle's hope chest. The evening settled into a sweetness that you could taste.

Cam stood. He cleared his throat. "I want to share one of my first memories of the amazing Morgan women." He winked at Molly. "At five Molly never went anywhere without a small, affectionate Silkie named Geronimo. He was a small rooster she carried in her arms like a baby. One spring day I noticed a commotion had erupted in the yard. Two of the neighborhood dogs had captured Geronimo and were shredding him in front of the verandah. Miss Delilah dashed toward the fray and whacked them with her only weapon at hand, a tennis racket, until they released that little bird. He was a pitiful sight, his neck nearly broken and half his feathers pulled out."

"As Molly stood cradling her bird, Miss Delilah shouted for Josephine to watch all the kids while she took the rooster to the vet. And at that moment I was the first Henderson man to succumb to the tenderness of a little girl's broken heart and the charm of Miss Delilah's compassion."

Cam's lop-sided grin emerged as he bowed to me. I gulped in a breath.

"You've been my compassionate, caring *real* mom," Cam said. "The mom who sewed the patches on my jeans, who taught me how to fry an egg. The mom who took pictures of me with my prom dates and taught me how to do a one-eighty in the school parking lot with the emergency brake and accelerator."

Lyle eyes widened as if surprised.

"Thank you for being a step across the street, for putting down your reading when I came in and acting eager to listen." Cam bent and kissed my cheek.

My eyes spilled tears.

The judge whipped out a fresh handkerchief.

Lyle excused himself to meander from table to table, shaking hands and acting as if he had been running his five miles all week instead of trying to die on us.

As the guests began to scatter, Mademoiselle Bousquet drifted in from the dining room. Mademoiselle was in a dress that barely covered her bosom with an inch to spare. She sidled up to Lyle and put her hand on his arm. Leaning into him she kissed his cheeks, first the right then the left. Lyle smiled down at her.

Meemaw took one look at the smooching French teacher and scrunched up her brow until it was all lines. "Who's that?" she asked loudly.

"Mademoiselle Bousquet is a French professor at the college," I answered.

"She that friendly with *all* the men?" Meemaw said in a voice that made heads turn our way.

"It's the French way of greeting." I patted her arm.

"I think shaking hands is friendly enough."

I was about to say good night to our host when Mademoiselle Bousquet put her hand on Lyle's chest, near his injury. His eyes narrowed with pain. My breath caught.

"I know you're leaving for Paris after the wedding. When you're in the city do look up the Duchamps." She slipped him a card. "They are dear friends and are expecting your call. I'll rearrange my class schedule so we can explore Paris together."

"Merci," he returned. "However, I have a friend who will accompany me."

I'd forgotten about my Paris dreams, what with the Paducah mess and sharpshooter Clarisse. I swallowed a big lump in my throat.

Some dreams have to die, I reckon. If I decapitated this one it wouldn't haunt me.

Maybe my brochures created a longing for the judge to travel to France. He would be seeing places he loved. I squared my shoulders and took Meemaw by the hand. Her fingers always had callouses. I rubbed my thumb over the quilting one on her pointer finger.

Her hand felt right in mine, like I had finally made it home.

Chapter Twenty-Nine

SLEEP SKIPPED AROUND THE BEDROOM. AT 1:00 I took the sleeping pill the doctor had prescribed. When the alarm jangled at six, my eyes couldn't locate the clock with the room zizzing like a merry-go-round. I should have taken half of the pill. My feet felt mushy and the shower didn't do much good in the wake-up department.

Thumping came from our basketball court. I stood barefoot on the verandah and spied Molly and Cam playing ball. Molly waved at me. When Cam turned away from the basket to see who she greeted, Molly took a shot. It arched over his head and swished in the net.

"Penalty to be exacted." He laughed. "An interfering fan distracted me."

"Ha," Molly returned. "Pay up, Henderson."

"Only two." He grabbed her around the waist, kissed her quickly, then slowly, as if tasting something sweet.

I left them so I could throw on my clothes and run an errand. While I slapped on my shirt Molly dashed up the stairs.

"Hey," I said.

"Hey, yourself. Thanks for the distraction, Mom."

"Anytime up to the wedding. After that, you're on your own."

Molly's laugh echoed in the stairway.

I headed for the car. I wanted to talk to Harry. With two bridesmaids sleeping on the library hide-a-bed, I'd have to make do with the Morgan plot.

George's patrolling friends were changing shifts when I walked down the back steps. The air was crisp and sharp as if fall had arrived. I waved to a burly man going toward the side of the carriage house, got into my van, and turned the key.

The dew was still on the grass when I stepped past the black iron gate that kept the Morgans in their places. I wasn't alone. Beside Harry's tree stood Lyle, vehemently talking to Harry.

"Hey," I said.

"Hey, yourself."

"You're up early."

"When Molly finished trouncing my son, I asked him to give me a lift. Thought I might find you here and you could give me a ride home."

"I guess I'm predictable."

"Not really. Last night I thought you'd have the courtesy to say good night before you left."

"Oh. Well . . . Meemaw—er—I had to ..."

I couldn't out-and-out lie to a judge. I looked at the tree above his head, the leaves glistening with their nightly coat of dew.

"I wrote a thank you note." I skirted the issue. "It was a lovely evening, Lyle. Meemaw had a wonderful time with George and Mamie. You were wise to put them together."

"Won't work, Di. Fess up. What's the problem?"

"I heard you are going away for a while."

"Yes." The word drawled slowly from his lips. "On Sunday. I'm taking Beau to the airport, heading to the farm in North Carolina, then Europe."

"Oh. Well . . . . that's wonderful." I tried to sound excited for him. "How will you carry your bags with your injury?"

"I'll hire a porter."

"I'll take care of your little dog if you like," I offered.

"Bartles will stay with the Salases. Mamie has taken quite a shine to him."

I took a deep breath. "You seem to have everything well planned."

"That was my intention. I don't like loose ends. There are a few things I don't have control over, but my travel plans are in order."

I studied his lime-green running shoes. They didn't match the bluer green of the grass on Harry's grave. Harry would never have worn lime-green shoes. He had been a muted blue-green man.

I needed to sit down.

I wished the bench was already installed, although I hadn't made up my mind where I wanted it placed. My eyes glommed onto the white plastic flowers thrown willy-nilly over Harry's grave. I sighed. I'd forgotten the bag for the grave detritus.

"Tell me about Harry's grave decorations."

"He has an admirer."

"She left a letter. I don't think you should read it." Lyle brought a hand-cut pink Valentine from his pants' pocket. He folded it neatly in two.

"Why not?"

"Mothers-of-the-bride have enough to worry about without obsessing over a letter from a nut."

"You keep it then."

"I've finished my talk with Harry. I'll hike over to Charles Wesley Brown's grave and tell him a thing or two." Charles Wesley, Lyle's former law partner, died of a heart attack at eighty-seven while windsurfing in Bora Bora.

Lyle stepped carefully around the humps in the grass, past the marble markers, and stood before a six-foot obelisk. He seemed to be having an intense conversation.

"Harry, I'm a hot mess," I said. "I'm overly fond of Lyle Henderson. The way I feel isn't becoming. He's leaving for Paris. It could have been anywhere but Paris, and I would be okay. But it's *Paris*. The next thing you know he'll be buying a flashy sports car and I'll still be putting fifty bucks worth of gas in the van. He acts like he's interested in me, but it's obvious he's not." I paused. "I don't know what to do, Harry. I never had a teenage crush. I just had you. It was perfect."

Tears clung to the inside of my eyes and burned

like hot pokers. I squatted near Harry's head and patted the fresh mown grass.

"I don't know how to say goodbye to Lyle," I choked out.

The day was all wrong without Harry. I'd turn around expecting him to be waiting to take my hand. Not having it to clutch made me cry. The judge would need a suitcase full of handkerchiefs before the day was through.

The wedding party left the house as florists finished the front yard and headed toward the back. Everything according to the clipboard.

I sashayed through the kitchen in my pumps and fancy dress. Esther ordered the caterers around like she knew the place. I nodded and exited through the back door.

As I aimed for the car my feet stuttered to a stop. Vans disgorging food, vans filled with flowers, and the security guards' vehicles standing nose to tail in the turnaround spot blocked me in. Leaving my car accessible hadn't been on my clipboard. I blinked at the scene, shell-shocked.

"Cutting it close, are we Di?" said a baritone voice behind me.

"I forgot to move my car," I muttered.

"May I say that you are particularly ravishing today. I've never seen you in such formal attire." I turned to look at the judge. Was he joshing? Lyle stared at me with unashamed eagerness.

"Mothers of the bride are supposed to be in the background, like a piece of furniture." My words were a bit stiff.

"This mother of the bride will put the bride to shame."

"I'd better not."

"Come, dear. It would appear rude in the extreme

for us to be tardy." We skirted around the clump of vehicles and walked across the street. His flashy BMW was in the drive.

"I took the precaution of putting the roof up, in case I had the privilege of escorting a lovely lady."

Police waving white-gloved hands guided traffic through the campus. We slowed to a crawl. Lyle hummed the wedding march as he braked. The car in front of us sat zombie-like as the cop waved her on.

"Moron, the gas." Lyle thumped the steering wheel. A laugh burst out of me. "'Better than you stupe, don't you think?" he said. "I've been practicing my taking-small-children-in-the-car manners."

"Austin will understand you when he's four."

"Perhaps," he allowed.

The lady driver in front finally crept down the street. We walked into the side door of the church with ten minutes to spare. There was a low murmur from the sanctuary. Molly was in the nursery-cum-dressing room, surrounded by attendants and family. I kissed her cheek. Mama put Meemaw's silk veil on my daughter's head then fluffed the netting.

As I stood watching the wedding party, another person grabbed my heart and held it. Josephine's daughter Savannah was a radiant, beautiful bridesmaid. The green dress accentuated her gray-green eyes.

Cam offered to escort me down the aisle, so I put one foot in front of the other. Everything was numb, and I didn't feel my feet as I walked on the scarred wood flooring. Our congregation usually was a sea of dark chocolate with a little cream floating here and there. Today it was freckled. Cam walking stiffly down the aisle made me remember Harry at our daughter Mindy's wedding. No ready smile or joke had been on his lips. "Covenants with the Lord," Harry said at breakfast that morning, "are to be entered into with deliberation and humility."

I glanced at our guests, and my children and

grandchildren all seated in the front. I faked joy with my mouth turned up and my heart broken that Harry wasn't here to see this. I wouldn't look at Mama. I never could fool her, so I shifted my gaze right and stared into Lyle's dark-lashed-baby-blues. He took one look at me and left his seat.

"Good try, dear," Lyle said into my ear. "However, your lip is quivering. Should we break precedent? May I sit with you?" He didn't wait for my answer but seated me and took his place by the aisle.

"Lyle?" I said quietly.

"Hush, Di. I think I hear the sound of little feet."

The music changed to Handel's "Water Music." When Cam saw Molly, he gave a goofy grin that told me all was well.

"Thinking about Harry?" Lyle asked as Molly lit the unity candle.

"No," I said, taking the handkerchief he offered. "Thinking of you." He glanced at me, unable to hide his surprise.

Everything went as rehearsed until Reverend Daniel asked the bride and groom if he could read a letter from the bride's father to the congregation. There was an audible gasp behind me. It was good I was sitting since my knees wobbled.

Dearest friends and family,

Reverend Daniel cleared his throat and wiped his eyes. Harry's special linen paper trembled in his hands. Reverend Daniel MacPherson had loved Harry.

I am with you in spirit as Cam and Molly enter into the covenant of marriage. I can say without reservation that marriage is a gift from God. It is holy. Without Him in the center it will flounder. Marriage is under siege today because it is the picture of Christ and the Church. Protect it, fight for it.

I challenge you, the hearers of this missive, to

support this young couple with your prayers and actions. A fit word spoken in love will encourage them.

I am not there to shake your hands and thank you personally for celebrating with Delilah and Lyle the joining of our families. Most likely I will be busy in the Lord's garden while you gather and feast. I hope He has some chickens to grace the lawns.

Harry

For once I wasn't crying, but Lyle used one of his handkerchiefs to blow his nose and wipe his eyes. The picture of all shapes and sizes of chickens sporting on the grass of heaven struck me funny. Only Harry would bring that up. Would they traipse after him like his old hen Myrtle?

I buried my face in my left hand to hide my laughter. I shouldn't be tittering or imagining Road Island Reds, Silkies, and a plethora of birds coloring the heavenly environs, but it helped me avoid thinking about missing Harry's hand in mine.

Reverend Daniel refolded the paper. When the vows were given, Cam lifted Molly's veil and took her face in his hands. I held my breath. His kiss was gentle, tender, solemn. When they were introduced as man and wife, lottery winners couldn't match the sheer joy that bounced from Cam's eyes.

We made the photo session short. "Really, Miss Dee Dee," Josephine huffed when I called her forward for the family photo. "I'm going to look like a raisin among a bunch of white grapes."

"Whether you like it or not, you're my best friend, *and* family. Mr. Harry would haunt me the rest of my days if I didn't have you standing beside me."

As soon as the photos were done Josephine skittered off to supervise the kitchen. Daddy, Mama, and Meemaw had taken off with the Salases. It wasn't on my clipboard or theirs. It flitted through my mind that something was odd about it.

I was about to comment about their vanishing act

when Molly teetered my way. The girl was an athlete but put her in high heels and a floor length dress, and she'd trip over a ladybug. When a series of car horns blasted outside, I helped Molly smoosh her wide skirt flat so she could exit the sanctuary door. Before us was a Stutz Bearcat, Model A Ford, 1932 Ford with a rumble seat, and two 1920's touring cars. The judge's solution to the carriage-less wedding party.

"Great idea, Dad," Cam exclaimed.

"Thank Carter," Lyle said close behind me. "He called up the old car club to see if they would help us out."

"It's perfect, Lyle," I whispered, as the bridal party climbed into the cars. "Are you all right?"

"Physically fine. My heart, however, is in that car with my boy."

I stood on tiptoe and kissed him on the cheek. "I know." I spoke quietly up to him. "No one told us that the first day of kindergarten would lead to the pain of letting them go in marriage."

He put an arm around my shoulder, hugging me benignly as men do in church who don't want you to get ideas.

That made me sad.

He's letting me go too.

It's not that I hadn't asked for it. I'd been pushing him away for weeks. We drove away from the church, up the hill and past the park. The parade of vintage cars honked their way along the street while the bridal party waved at the crowds heading to the park.

"Is that Meemaw?" I asked, spotting a vivid purple hat.

"Could be," he replied. "We'll get home sooner if we avoid the traffic jam." He turned the car to a side street.

"But whatever would Meemaw be doing walking down the street to the park?" I craned my neck to peer behind me.

"Checking up on the mayor's fiasco, I imagine,"

Lyle said.

It was a silent drive. Lyle was lost somewhere in the regrets of parenting.

Chapter Thirty

WE WALKED TO MY HOUSE FROM where we parked at Lyle's. A dance floor filled my driveway instead of cars. A raised bandstand was behind the dance floor where the musicians tuned up, sounding like a zoo at feeding time.

Daddy and company should have been here before me. I was looking frantically in my cell phone for George's number when I heard chattering in the Salases' front yard. I scooted that direction.

"Cain't say I'm sorry to have interrupted the mayor's little love fest," Mama said, as I marched through the connecting gate. Meemaw and Josephine's mama were linked arm and arm. They teetered like unstable toddlers behind the rest of the party. Above their fragile frames, their wedding hats bounced like flowers perched on thin stems.

"What have y'all been up to?" I asked.

"Helping out Mamie's friend," Mama stated. "Olive Lorraine Patrick has enough on her shoulders without adding the mayor's frolic, so we volunteered to help. The missionary society from your church, Delilah, brought over food. I gave a little speech."

Mama never gave a little speech, she pontificated.

"Your mother complimented the whole town for the way they treated Harry and you," Mamie Salas blurted. "She was so tactful no one knew they'd gotten a tongue lashing. She said straight out that having a Pulitzer Prize winning author in residence put the town on the map. She thanked the mayor for the opportunity to inaugurate the ninth of September as the first Harry Morgan Day."

"I thought the mayor was going to choke to death on Josephine's mama's barbecued ribs," George interrupted. "Charlene kept hitting him on the back until he could breathe again."

"Then Meemaw hauled herself onto the stage and stared at the town council," Daddy said. "She said it was kind of them to declare a holiday on her great-granddaughter's wedding day. Then she stuck it to them when she added, 'the food donation was a thank you from the friends of the Morgans.'"

Words were flying through my brain, but nothing came out of my mouth. All my plans to bless the town had frizzled away. Instead, the Lord put His hand in and let others lavish the kindness. I was all kinds of grateful.

Dancing began after the best man's toast. As the band played softly Lyle appeared and offered me his hand.

"I haven't danced in years and will probably tromp on your feet as I did on Cam's," I said to him when we began.

"Keep your eyes on mine. I'll guide you."

We spun across the makeshift floor, his hand on my mid-back. I stumbled, apologized, stepped on his foot, apologized. He waltzed me off the floor, kissing my hand as he released me. I'd had my hand kissed once or twice before but not like Lyle kissed it, with a little press from his lips at the end. I watched as he sat down beside his sister, his breath too rapid. About the same speed as my heart rate.

As soon as the music stopped my publisher appeared. I'd been avoiding Max. I knew he would follow Harry's instructions to the letter by "outing" me as an author.

"I figured you'd be peeved at Harry and my plans for your future." Max shrugged. "Give it up, Delilah. Not much point in arguing. The world saluting your talent is something Harry wished."

"Max, I love you. You've done amazing things for my career. But we are not going to kowtow to Harry's wishes. D.B. Burns is my secret. If I want to tell, it is for me to decide. Not you or Harry. If you so much as make a hint that I am D.B. Burns, I will take my next manuscript to Random House, Putnam, or Ballantine. I might even see what kind of bidding war they get into."

Max's eyes twinkled. "I can't say I'm surprised. You never liked the spotlight. I'll let you call the shots, Delilah." We shook on it.

Max could look you in the eye and manipulate things like a slight-of-hand artist.

Was he telling me the truth?

"Thanks," I said, kissing his cheek. His smile slashed across his face. We began to dance.

"When do I get your next manuscript? I believe the contract states in February."

"I've not had time to do anything since Harry's diagnosis."

"Harry said you wrote while he slept."

"Scribbling down a story is one thing. Rewriting it five times is a whole other country. I need solitude, no pressure. For Pete's sake, Max, people have been shooting up my house since July."

He swung me sideways. We almost collided with the judge who was sashaying across the floor with Mademoiselle Bousquet. He should be sitting down and practicing breathing. The judge grinned at us. I nodded back.

As we finished, Lyle leaned over Mademoiselle Bousquet. She elongated her neck, like a sociologist reported women do when they flirt. Turning away I saw Meemaw yawn. The temperature had turned from crisp to a warm 85 with a coat of humidity wrapped around.

Taking Meemaw and Josephine's mama in hand, I escorted them inside where the air conditioning would revive them. They toddled through the house to the downstairs bedroom and promptly took up residence in the twin beds. As I closed the door, Josephine's mama began to snore.

When I returned to the kitchen, I spied our

preacher through the window. Since he'd arrived from the church, Reverend Daniel had been glued to Josephine's side. Maybe she would give up her, I've-got-no-business-marrying-a-man-of-the-cloth attitude. When she would forgive herself for birthing a baby without a father in attendance was beyond me. The good Lord had forgiven her long ago.

Someone tapped on a crystal glass.

The crowd quieted. I walked over to the Salases' table to grab an empty seat, settled into a gilded bamboo chair, and slipped off my heels. My feet were hot and the brick patio comfortable.

The judge and Cam climbed the stairs leading to the back door then turned and faced the crowd. Cam saluted his bride. "To the woman I cherish. May our lives be as rich as your parents' marriage." He jogged to her and planted a kiss firmly on Molly's lips.

"Bravo," agreed a male behind me.

The judge lifted his glass.

"Another toast is in order. Please join me in raising a glass." The judge's resonate voice carried over the noise of the crowd. Heads turned his direction.

"To my first-born son and his bride," Lyle began. "Cam, you have chosen to marry a daughter of the King. Treat her with an eye toward eternity. I salute you for your choice and for your character. Molly, whom I have grown to love like a daughter, may you share your tender heart with Cam. You both have my blessing and love." His smile radiated to his eyes.

I rose and lifted my ice tea to that, then fumbled for my chair. Suddenly Molly was beside me, wrapping an arm around my waist and keeping me upright. I hoped no one could see my sassy pink-lacquered toes under the hem of my dress.

"Mom," Molly whispered. "Why are you fidgeting?"

"Sweetheart, this is your day, so I need to sit down."

"I'll share," she offered.

"Before I finish and you all head home, I have

something else to say," the judge continued. "Delilah, I've a get-out-of-town-free card in my pocket. Two tickets to Paris leaving next week." His smile broadened. He walked down the center staircase.

I took a backwards step. "Lyle," I said in a shocked voice. "I can't go off with you and gallivant all over Europe."

"I don't see why not. You want to see France. I'm available as a tour guide." His expression softened as he stopped at the bottom of the stairs. He put his right hand in his pocket.

"It's not proper, Lyle Henderson."

He drew a forefinger over his upper lip.

Stalling. Letting me breathe.

"I thought you'd say that. So, I'll up the ante."

He sauntered my way. Cam was on his left, Beau on his right. Molly kept her arm around my waist so I couldn't high-tail it through the arborvitae. Right in front of God and everybody he dropped to his right knee and reached for my hand.

"You are a loving mother, great friend, and Harry's wife. One ticket has my name on it, the other, yours. Before July seventh I was prepared to ignore Harry's letter. But when I saw you moseying down Washington Avenue in your little green dress, chin high, eyes wide with fear, I had no choice but to rescue you from Charlene Higgenbottom. When we walked home, you took off your shoes. Then and there I decided my sabbatical from women was over."

He took a deep breath. "Delilah, I'm asking you to marry me."

I burst into tears.

He stood and wrapped his arms around me.

"I thought you didn't want me," I mumbled into his chest. "That you were going away and I wouldn't see you for months."

"Months, eh? Then what did you imagine would happen when I returned?"

"You'd live across the street and I'd see you

sometimes walking Bartles." The tear faucet went hyper.

I snuffled. He fished for a handkerchief.

"No, my dear. I'm here. I'm here for a good long time."

I wiped my eyes and blew my nose.

"Autumn in Paris, Di? Hard to resist." He waited for my response. "There is one minor thing that needs fixing. The name on one ticket is mine, the other says Delilah Morgan-Henderson." He paused, then said softly, "I won't marry you if you don't love me, Di. I couldn't bear it."

"Oh, Lyle," I croaked. "Since we had breakfast at Carter's I've argued with Harry about you. He says yes. I say it's too soon. Harry says get over it." If my hands had been free, I'd have been wringing them. "I'm in love with you, Lyle," I whispered, hoping only he could hear. "But I can't drop everything and take off. I've breakfast to cook for my guests and my garden to winterize."

Lyle smiled and leaned close. "Molly has a clipboard with legal-sized paper attached. The paper's filled out with all your objections and how we have fulfilled them. Care to look?"

Our children surrounded us. No room to wiggle out.

"Give it up, Mom," Molly said. "Dad talked to each of us in June. He wanted Judge Henderson to court you, asking each of us what we thought."

"No objections from any of us," Beau Henderson added.

"Just because it's now instead of a year down the road doesn't make it wrong. We think it's right. Right for you both, and for the family." Cam smiled as he spoke.

"One doesn't simply run off and get married," I mumbled. "There are financial discussions. Which house to live in decisions. Let alone all the weird little things that we haven't talked about yet." I looked up at the tall man beside me. "Do you like milk in your tea? Do you even drink tea? Shoot, I know diddly squat about you, Judge-er-Lyle."

Lyle's eyes glimmered with foreboding.

"I pray you'll understand my answer, Lyle. I can't marry you before I've mourned for Harry. It wouldn't be right." I nodded firmly. "And *you* need time. We've been thrust together by a ghost. For your sake, go to France, be with friends, enjoy life. Then come back to me. I want us to work, but it's a little too soon." My voice faded like a silent picture screen.

Lyle tilted his head looking deeply into my eyes. He nodded once.

I put my hands on his cheeks, pulled his face toward me and kissed him softly. In front of everyone. Then dashed up the stairs to the house and to my bedroom sanctuary.

I reached for a tissue from the nightstand on Harry's side of the bed. Its small drawer was slightly open. Funny, I hadn't noticed it when I dusted. Had Clarisse gotten this far in her snooping or had my daddy looked for something and opened the drawer?

I opened the drawer and spied Harry's latest journal. I reached in and fumbled with it. It was stuffed on top of another journal. A black one. My hands started shaking.

I threw the latest journal on the bed beside me and dove into the old black one. There was a red bookmark between pages marked October sixteenth and October seventeenth where Harry relayed all the rest of the details. Where he had gone that day, what he had done. He even stated that he saw the weaselly detective Lyle hired skulking around Paducah. It was the seventeenth I found most enlightening. Lyle hadn't remembered what he had done that day. I couldn't recall if the boys had been with me, but Harry chronicled it.

I had Delilah put Lyle's boys up for the night after

explaining to her I needed to waylay Lyle. A man shouldn't be alone with the kind of misery a wife's betrayal brings. Grabbed a bottle of Woodford Reserve from the cupboard and told Lyle I had need of him out at the farm. We nearly finished that bottle. Hope Delilah isn't counting on it for her Christmas cookies, 'cause I'll have a bit of explaining to do. It may be necessary to sit on Lyle for a bit. So, I'm hatching plans. Think the fish are calling us. Friday seems a good day to try out my new rod.

We fished for two days, catching trout at the stream by the corn field and hiding out in the old share-cropper's cottage in the woods. Finally hauled him back to town on Sunday afternoon, sober, but with a fractured mind. Man needed to be with his boys and show up by 8:45 for the Johnson case on Monday morning. Hope old Johnson wins against the Higgenbottom crowd. No one should force a man off the land his family plowed for four generations.

The tension around my lips vanished. So like my beloved husband to gather up his wounded friend and bring comfort via fishing rod, trout, and a campfire. I laid the journal on top of Harry's night stand as if it were a fragile piece of glass.

"This means, Harry, that Lyle is in the clear with the authorities." I blew my nose. "I'll show Lyle your journal in the morning. It will ease his mind." I chewed on my lower lip. "If he wants to see me." I breathed out the words like a prayer, remembering the sadness in Lyle's eyes when I'd said no.

I regrouped and returned to the backyard. As I filled the air with social inanities, I caught a glimpse of Madison striding up the drive. He clapped Lyle on the back, spoke to him at length, then they both looked my way.

Madison grabbed a drink from a passing server as he stepped onto the deck. He lifted it my direction and took a swallow. "Off duty," he said when he reached me. "This is good, do you know the vintage?"

I smiled. My fake champagne punch had fooled another person. "A modest little house."

"Thought you'd like to know that Neely Patrick has told us quite a tale. Says he was in Paducah and saw the doctor and Darlene get shot by Clarisse. Claims it was all her idea. He only helped get the bodies into the lake." When I didn't look surprised, he added, "Seems Clarisse found something in the doctor's room at the hotel and she went crazy. I suspect it was a package or two of the diamonds, because Neely said she came out of the doc's room with her purse bulging and murder in her eyes."

"Our investigation gives her motive and opportunity. This morning's interrogation had Clarisse pointing the finger at Neely. My gut says both. I think this one just needs a bow to decorate the legalities."

I kissed Madison's cheek. "Stay and enjoy the evening." I signaled for a server to refill his glass.

I reached for Lyle's hand as the kids were rattling out of the drive in the family's car festooned with cans stuffed with rocks.

"Lyle, my heart is breaking into little bits."

He put his arm around my shoulder. I eased into him. We fit like pieces of a puzzle.

"I need time to stand on my own two feet, Lyle. Embracing the loss of Harry and preparing to marry you won't happen if I trot off to the altar. I don't know how much time I need. Six months? A year? Two? But I want to say it again. You mean the world to me. There isn't another."

I reached up and took his face in my hands and gave him the kind of kiss you see at the end of a Hallmark movie, long and tender with a hint of a promise. Lyle took a step back and looked deep into my eyes. "Then you'd better be ready when I return from France for some old-fashioned courting. I've been known to be persistent." His eyes glimmered with love.

I smiled up at him. The pain in my heart wouldn't

disappear like a wisp of smoke, but there was room for me to love Lyle. And who knew, Paris would still be there, right? I smiled. Maybe my dream would come true one of these days—and I wouldn't have to see it alone.

Author Note

Courtship began as a short story contest through Free Expressions Literary Agency. A series of writing prompts were offered. I choose, 'pliable as iron,' which was the expression on Charlene Higgenbottom's face. The story began to soar when I added my grandmother's name, Delilah Belle, her Appalachian origins, and her beloved husband, Harry Morgan. Yes, he was named after a favorite actor who appeared on *Dragnet* and *Mash*.

My husband loved the short story, and as the tale grew, he laughed with me, grew teary over Harry's letters to Delilah, and cheered me on as I wove Lyle, family, and prejudice into the mix. This is a novel about love, loss, everyday life mixed with humor, and the machinations of petty minds in a small town.

The entire jumpy castle plot twist still makes me laugh. We celebrated a grandchild's birthday with an adventure at a jumpy castle gym, and it was so much fun I'd like to do it again. I suppose you could call my giggling as I flopped around with little kids my research.

The Thunderstorm grew from an idea my husband had while we were working in Kenya. Our daughter, who was stateside, had many wedding showers before her nuptials, but what about the groom, my husband lamented. Rod concocted the Thunderstorm idea and sent invitations from Africa to our friends and family in the U.S. After he flew home for the wedding, the Thunderstorm was held. There was manly man food, laughter, Craftsman tools, and sharing of scripture and memories. It has been incorporated by others to bless the men of the wedding gathering with wisdom and joy.

Characters inhabit my mind. They grew like weeds in spring, populating the small Kentucky town where the story takes place. I purposely did not name the town. I wanted it to be every village, burg, small place where stuff happens, and we get to choose how we respond. In my next novel, *The Last Roses*, the name is revealed. I grew up in a small college town in the west and now live in a small college town in Kentucky. I've lived in villages in Thailand, Africa, and Michigan and in large cities, from Portland to Santa Monica. I love being part of a community where loving and serving those in need is part of the DNA. I call wherever that happens, home.

Ways to connect with me:
Find my blog at: www.jeanettemariemirich.com
Follow me on Twitter: Jeanette-Marie Mirich
Follow me on Instagram: Jeanette-Marie Mirich
Follow me on Goodreads: author Jeanette-Marie Mirich

Discussion Questions

1. Delilah was grieving deeply over her husband's death and needing the support of friends and family, but she also had people in town who were determined to pull her down. Have you ever been in this position where you're battling people who show no compassion for the situation you're in? How did you handle it? Have you ever helped a friend who was struggling with negative feedback due to their circumstances?

2. Lyle has reoriented his life after his wife Clarisse deserted him and her sons. Abandonment is one of our core fears. Have you had a friend who has been abandoned? Did you walk with them through the crisis? What advice was helpful? What did you learn through the experience? Does a widow or widower feel abandoned?

3. Harry is never seen but remembered and heard. Harry's letters to Delilah reveal his character. When you write, do your words reveal who you are? What is the response you receive when you communicate by writing?

4. Delilah and Lyle both use sarcasm. Have you met people like this? Is there a way to use sarcasm or humor that's helpful instead of destructive?

5. There are several levels of prejudice exposed in the story. Have you personally experienced prejudice in your life or town? What kind? How did you respond to it? Have you ever needed to help a friend deal with prejudice?

6. Josephine is a unique voice in the story. Are there people in your life who express their views in ways that give a direct, no-holds barred answer? How did you handle the interaction and maintain the relationship?

Have you ever helped restore a friend who has been wounded by someone 'telling them the truth?'

7. Lyle is a man who makes friends easily and serves others with joy. He also found simple ways to meet Harry's needs as Harry was dying. Are there people in your life who show love by quietly serving others? How does that affect the people being served? Does it draw people to the person serving them?

8. Olive Lorraine has a bitter attitude toward Delilah. When Olive choses to turn away from her past and embrace Delilah as a friend, Delilah forgives, but is cautious. Have you ever had an experience where someone who has kept you at a distance changes the way they treat you and becomes friendly? How did you respond? Did the relationship grow or did it wither? Did you feel safe with that person or were you waiting for the other shoe to drop? What would you advise someone who is having a similar experience?

9. I have laid a word path for an Easter egg* hunt for expressions related to chickens throughout the manuscript. There are more than fifteen.

*A search for words or puns in a film or book.

Now, a Sneak Peek at Book Two
THE LAST ROSES
Coming July 1, 2020

Chapter One

I SPED DOWN THE INTERSTATE LISTENING to the local channel. The drive from Raleigh-Durham had been easy, little traffic and clear skies. Easing off the freeway to take a two-lane road toward my cousin's, I grimaced when an Amber Alert blared from my radio. "Eleven-year-old Drew Albert is missing from Hendersonville. Four-foot-nine, Caucasian, dressed in jeans, a gray T-shirt, and an orange, hooded sweatshirt. A silver van with a Tennessee license plate was seen where Albert waited for the school bus. Please contact the Hendersonville Police Department or call 911 if you sight Albert or the van."

"Lord, bring that boy home to his mama," I whispered, unable to imagine the agony of a child vanishing. It was hard enough when my beloved husband's gaze had fixated on heaven and never looked back.

Tears erupted from my eyes. The littlest things made me weep. They'd predicted that in the grieving information hospice had sent me. I fumbled for a Kleenex and wished for the soft, linen handkerchief of my across-the-street neighbor. Over the last couple of months, I'd learned to appreciate his initialed and pressed handkerchiefs. I chewed on my lip.

"Life would be a lot easier if evil didn't jump out and grab you by the throat." I did a lot of mumbling these days. Being alone would probably turn me into a woman chatting to herself and answering back. A shaft of sunlight blazed through the trees, momentarily blinding me. When the asphalt was black again, I forced myself to smile.

"Gratitude, Delilah," I quoted my Meemaw, "is practiced when you get a sweet cherry or a sour one." Of late I'd had a handful of pucker-up-your-lips cherries. From my husband's death to the man I'd grown to love disappearing like a jet's vapor, I'd been through a bit of trial.

I caught a glimpse of four deer hightailing it from the woods to the asphalt. Three turned back, but the yearling leaped over the grass verge to my left. I straight-line-braked. In three strides he collided with the hood of my van then did a somersault off to my right, disappearing into the valley below. I managed to keep the van with trailer on the asphalt.

Shaking so hard my teeth clinked like ice in a glass I glanced in the rearview mirror. The trailer was still attached to my vehicle. Although my van shuddered with death-like spasms, the trailer was upright. A staccato sigh escaped from my lips. At least this time no one shot my direction.

My hands gripped the lifeline of the steering wheel as the van began to steam. I wrinkled my nose. Something smelled like innertubes in an August heat wave. Does rubber melt with heat and ooze around the engine?

Easing to the side of the road, I stopped beside a dogwood strung with kudzu. I stomped on the emergency brake. Just in case.

Prying my fingers loose from the plastic, I wiped my hands on my skinny jeans, and glanced at the empty road. Route 18 was not a popular bit of highway, only a little squiggle on a North Carolina map that led through the mountains toward the house of my cousin. I was an hour-and-a-half away from her house in Piney Creek and farther from the kids' apartment in Raleigh.

An old GMC truck lumbered past.

"Hey, stop for a lady in distress, will you?" I shouted in my head.

The day didn't look promising.

In a few seconds a semi sped in the opposite direction. I stared at the truck's red shield logo until the semi disappeared over a hill. Mental telepathy didn't work worth beans. I picked up my cell phone and called my insurance company, the one my late husband Harry had used after he left the Marines. A sweet Texas voice greeted me.

"I've been in an accident," I reported. "A deer crossed the road ignoring the walk signal."

"Are you all right?"

"A little shaken is all. My car is steaming and . . ." I creaked out of the van to investigate the damage. My body, reluctant to cooperate with my brain, was as stiff as an over-whipped meringue. "It appears I've a pool of iridescent yellows and greens growing on the asphalt." I took a deep breath. "You need my info. Delilah Burns Morgan, policy number #38756, and this vehicle is the 2010 silver mini van, not my husband's truck. Do you need my Kentucky address?"

"No, ma'am. I've got you right here." Her voice sounded like she was reading from a teleprompter. There was a pause. "I see that everything has recently been transferred to your name." Her words trailed off. "Oh, I'm so sorry for your loss."

I fought the tears that emerged.

"I will contact a tow-truck to come and get you. Stay near the car, but away from the road," she directed. "You need to have a doctor check you out, Mrs. Morgan."

"I didn't hit anything but the deer. Actually, I think it hit me."

First car accident.

Probably ruin my record and the premiums would go up.

"I'll stay on the line until the tow-truck arrives." The woman on the other end was more than accommodating, but I had a list of things to do.

"I've got some calls to make. I'll get back to you when he appears." I got back into the driver's seat and searched for a pen to make a to do list.

"I really think you should see a physician. Whiplash happens in a deer-auto misadventure. You won't know until tomorrow when you can't move your neck."

"Thanks. I'll keep that in mind." I hung up and called my daughter.

"Er, Molly," I began. "I've had a little car trouble."

"Where are you, Mom?"

"Near Hendersonville. Someone's coming to haul the car to a repair shop."

"You have a flat tire?"

"No. A venison collision." I laughed.

"What?" Molly's voice cracked.

"A deer decided to cross the road. We met in the middle."

She sucked in air. "Are you okay?"

"I'm fine. The car's life's blood is all over the road. I'll get a rental car, then head to Linda's."

"Mom, there probably isn't a rental car company in a hundred miles. Let me talk with Cam."

I rolled my eyes. "You're *not* coming to get me. Cam's got classes, and you've got a job interview. Linda can get me."

"I'll speak with Cam," she said firmly as she hung up. Three weeks married, and my independent Molly checking with her husband was out of character.

I phoned Linda. No answer. I glanced behind the car and got out. Uneven bits of gravel crunched under my tennis shoes as I walked south to examine the trailer hitch. I looked east where the little two-point buck lay still in the tall grass forty-feet below. Was he kaput or simply stunned? I sighed and turned to my next problem. I'd need something to put by the tires so the car wouldn't join the deer in the netherworld. Maybe a big rock.

Scouting the area for a hefty bit of granite, limestone, shale, anything with weight to it, I sighed. "Not fair, Harry," I said into the humid air. "What were you thinking leaving me behind to fix every mess that jumps out at me."

Shouldn't quibble with a dead man, but dad-rat it, Harry knew everything, even how to unhitch a trailer.

I squatted to examine the hitch's underside. Kneeling on the pebbly surface of the shoulder for a closer look I winced as small bits of gravel imbedded into my worn jeans. Things appeared fine on the underside of the hitch and trailer tongue. I rose and rubbed the stones from my knees.

Hunched over the ball on the car where the hitch sits, I tested the metal with a finger. Without a by-your-leave a black cloud above me wrung itself dry. Water ran down my neck and into my shirt until I was wet to the skin. I looked toward the hills. The horizon cavorted with boiling dark clouds waiting to empty themselves. I scurried for the van. Before reaching it, my cell phone chirped. As I pulled the small phone from my jeans pocket, the phone slickered out of my hands and tumbled into the soggy grass.

"Erg!" I swiped a hand across the hair plastered to my face and began to search the wayside for the phone. From the look of the jungle of weeds and tin cans the grass had grown unabated since August. Now the days leaned into October, and I couldn't see the ground, let alone a small dark object. The thigh-high blades of grass wiped themselves dry on my jeans. The phone kept ringing. I located it by sonar.

I dashed for the passenger side of the van as I said, "Hello."

"Bon jour, to you too." The baritone voice of my across-the-street neighbor made my feet slip in the soggy grass. I caught myself from falling by grabbing the door handle. "Cam tells me you're having a challenging day."

I flung myself into the front seat. Chilled, I vibrated against the seat like a half-drowned cat. "You called all the way from Paris to commiserate?" Jealousy crept into my voice. After Harry died, I'd wanted to go to France and hide out in a little apartment, continue to learn French, master the art of sauces, and get so busy I could ignore the painful throb in my heart.

"I'm not in Paris," said Lyle's reasonable male voice.

"Last I heard, you were heading toward Provence."

"Keeping track of my comings and goings?"

"The kids mentioned your travel plans since you didn't." I grabbed the pillow on my passenger seat and squeezed it tight.

"An oversight."

Turning the car on from the passenger seat seemed a good idea. I pulled my purse out from under my bum and scavenged for my keys in the bottom's black hole. "After I refused your marriage proposal, you up and disappeared." My lips scrunched up tight when I finished.

He laughed. "I couldn't escape after all. Everywhere I looked I saw your face. You were in the Louvre, in Da Vinci's lady's mysterious smile. I caught you nibbling crepes on the Champs Elysees, then you had the audacity to invade my dreams. So, I came home."

"Oh." I chewed on words that wanted to exit my lips.

"I'll be there in a half-hour or so."

I blinked with shock. "I thought you were home in Kentucky."

"I'm at my family's farm in the Piedmont. Just an hour from you. I began driving as soon as Cam called. Shouldn't take me long to reach you."

"I don't need to be rescued. I'm fine. The car will be fine. My cousin Linda can get me when I'm at the repair shop."

"I'll turn around then." There was a hint of disappointment in his voice.

My heart skipped a beat.

"Well." I wrinkled my brow. "It would be nice to see you." Should I let him know hearing his voice made my toes itch? That kind of brazenness was unseemly in a grandmother. But it was the truth.

"Okay." His voice was bland.

"Fine." I removed the pillow case and dabbed it over my soggy locks.

"Can you give me directions?"

I did.

Then, just like that, he hung up.

The van's windows steamed from my damp clothes. I rubbed a circle in the windscreen. My small aperture showed trees with mountains in the distance. With nothing to do but count raindrops I dialed my cousin's phone again.

She answered on the third ring. "Hedow?" she snuffled out.

"Linda? You sound like flannel is stuffed up your nose."

"Got an awful bug. Came on all of a sudden." A paroxysm of sneezes concussed my ear before she said, "and I'm living in the bathroom." She blew her soggy nose. "Don't come if you value your life."

"I can help."

"Declined. Some things should not be shared. Hank's got the shivers too. So, head on home." Being a nurse Linda had a corner on direct. "We'll catch up when I get my head off the pillow."

"Love you, bunches."

"Love you back." She disconnected.

Drat! I couldn't use her as an excuse to avoid the judge.

9 781943 959693